FOREVER

———————————

STRANGERS

By Eleanor Mayo

TURN HOME–1945
LOOM OF LAND–1946
OCTOBER FIRE–1951
SWAN'S HARBOR–1953
FOREVER STRANGERS–1958

FOREVER

STRANGERS

ELEANOR R. MAYO

REBEL SATORI PRESS • New Orleans

Originally published by
W.W. Norton & Company

ISBN: 978-1-60864-130-7

Published in the United States of America by
Rebel Satori Press
www.rebelsatoripress.com

FOREVER

STRANGERS

PART ONE

BARNEY Cousins was feeling pretty well pleased with his week's work as he drove down the shore road from Port Kezar toward his brother's house. He'd wanted this car ever since he set eyes on it last week end, the first day he'd been home, as a matter of fact. It had taken him the whole week to beat Pete Gonsalves down into selling it to him at the price he wanted to pay for it.

He'd wanted to get it on time; but he discovered he couldn't do that without having somebody else's name on the note and he could picture himself asking Sam to go on a note with him. He had the money all right, and to spare, out of the allotment Jude had been banking for him for four years, but paying cash for the car didn't leave as much to pull and haul on as he would have liked even after he got Pete down to reason.

Pete wasn't too interested when you didn't have a turn-in and Barney's thin, high-cheekboned face twisted into a reluctant grin as he recalled Pete's scream of anguish when, after three days of talking around it, they'd finally got down to dollars and cents. That was the trouble with those Portuguese guys. They got emotional over everything from the price of a car to death and destruction, and the minute they started getting excited, you knew you'd won. If you could only hang on, you could get them on the run every time.

Bulldog Barney, he thought admiringly, feeling the quick lift

7

of power under his seat when he touched the accelerator. The way
to get what you wanted was to wear them down.

It was nearly dark and the sun, long gone behind the humped
glooming shoulder of Mount Hagar, had left behind it only the
memory of color outlining the top of the hill. There was a warm
northwest wind blowing, but the ocean was stirred into a deep, almost wintry, savage blue and the islands had taken on their night
look of anonymous strongholds, black between the town and the
great eastern expanse of heaving, glistening, dangerous water. Even
in summer it was a savage landscape to the east; although in summer there were a few lights still left. But for nine months of the
year the islands lay dark, alone, and threatening in their loneliness.
The sea still creamed whitely on the ledges; but the ice in winter
bothered nobody now and the cries of gulls and sea birds was the
only sound in the steel-bound stillness.

His brother Sam's house was a big old white place set on a little
rise across the road from the water. Not Sam's, really. Judith's.
Because it was the old Cameron homestead and Camerons had
built it and lived there practically forever, until Sam and Jude got
married and went there to take care of the old man, Jude's father,
in return for the place. James had been an old man then; he'd been
an old man trying not to be, ten years before that, when his young
wife ran off and left him for a Portuguese fisherman, and after she
went he stopped trying and *was* old.

James and Barney never got along well; but it wasn't an active
not-getting-along. They bore with each other because they were
together under the same roof, each one trying to pretend the other
one wasn't there. Jude's letter saying he had died caught up with
Barney in Germany, and Barney could remember now not being
glad, but relieved, the way you'd be when a grumbling tooth
stopped and you knew it wasn't going to develop into a jumping
toothache.

It was probably all to the good that James had been the way he
was, hauled back into his shell like an old turtle in the sun. There
had been plenty to upset him those last years, if he'd been willing
to let it. There was Cliff. Barney had never been able to tell what
the old man was thinking, but it must have been kind of hard for

him to have his own wife's Portuguese bastard facing him across the table three times a day.

Barney slowed for the driveway, feeling his shoulders begin to stiffen for what was coming. He didn't doubt it would be something. The tires spat on the clamshells and Jude, who was coming in across the field from the garden, stopped to look at the strange car, wondering. He parked between Sam's truck and Cliff's old Ford and climbed out. The minute he poked his head out of the car, Cliff, who had been standing in the kitchen window eating something from a big yellow mixing bowl with a tablespoon, let out an excited yawp and came galloping out the door, his young, punkin-devil face grinning, his light hair on end, the bowl still in his hand.

"Hey, Barney! Barney! Hey, Barney!"

"Matter with you?"

"New car, hanh?" Cliff, his momentum enough to keep him going, had circled the car twice before Jude got within hailing distance.

"New to me," Barney said. "What you think of her?"

"Boyoboy! What'll she do? Can I try her, Barney?"

Barney didn't answer. He didn't really hear. Cliff's yodeling went on so constantly it got to that point. Instead Barney was watching Jude's dark face, hard to make out in the dusk, for the disapproval he expected to find. She was doing pretty well at keeping it hidden if she felt it.

"Pretty handsome, Barney. Is she yours?" Her low voice was pleasant, but he could see she was a little upset. Instead of coming over to look at the car, she reached out and grabbed her young half-brother on his next circuit and glanced into the mixing bowl he was clutching in one big hand. "Cliff Gonsalves! There must be a quart of ice cream there."

"I was *hungry*," Cliff protested.

"I don't see how you could be. You just got up from the supper table an hour ago."

"Well, I was." His grasshopper mind went back to the first excitement. "Hey, Barney, you get her from Uncle Pete?"

Barney nodded, still watching his sister-in-law.

"Where's Sam?"

"Oh, he's in the living room writing his annual sales letter," she said.

"Kind of previous this year, isn't he?"

"I don't know," Jude said thoughtfully. "It's July. Be hunting season before we can turn around."

Cliff relaxed enough to lean against the front fender of the new car and start spooning down his ice cream; but his eyes never left off their admiring catalogue of its high points. Jude started for the shed door and Barney followed her slowly, against his will feeling like a kid who'd done something he shouldn't have.

He didn't have to go down the long hall to the living-room door to know what his brother would look like, sitting at the fumed oak library table, his light hair standing on end, his dark Indian face contorted with the effort it took to produce that letter. Or sound like either, because letter-writing with Sam was an audible process too. He would sigh and wiggle his feet and thresh around in his chair until the rungs squeaked in their sockets, and when he got all through and tossed the pen down with a last long sigh of utter relief, he would have produced exactly the same letter he had every year for the last fifteen.

They didn't sound like Sam. They sounded more like a thirteen-year-old kid without much imagination. Barney had seen them before and they all read the same way:

Dear Sir: I have some pretty good deer country lined up for you this fall. Some pretty good hunting. Some pretty good coon country. Yours truly, Sam Cousins.

Barney couldn't see how Sam could do it, pick up a gun again and shoot at anything to kill it. Because Sam had been standing right beside that other man named Barney Cousins when he died. Sam was twenty, and it happened in a brushy clearing in on the Allegash one gray November morning and there might have been a smell of snow in the air because it was late, the last day of the season, when some guy took a snap shot with a high-powered rifle at a sound in the woods and got him.

Sam didn't talk about it, didn't tell Barney about it for four years, until Barney was nine, and then he told him how the slug got the old man right through the throat and he never spoke another word. Sam said something about the noise, kind of a bubbling noise, he said. When he told that it came out of him fast as if he had to get it out or he himself would never be able to speak again. Barney went out into a patch of burdocks behind the woodshed and threw up after Sam told him and Sam came and held his head until it was over.

But he still couldn't see how Sam could ever touch a gun again, standing right beside a thing like that, watching it happen between two breaths—a life going out like a match when you blow it and it being your own father.

And what a hell of a way to make a living! Every fall when the sports started writing to him, Sam must remember, must sit and think about it when he was answering their letters, and maybe that was why he made such heavy weather of it.

Barney knew that first Barney Cousins had been a good man because everyone was always saying, whenever he turned around, how *that* Barney was a big man and a good man and Sam was just like him and what's the matter with you, anyway? Why can't you? Why don't you?

So by the time Barney got to the living-room door and saw Sam sitting there looking and sounding just exactly the way he'd known Sam would, he was beginning to be mad because everybody said Sam was a big man and a good man and he was just that, so where did that leave Barney, with Sam taking up all the room there was.

"There, by god!" Sam said. He signed his name with a flourish and threw the pen. "There! I feel like those guys in the newsreels, like I ought to have a bunch of characters standing behind me waiting to fight over the pen for a souvenir."

"Well, haven't you?" Barney said. "Here *I* am. Jude and Cliff are right outside. I could call them in."

"Hanh?" Sam glanced at him suspiciously. "Whatta *you* been up to?"

"What makes you think anything?"

Sam snorted. When he asked a question he liked a straight answer, and it always made him impatient to be answered with another question.

"Hell, I can always tell when it's something. When you begin to get sarcastic. What is it now?"

"I bought me a car."

"Oh." Sam reared back in his chair and straightened his long legs. The chair creaked hopelessly. "What for? To go back and forth to work in?"

"Yeah. Something like that."

"Well, that's just fine. Now all you need is a job."

I sure handed him that opening, Barney thought.

"I've only been home a week," he said.

"I don't know how much dough you've got," Sam said thoughtfully, "but if you spend that much every week, it won't last long, whatever it is."

"There's plenty of time."

"Barney, there's *never* plenty of time for anything. The sooner you find it out the better. Before you know it, time's going to be the thing that's behind you and then you'll see there's never enough."

"Christ almighty, anyone'd think I was beginning to dodder, to listen to you."

"Twenty-two ain't very old, true," Sam said pontifically. "But it's old enough to make a beginning and you haven't even done that."

"Haven't had much chance, have I?"

"Nope. But you can start now. You got any ideas?"

"I thought I'd head down East," Barney said. He hadn't thought anything of the kind; but he had to say something and it was the first thing that came into his head. Once he'd said it, it sounded like a good idea too.

"What's the matter with Port Kezar? *I* could always find plenty to do here."

Matter with it! Barney thought. My god, with you spread over it like the lid on a kettle! All there'd be left for me to do would be tend the fire under the pot.

That business about Jack-of-all-trades-and-master-of-none might as well never have been said when it came to Sam. Whatever he did, it turned out right. He had to do it well. And if he started out doing it well, he had to do it better before he was satisfied.

Take those damned hens! They'd lived hens for four years and by that time they were getting too easy for Sam, so he turned them over to Jude and Paul. Sam, he had to try something else.

He ran a string of traps all summer, not inshore where the shedders crawl, but fifteen miles out where the hard ones were. He made Barney get a lobster license and go with him. Barney hadn't liked it much; but he'd kept his license renewed, for some reason. Maybe he was more like Sam than he thought and had to have a few strings too.

He'd always felt that's what Sam was doing, spinning away like a god-damned spider, as if he had to have as many attachments or points of reference, or whatever damn thing you wanted to call them, as a spider web.

Sam was a registered guide, too, and good at it, and the sports had got to know him. Come fall, half the rest of New England was after Sam to take them out to where they could sit on their fat arses and let him drive a deer in so they could shoot it without having to do more than lift the gun.

Then he had all those pulp operations going that he had to go off and see to every now and so often.

When you stopped to think, Sam probably had his finger in as many pies as any man in Port Kezar. That made him a big man. As well as a good one. But, whatever it was and whoever he turned it over to when it got too easy for him, he never really let go. He was always the one to decide, because it was still his. He had to be the one to say.

And there he sat asking what was the matter with Port Kezar! Barney shook his head.

"I want to see a little more country first."

"I should think you'd seen plenty, the last few years. You've seen a hell of a lot more than I ever did."

The front legs of Sam's chair hit the floor with a crash and he stood up; but whatever else he'd been going to say didn't get said because Jude appeared in the door behind Barney and both men turned to look at her. Under the barrage of those two similar pairs of eyes, her smile didn't fade, it simply grew fixed.

They looked so much alike, each with the shock of light-colored, heavy hair, each with the same sharp, dark-skinned features, each with the same big spare bony framework of body and no extra flesh to conceal the bone. It always startled her a little to come on them together like this. It made her feel as if they should *be* as well as look alike, and she knew they were completely different. The difference went beyond and deeper than the simple one of age. They should have been father and son, not brothers, and Sam had nearly the age but none of the authority.

"Barney's leaving us," he said abruptly.

"I'm sorry to hear it." She looked at Sam, not Barney.

"He seems to feel there ain't enough to keep him busy in the Port."

It was characteristic of Jude that she didn't ask Barney where he was going. Only when.

"I think I'll start out tonight. Matter of fact, right now, as soon as I get a clean shirt."

After he'd left the room, Sam stood looking after him and the puzzled wrinkle between his eyebrows made Jude want to say something to comfort him; but the whole thing had happened so quickly and before she was expecting it that she couldn't think what to say.

"My god," Sam said. "What ails that kid? I thought as much as anything he'd be ready to settle down when he got out of the Army. You'd think the jaunting around he'd been doing, he'd be glad of the chance."

"Did you offer him the chance?"

"Well, hell, not in so many words, I guess. But I told him there was plenty of room for him here. He never gave *me* the chance to tell him anything more."

"Oh, Sam!" Jude began to laugh helplessly and when he turned the same uncomprehending stare on her, she could only shake her head.

"Am I dumb?" Sam began to sound angry. "Should I have

rolled out the red carpet or something? What did you want me to do, just say to him: Here, I'll step out and you step in?"

"It probably wouldn't have done any good if you had," Jude said soothingly.

She wanted only to comfort him, to make him stop looking as if somebody had hit him in the stomach, but this had happened to him so often she couldn't dredge up the lying words to say: It won't happen again. Jude herself had hoped that Barney would be ready to settle down and go to work when he came home. He wasn't ready and it seemed to Jude now, in the sharp light of hindsight, that he never would be. He wasn't the settling kind.

But he would always be coming back and Sam would always be hopeful and willing to take him in and then there would always be the disappointment and surprise. Sam's capacity for surprise when an established pattern kept repeating itself sometimes astonished her. She knew he wasn't stupid, but occasionally she felt that a reasonably intelligent man with well-developed blind spots could be worse than a stupid one.

"Barney's a hunter," she said finally, and knew from Sam's blank stare that he had no idea what she was talking about.

"What's *that* mean?"

"Only that he'll always think what he has isn't as good as what there might be, if he keeps on looking."

"That's damn foolishness," Sam said impatiently, cocking his head to listen to the steps coming rapidly down the front stairs. Barney was whistling when he went past the door. He looked in at them, grinned, waved his hand.

"See you later," he said blithely into their silence, and disappeared down the hall.

"He will, too," Jude said, more to herself than Sam, hearing the car start and the sound of the motor fade into the still summer night.

"Maybe he'll get it out of his system." Sam turned his back deliberately and went over to the window to watch the conical glare of headlights die through the trees.

"Hell," he said. "After all, he's only a kid."

"He's twenty-two," Jude said dispassionately.

"The service doesn't let them grow up. It takes care of them and they don't have to think about where the next meal's coming from. They don't have a chance to think for themselves. Christ, they're nothing but babies when they get out."

"All right."

"It's *not* all right." Sam didn't turn around, and the set of his wide shoulders told her that he didn't want her to come over to him. "I know it as well as you do, Jude. Not all right at all. Just, I don't know what to do."

If any of them had been different—Sam or Barney, or Jude herself—she might have been able to tell him. Not what to do, but what she might have done in his place. But they were all as they were and she was as helpless as Sam was, and this was the first time he had ever come close to admitting that he had failed in anything he'd ever tried to do. He wasn't admitting failure now, he was simply saying he didn't know.

"Nothing," she said. "I suppose there's nothing you can do."

A few minutes after she'd gone upstairs, she heard Sam go out in the side yard to the kennels and the dogs began to mutter at his approach and a moment later Bruce, his old black coon dog, bayed once before Sam's quick steady voice turned him off.

Hearing him quieting the dogs, Jude thought suddenly: He's a hunter, too, but his quarry has fur and teeth and talons and can fight back and that's hunting he can understand. And he can put them out of their misery and have a hide or a side of meat to show for his labor. But Barney was looking for something you couldn't hold in two hands.

She heard Sam walk slowly around the house and knew, as well as if his mind were an extension of her own, what he was thinking. Not about Barney. Once he was out of the house, Sam was sensible enough to put him out of his thoughts too.

He was thinking now of the fall before the spring was barely past, was wishing away the summer when no prime pelt went on four feet, was wondering if Bruce was too old this year to stand another fall of shouldering through the blowdowns and the tangled pulp slashings, and, if he was too old, would he have taught the two young dogs half what he knew?

Heading north and east through the summer night, Barney had forgotten Sam, too. It was pleasant, driving through the little coast towns lost in summer, lost until he came into this flash of neon with the whole life of one of those small towns pin-pointed down to one-syllable words in red fire against the sky: Coke. Ford. Gas. Clams. Eat. And then gone again, in a flash, as the souped-up engine hauled him through the main street, up the hill, and out into the endless night waiting for him.

He liked the feel of that motor. He knew it would let him break a hundred on the straightaway. Not that he wanted to go that fast, especially not knowing where he was headed.

He'd always had a feeling that things were going by too damn fast for him ever to catch up with them and if he could only get to a hundred miles an hour, he might do it. Now, though, by the time he could do it, he'd found out, too, that when he went that much faster, everything else speeded up accordingly and was just that much ahead of him still.

The wheel of a good car under his hands reminded Barney of Joe Samuels, because Joe, all his life, had had to have a car and to be going, too, and they had done a lot of going together.

Joe was the big jewboy whose father ran the secondhand store— my god, and that was all different now, too, because Joe was dead and the old man wouldn't touch anything second hand unless it was a hundred and fifty years old; and he was really right up there, leading citizen and all that, as if he'd planned it for Joe and when Joe was killed, Jacob had to do it himself to prove it could be done.

Barney wondered sometimes what Joe would have turned out to be like if he hadn't met a Chinese sentry that night on a Korean hill. Joe was so different from what his old man thought he was; but not afraid of man nor devil. Once when Barney was home on leave he'd gone in to see Jacob and the old man had talked to him about Joe. He didn't want to talk about Joe in the war—that was something he'd never had with him—but around home and a kid again. That was when Barney had first begun to see that one person was really a lot of people, a different one for everybody who knew him, because the Joe his father talked about wasn't anyone Barney had ever known so it was easy.

Barney could remember as clearly as if it were happening again the night the two of them in that old Ford phaeton Joe pieced together off the junk yard started in through the Parry Hill Crossroad after a deer. About halfway up the shoulder of the Hill there was—it was starting to grow up to pucker brush even then and that was eight years ago and Barney hadn't been in there since and pucker brush grows fast—an old apple orchard. The big spotlight rigged on the hood picked up the shine of eyes and Joe hopped out of the car and let go. The eyes went out.

They put the car in across the field and when they got to it, they found the doe lying there and right alongside her, a lamb. They hadn't even known there were two of them. The lamb was standing just the other side of its mother at the crashing minute when she turned her head to the light, and Joe's slug went all the way through her chest and took the lamb in the temple.

They didn't stop to bleed the deer because they were so near the main road and Joe's gun made a sound like the end of the world. They stuffed both carcasses into the back seat and lit out. As they jounced out of the orchard a pair of headlights came on, out of nowhere, and showed them up like flies in a butter dish. The only way left was on through that old road that had been impassable for years. Barney shoved his foot down on the accelerator and the Ford lurched into ruts deep enough to grab her wheels and hold them like a trolley track.

Joe was in the front seat beside him, looking back. It was like something out of one of those old Western serials in the movies; but in them the reel always stopped when the bandits were chasing the stagecoach and just about to catch it—this reel kept right on going.

"Jesus, Barney, keep her coming!" He could hear Joe laughing. "It must be the Warden. He's still there and gaining fast. Keep her coming, son! Give her her head! Ride him, cowboy!"

Barney let her have her head all right. He couldn't do anything else. Frozen into those ruts, all he could do was either step on it or let up. He thought his own head would bounce off his shoulders. The road wasn't any better than a brook bed where ten years' spring rains had washed the gravel out and there was only bedrock left and nothing ever put back because there was no reason. The people had all sold out or died or gone away and only the old graveyard remained to hold the land and that was full, so there wasn't any reason to keep even a hearse road.

One place they came up over a little hill and as they broke over the top, the lights hit a sheet of water where beavers had dammed what used to be a good trout brook and flooded it across the road. Barney thought: Good god, if I hit that fast, I'll drown her out. If I don't, he'll get us. Either way, there wasn't much choice. So he hit it fast. Solid water shot out each side of her and up over the windshield. It soaked him, not only splatters and a little at a time, but exactly as if he'd jumped down a well, and it was cold water.

Joe let out a yell that nearly blasted his eardrums.

"Hey!" he roared. "Raining hard, hey, kid?"

It was then the lamb in the back seat came to. His feet began to drum against the floorboards. He'd been lying partly underneath the doe and that was the only thing that saved their bacon. It gave Joe time to get over the back of the seat before the lamb could gain its feet. Barney wasn't sure to this day why Joe hadn't shot it. He was just crazy enough and Barney was sitting there holding his breath and hoping to christ Joe would get the deer and not him.

Maybe Joe didn't want any more of a hole in the old jalopy than he already had, although there was room to let go with a howitzer and not do any harm. You could look right down between your feet and see the road going by underneath.

Anyway, he didn't shoot. There were a couple of quart bottles of beer in back and Joe grabbed one of them. He got kind of crazy anyhow when he got excited and he was sure excited then. Barney could hear him yelling something at the top of his lungs, but not what it was. He heard the thud when Joe hit the lamb between the eyes with the bottle, not hard enough to break the glass, but just hard enough to stun the lamb back to its knees. Leave it to Joe to judge that right. *He* wasn't going to waste good beer on a little thing like a deer that might only cut him to ribbons if it got a good clip at him.

By that time they were through the pond and the Ford hadn't drowned out and the following lights had stopped. Barney could see in the rear-view mirror what looked like a long green tunnel behind them with those lights fading at the back of it.

He was laughing so hard he felt sick and he could hardly hang onto the wheel. He was bent forward over it, and at every bump in the road that hard old rubber gave his stomach a hell of a drubbing, but he couldn't straighten up.

In the back seat, Joe was singing. He had the cap off the bottle. Every now and so often he'd put his finger over the top, lean forward and take a two-handed swing at the lamb. The warm beer would shoot a foaming fountain up into the air and Barney got some of it that way before Joe shoved the bottle into his mouth again.

"Got to stop pretty soon, Barney," he yelled. "Got to kill this little bugger before he kills me. I'm nearly out of beer."

He was, too, the damned hog! He'd nearly finished the second quart and Barney was drier than a wooden god on a frosty morning, but he never got any of *that* beer.

Next day on his way to school, Barney stopped into the drugstore to get a pack of cigarettes. When he came out the Warden was standing on the sidewalk waiting for him. He wasn't mad at first, but when he got thinking about it and remembering it, he started getting red around the edges of his cap.

"Look, son," he said. "Don't think I didn't recognize you two jokers last night. The next time you'll get more of a surprise. I don't know how the hell you got through that road, but I've got a couple of men in there this morning taking out the culvert by that beaver pond. You won't do it again!"

It was pretty decent of him to warn them. Barney was still too sore across the ribs to laugh, just grinned.

But stuff like that was all they ever did, kid stuff, because the Army caught up with both of them when they were eighteen.

Somebody told Barney if he ate soap before he went to take his physical, he could make a pretty good stab at being sick. He ate enough so the Procter & Gamble people should have declared him a special dividend, and he wasn't pretending anything. He *was* sick!

The doctor gave him one of those I-know-you looks, glanced at the other two guys in the line who were holding Barney up to make sure they were watching and listening and he wasn't wasting his brains on one alone because that wasn't enough of an audience.

"You're foaming at the mouth, young fellow," he said. "You must be mad and the infantry sure as hell needs mad men."

The last time Barney had seen Joe was that fall. They both got home on leave at the same time before they shipped out. Joe made it a couple of days sooner, but they were in Port Kezar about a week together. They didn't seem to have too much to say to each other. Joe used to have to have noise and racket and things going on; but that fall he never seemed to want anything but silence from anyone. He didn't even want to go hunting and they could have gone legally for a change.

Then one night, bright moonlight and like day, Barney had been out somewhere on a date and had just got back to Sam's and into bed when a car drove up and stopped. He was curious enough to get out of bed again and go look and it was Joe, driving that big Packard convertible that belonged to his old man. It was a chilly night, but he had the top down and was sitting there looking up at the window with a funny thoughtful expression on his face— not quite as sharp as puzzled—as if something was bothering him and he didn't know what it was.

"Hey, Joe," Barney called down to him.

"Hey, Barney," he said, calm as if it had been two o'clock in the afternoon and Barney waiting for him to turn up because he'd said he would. "Come on down. Let's ride around."

Well, hell, what could he do? He was sleepy and there was the bed; but he didn't know when he'd see Joe again and Joe'd been so damned queer! That was all Barney thought about it then: What the hell. It wasn't any later than ten. Might as well go along with him.

That turned out to be another night for the books. There wasn't a joint within twenty miles either way they didn't hit that night.

They were all familiar places. Joe would stop, go in, take a look around, maybe order a glass of beer. He'd sit for a minute with the beer in front of him, get down one swallow, start to fidget, and they'd be off again.

He didn't even want to talk. He just wanted to go. It got to be nerve-racking after a while.

After midnight when you couldn't get beer, Joe started driving. They went fifty miles up along the old Airline Road, way out beyond Lead Mountain, and then turned around and came back. They went down the Estuary, way down below Verona where they used to go duck-hunting. Got there. Didn't stop. Turned around and came back. Every place they'd ever gone hunting or helling around, they hit. But it was just like touching first base and lighting out hellity-hoot for second. Barney began to feel like some kind of a god-damned yo-yo bouncing around on the end of a string.

When they finally headed home it must have been nearly five-thirty in the morning. It wasn't even showing daylight, but there was a late feeling to the night.

They passed the Parry Hill Crossroad and the Packard was doing eighty; but Joe remembered the same thing Barney did, because he slammed on the brakes and started up the road as if he was still trying to do eighty to get back to something in time.

Barney said, "My god, Joe, you can't get in through that road now. Not in this car!"

Joe sat looking where the lights fell and it wasn't any more than a memory of a road, with the alders head high in the middle.

"No," he said finally. "I guess I couldn't. Well, hell with it. Might's well leave one place to be the way you remember it."

Five minutes later he stopped in front of Sam's house, waited for Barney barely to make it out of the car, said:

"Good night."

The wheels spun in the gravel before they had a chance to take hold and Joe was gone and the darkness flowed like liquid back into the hole the noise of the engine had torn in the night.

Barney never saw him again. He went down the next day, as soon as he crawled out of bed, but Joe wasn't home and Jacob didn't know where he'd gone. Barney tried once more, the day after that, but that time Joe had gone for good.

Joe got his pretty quick, but Barney didn't hear about it for nearly six months. When he did, he remembered that night and decided he knew what Joe had been doing, though maybe Joe himself hadn't known.

It was something the old folks around had to do and Barney had never seen anyone young have to do it before, so he didn't recognize the symptoms at the time.

The old people sell their places and move into town, maybe to live with a married daughter or son. But they hang onto the memory of "the old place" the way a terrier will to a rope once he's got the end of it tight in his teeth. They never want to see the old place again, because there's too much tied up with it—death and misery and hardscrabble. They remember it, though, and along toward the end, there's a time when they have to go back to it once more to find the spring. Because, of course, that was the heart of the whole setup, the source of life itself. Without the spring and the clean water welling up in the old wooden tub sunk in the ground, or up through the mossy rocks lining it, there wouldn't ever have been anything to get to be "the old place" someday.

It isn't anything like premonition. No matter how old you get to be, you never believe *you*'ll die; but still it's the last thing a lot of them do, as if there was some hope of life eternal for them to hold to when the choking leaves are cleared away and the water bubbles up as clear as it ever did from the sandy bottom.

Then, in a week or two, you hear they've died. Barney had known five or six cases like that so when he got thinking about that night with Joe, he figured they'd gone out to find him his spring.

For Joe the Army took everything there was. For Barney it took only four years. They hadn't been a total loss. He got around. He didn't see much of the States, but he saw some foreign countries. He saw enough of the tropics to know he didn't want to live anywhere near them again. As for the gooks, you could put them all in a sack if you wanted to bother. They were *really* backward, and filthy! As far as he could see, they'd never even heard of a backhouse, let alone a real toilet. Right in the street, that was good enough for them. After all they'd seen of civilized people during the First War—or the Second War or whatever the hell War you wanted to call it, the First for him—it hadn't done them any good.

Germany wasn't bad. And Japan he really liked. The American soldiers could get anything they wanted there and those Japanese girls were like toy dolls, some of them. Not the ones you saw on the streets trying to dress like any steno from Forty-fifth Street; but the ones you had to hunt for. He came close to bringing one home with him but she got scared at the last minute at the idea of all those miles and all those strangers waiting for her across them.

Funny, the things that came back to you just riding along like that, not trying to remember anything, but letting whatever there was come to the top the way leaves float on a brook.

Barney hadn't thought about that little Japanese girl for nearly a year now and there'd been a time when he couldn't think about anyone else.

There was another time when he couldn't think about anything except how god-damn good it was going to be to get home and be with Sam and Jude and Cliff and settle down and know he'd be there as long as he wanted to, not just until some old kooter loaded with gold braid looked at the toy soldier named Barney Cousins and thought: You'd better be sent somewhere else.

That lasted one week. One week, and he'd been ready to go again. Funny. He hadn't been able to sit still. All that go to work; get a job; settle down; you're a man grown. It was exactly what he'd been telling himself and looking forward to doing, until the time came to do it and he found he had to up and go.

He was on his way all right, and he could have got there fast if he'd only known where it was he wanted to go. He had the world on a string and the string in his hand and it seemed to him you couldn't be content with what you had for sure, you wanted different skies, or something.

A Maine man had to see California skies, or New York skies, or Minnesota skies, before he was reasonably satisfied with his own, and even then he was always remembering the others, homesick for a blue he'd conjured up out of time and memory and that never was over the earth. This country was too damned big. You knew there was too much of it you hadn't been to that might be different —not better, nor worse—just different. And then you had to go and see or be forever half sick with something you couldn't name and you knew god-damned well you wouldn't find, even if you got where you were going; but you kept going in case it might be down the road a piece.

You wanted to see the places with the names that always pulled at you—and then they turned out to be nothing more than another wide place in the road because the people who named them and meant something by it were gone, and the names weren't anything but a familiar sound to the new ones.

Barney'd heard about a place in the Carolina mountains once and he always wondered what it was like. High Lonesome, it was, and he even looked it up in the postal guide and it wasn't there. So he never even thought to try and find it in case it might not be a place at all.

This wasn't a country for a man to own, or to own him. He could have a claim on one little corner of it, or it on him, which-ever way it worked. But there was too much. You might think it was all tamed and the trees cut and the wild feet that made the tracks through the old forest gone for good. But no foot ever stepped on a square inch of American ground that didn't leave a ghost or a seed or some such thing to grow and live again, either in itself or whatever came next to sense it and leave its own ghost or seed. Memory? No. Stronger than that. Something, in some places, as strong as a hand at your jugular; but never a personal hand at your personal jugular—just you happened to be there and it did, and that's all.

It was a country unhappy with its ghosts—too big, too new— ghosts need old and little places because they can't fill up forever, not and be peaceful about their haunting. Ghosts here were rest-less like the people that went hunting them.

Barney headed down East first, thinking: Maybe Canada. It was fun, jogging along the coast, seeing the towns he hadn't bothered to look at before, with summer on him and money in his pocket and nothing he really had to do. It was a good way to begin.

He was looking around for something else too, and he didn't know, for a week in late July, but what he'd found it.

There was a girl working in a diner in Lubec who looked pretty good to him. He got talking with her the first night he hit town. That night it was only talk, but the encouraging kind, and good enough to make him decide to stay a while to see if he'd been right or wrong.

He found himself an attic room, cheap and not much to look at. He had to bend double to get in through the door, but he could straighten up, once inside. The house was run by an old girl who was really a character. Talk! Words poured out of her the way water does out of a tap and all the time she'd be chewing as if she'd been interrupted in the middle of a perpetual meal and she couldn't take time out to swallow for fear Barney would get away from her before she said whatever it was.

She used to follow him up three flights of stairs, talking steadily, and all the time she'd be pushing at the wig that looked exactly like a fish-hawk's nest and didn't quite touch at the back of her neck. She used to hang onto it and push at it the way a lot of women keep jabbing at a hat that doesn't feel comfortable.

The morning after he settled in, Barney went out and walked right into a job at the factory. Their general handy man had gone on a bat three days before when he got his paycheck and they were tired of waiting for him to get over it. Barney had some experience at it, working summers in the factory at Port Kezar, and he could make a pretty good show of knowing what to do without having anyone lead him around by the hand.

He was there for four days before he could even get that girl to go out with him. He began to think he'd lost his touch, but on the fifth night she let him take her to the movies. And she spent a whole hour afterward, sitting in the car beside him saying in one way or another: Oh, dear, I don't know what my boyfriend'll say if he hears I went out with you!

That was pretty discouraging, but Barney thought he could wear her down before too long. He might have, too, but he got into a little trouble.

Part of his job was to haul the barrels of mash down to the big room where they made fertilizer and where the fishermen came to get cuttings for bait. He worked out quite a system. The cart he used was heavy two-inch lumber with flat iron wheels, and the barrels made it heavier and there was just enough slant to the floor to give it momentum. He'd get the cart going at a good clip and once it really started there wasn't any stopping it. Then he'd jump aboard and ride with it.

The damn thing would go roaring down the long cartoning room, through the door, make a wide turn, and come up against the bin with a crash loud enough to wake the dead. God only knew what would have happened to anyone who got in its way—mincemeat, probably.

The first time he did it to get a rise out of Hacky Webster. Hacky tended the mash and it wasn't hard work. He was too old to do much and it looked to Barney as if they'd put a chair there and said to Hacky: You sit down and go to work.

He was sitting there when Barney made the turn and came up against the thick planks the first time, and he came up out of his chair like a flock of hens off the roost. He let out a screech, it was hard to tell whether it was an old man or an old woman.

"You damn fool, if you don't look out you'll knock the living hell right out of that bin. Now—you do it again and I'll tell the boss."

"Go ahead," Barney said. "Go ahead. Go ahead and tell him! Why don't you do better than that? You have old Ped right down here the next time I'm passing through and I'll give you both a ride. Do you good to stop polishing that chair with the seat of your pants and get a little change of scene."

"I *will* tell him, by god! I'll tell him he's hired him a crazy man!"

Barney knew he wouldn't. Hacky was already feeling behind him for the arms of the chair so he could lower himself back down into it slow and easy, the way an old man sits down when he intends to get settled on the first sit and stay there.

Barney had all he could do to keep from laughing out loud, seeing Hacky sitting there hanging onto that chair, with his old wattles red as a turkey cock's and breathing hard through his nose, every bit as mad as if he were young enough to do something about it.

By the lord, Barney thought, it's the old men who really get the gravy handed to them in a bucket, when they're too far gone to either need or want it, while us young ones who could really get some good of it have to scrape it up off the floor with a sieve.

He could see to it, though, that Hacky's soft snap was a little more interesting, as long as he stayed around. He didn't want Hacky to get expecting it, so he didn't ride the cart too much. Just often enough to keep Hacky coming and not let him get there. The first trip he made that morning he rode her, and either Hacky had guessed right or it was pure bull luck; but when Barney came through the door, the old Wabash Cannonball in person, there was Ped standing right beside the bin. Barney was too surprised to make the turn and when he came to and grabbed the handle, it was too late.

The juggernaut shot out through the open door onto the head of the wharf with no turn to slow it, and came up against the heavy balk with a jolt that shook Barney's teeth. The bed of the cart was good and greasy with slopping oil and mash. When the flat wheels hit eighteen inches of solid timber, the cart stopped, but the two barrels kept right on going and so did Barney.

There wasn't time then, but afterward he got cold chills thinking what would have happened if there'd been a boat tied up to the head of that wharf. Christ, he'd have broken his neck! As it was, he hit the water flat just behind the barrels and knocked his wind out. He felt as if he was under forever in a sort of cloudy green milk with pieces of cooked herring swirling around in it and that god-awful feeling you have at night sometimes when you dream about drowning—about being under water forever and your lungs begin to crack with trying not to breathe and finally you can't stand it another minute and gulp in a great mouthful of what you know in the dream will be water. But it turns out not to be, it's air, and the relief is always enough to bring you awake sweating.

This time he wasn't dreaming and it was water and he thought to god he'd go down till he hit China. When he did come up there was something that felt like a baseball in his chest and nothing would go by it but a little trickle of air, enough to let him give a whooping gasp for more. He nearly sank again—and he would have. He would have drowned right there before he yelled for help at the two balloon faces staring over the edge of the wharf. For a minute he thought he was going to. Then he got down the first full breath and found he could swim. The *Polly Doodle* was tied up alongside the tower where she'd been unloading that morning and her stern line was the only thing that saved him.

He got both hands around it and hung there still whooping, hearing that noise as if he hadn't been making it himself. Twenty feet above his head Hacky let out a high thin hoot of laughter.

"Well, Barney Oldfield," he yelled. "When you going to start racing again?"

Barney was red-eyed mad when he started up the rope. He didn't even remember coming up over the wharf head. But he scrabbled up there somehow, and at the sight of his face Hacky stopped laughing as if it had been cut off with a razor, turned around, and began to run, his bony old elbows pumping, his knees nearly hitting his chin.

Barney climbed his back the way he'd have climbed a tree, knocked him down and was pounding his head against the planking as hard as he could and intending to do as much damage as he could, when somebody got him around the neck and hauled him off balance, backward. He really saw stars and Hacky lay whimpering and motionless.

"All right!" Ped said. "That's it!"

"Well, keep that old bastard off my neck," Barney shouted, feeling as strangled as he sounded. "Look what he did to me!"

"Did to *you*, hell! What kind of a damn outlaw are you, anyway, beating up an old man couldn't kill a fly with a baseball bat," Ped said. "You get out of here. You're through. I've lost enough out of your damn foolishness this morning without having a murder on my hands, too. Get up to the office and get your pay."

"I'll do that. And you know where you can stuff your factory!"

"I know I'll have more of it left to do it with, once you're gone. And you better step on it too, before I get mad enough to swear out a paper for you. My god!" He shook his head unbelievingly. "I thought I was getting a damn good hand when I got you. And look at you! What ails you, anyway? Your brother's a good man. If it wasn't for him, I *would* slap you in jail."

Barney didn't wait to hear any more after that. He went up to the office and got his pay, and thinking: Well, the hell with everything! started back down the coast again, retracing his steps through the lost, neon-lit towns. It was clear he couldn't lose Sam just by going away from where he was, because wherever he would go along this coast, Sam had been there before him.

It was in a truck stop on Route One, two nights later, that Barney met Sabra. He was nearly back to Port Kezar, only about fifty miles to go, and wasn't hurrying. When he came to the all-night stand where the sign said Eat, he stopped.

Sometimes it seemed to Barney you built your life on the mistakes other people had made. A man gets an idea in his head—god knows where from—but he gets it. Then he tries it out and finds out he's wrong. But something happens to him and he can't admit he's wrong. He has to feel that the idea was all right and it was just luck it didn't work out that way for him. So he goes around telling everybody about the idea and not about the proof. He forgets what he wants to.

The funniest part about it is how you go on believing what he's told you even after you disprove it for yourself, like that bull about the truckers always knowing the places along the road where the food's good. Barney had had better food in an automat. Some of those roadside joints were nothing but ulcer factories. But he'd read something in a magazine once about ideas making grooves on your brain if you hung onto them and once the groove was there, it worked like a railroad track.

This didn't look like much of a place and he stopped only because he saw a couple of big trailer trucks hauled off to the side with their parking lights on and their motors running.

There was a sick green light over the parking space, flashing off and on, from the neon sign that kept screaming Beer on Draft, and every time the sign flashed on the stars went out.

Inside, the room was long with a low ceiling and not many lights and a row of booths down the left-hand side. He wasn't going to sit there, it took too long to get waited on this time of night when the girls were tired and didn't give a damn whether you ate or not. If you were sitting up at the counter staring at them, they had to make a move of some kind.

The jukebox was going steady rip and so loud it was hard to tell what the song was. The air was coiling with smoke from the grill and all day's cigarettes. He couldn't see too much so he went over to the counter and sat down until he could make out a few landmarks.

There was a sour beer smell under the general stink that made him change his mind about having a beer himself. When he finally located the counter girl through the fog, she was way down at the other end and the minute he looked at her he knew she'd been behind that counter all day and was just waiting out the time till she could close up shop.

All day? She looked as if she'd been there all her life! She must have been about thirty-five and she had hair the color of a new penny, in streaks—in streaks, darker. It didn't look like anything as fine as hair, but as if it had melted and run together. She kept putting one hand under it where it was long in back and flipping it out over her collar. All the time he was sitting there, she kept at that hair with one hand or the other, flip, flip, flip.

She came down toward him walking with a hip-sprung, spavined lurch that made him wonder if she was even bending her feet or just picking them up and laying them down solidly like two blocks of wood, and made a pass at the plastic counter top with a wet cloth. When Barney looked down there was a trail of water drops following after the cloth and she hadn't even damaged the puddle of coffee the guy had spilled who'd been sitting there before him.

Barney pointed at it.

"What's the matter?" She gave him a hard-looking eye. "You particular?"

She made another sweep with the cloth and this time spread the coffee around and it wasn't so easy to see.

"Your sign didn't say anything about a swimming pool," Barney said. "I forgot my bathing trunks."

"Don't blame it on me." She was looking over the top of his head when she yawned. "*I* don't own the joint. What'll it be?"

"What you got?"

"Well, if you want steak and champagne, you're out of luck."

"Hamburger and coffee beyond your reach?"

"I'll go see if we're all out of horsemeat."

That was a big joke and she was laughing at it, but without making any noise, when she thudded away and slapped a hamburger on the greased surface of the grill. When she came back, she looked at him as if she'd never seen him before, and set the coffee and hamburger down about a foot to the right of where he was sitting. Sometimes you ran up against people like that and maybe they've got plenty of reason for being that way—she looked as if she had—and Barney wished he could leave it alone; but it always raised his hackles.

"Gosh," he said, making it really admiring. He reached out and retrieved the coffee. "You must be a big drawing card here. Customer relations and stuff like that. You're wasting all that talent. And a sense of humor on top of it."

"I know it." She gaped at him again. "All the B.T.O.'s come in here and tell me I ought to be on the television."

"Can't think what's stopping you."

She got tired of it all of a sudden.

"Sonny, I ain't got the time to tell you. Come around in another fifty years."

He watched her walk away again, hair going flip, feet hitting flat. She stopped halfway up the counter and said something to a big guy sitting there over a glass of beer that had been in front of him so long it didn't have a bubble left. Out of the corner of his eye, Barney could see him lean his head a little to listen to her. Then they both looked down the counter. He was a big meaty guy with a face like a skun side of beef and there was a bulge around his waist just above the belt where the soft fat rolled out over.

Barney could have taken him all right; but he wasn't looking for it tonight, so he didn't hand back the danger signals that were being passed around on a platter. He picked up the hamburger, started to take a bite, staring aimlessly into the cloudy mirror behind the counter, and saw Sabra.

She was sitting alone in the last booth at the back but there were two glasses on the table. She was drawing lines on the plastic surface with the wet bottom of the glass, but Barney had that second-sense feeling you have sometimes when you look at somebody and know they were looking too, until the second before.

She had a narrow, handsome—not pretty, handsome—dark face and she was sitting absolutely still except for that slow movement of her hand holding the glass. Too still. Looking down.

One morning just at sunrise, Barney had seen a volcano. He hadn't ever seen one before, but he knew what it was. It didn't look black the way he'd thought one would. The sides of it, going up smooth and straight, were almost pink in the new sunlight. It looked shining and high and peaceful. But it was a volcano and he couldn't get out of his head what it could do if it had a mind to.

While he was still staring at Sabra, she got up and there was none of that flopping women usually go through getting out of one of those booths, no pulling at the skirt, or smoothing down this or that that's come loose. She got up and came across to the counter and she didn't lift her head until she was standing behind his shoulder. Then she looked up, not at him even then, but at him in the mirror. He'd been right on both counts, the volcano first, and she *had* been looking at him before.

She was tall, and the rest of her, now he had a chance to get a look at it, matched the face. She really had it, whatever it was, and she knew it, too; but she wasn't making a fuss about it because she didn't have to.

With some people, the first time you ever see them there's a spark like when you take the plug out and hold the wire down against the block to find out if it's alive and the spark jumps. And you know this is going to be one of the people you're going to have to see if you can't do something about, because it's alive and the spark jumps. It's not love, love, love. Hell, it could happen with a man. Only when it *does* happen with a man you know you're going to have a fight with him. It's like men can't figure it out and it's something to fight about and it's usually a hell of a fine fight too, and one of you gets carried out. When it happens with a woman, though, you're really up in the air and you don't know which way the cat's going to jump; but you can feel yourself gathering to get ready to jump with it.

"Look," she said and she was still holding Barney's eyes in the glass so he didn't have to turn his head to look at her, and he found himself trying to think what her voice was like and not being able to. It was just her voice and he had never heard one like it before. "You look like a decent guy. Would you be willing to help me out a little?"

"That depends," he said.

The counter girl was already watching with one corner of her mouth drawn up.

"Oh, it's easy enough. I won't get you into any trouble. Have you got a car?"

Barney nodded.

"Well, I'm stuck here with a fellow who's trying to get mean. I want to get out of this place and I haven't any way to do it. You could take me down the road a piece and let me out—if you wanted to. You wouldn't have to take me home."

He thought suddenly of whatever it was he'd been hunting for that was just down the road a piece. He was still watching her and she hadn't dropped her eyes. He'd thought at first she was only a kid and too young to be fooling around in a beer joint at this hour of the night. But she wasn't all that young. If anything, she was a year or two older than he was. It was hard to tell. That voice wasn't a kid's voice.

"Hurry and make up your mind," she said. "I can't be standing here talking to you when he comes back."

"Okay." Barney said what he'd known he would say. "Go on out. I'll pay my check and be right along."

He watched her reflection turn and grow smaller down the dark tunnel of the room. She reached the door and went out and it didn't make any noise closing behind her. He jerked his head at the counter girl who wasn't attempting to hide her interest by this time, but she came slowly. When she took the dollar he held out to her, she gave him a wise look.

"You got asbestos fingers, sonny? You're going to need them!"

"I sure as hell didn't need them to hold that cup of coffee."

He scooped his change off the clinging rubber mat where she'd tossed it and held out a quarter to her. Before she could stop herself, her hand came up to take it.

"Here, for your pains," Barney said. "For christ sake, buy some aspirin!"

And that was the way it began.

Or did it? Come to think of it, Barney didn't know how anyone could ever put his finger on a thing that happened and say: This is where the end began. If you could, you'd know what the end would be, and you didn't. Was there ever a place that was really the beginning and, if it existed, was there any way to change it? Or was it just an incidental and little thing that might have turned out not to matter; but did matter because it was the beginning?

If there really was ever a beginning to anything, would it have been his beginning, or hers, or one that went way back to some old guy neither one of them ever knew or heard of?

Be nice if people could be like apple trees you can look at in the spring before the leaves come out, twiggy and barren, and pick out the fruitwood spur that in October will hold the result, good or bad. And if you don't want the fruit right there all you have to do is cut off the god-damned branch.

Maybe that was asking too much. What he was really asking for was a pilothouse like a ship with a little bell to ring whenever it was time to change course. But he knew, unless he wanted to, when the bell rang, he'd bull it right ahead and think: To hell with it! Whatever's in the way, I'll run it down.

The fate boys had something—the beginning was too far back to bother with and the end too far away to see—so you might as well simmer down, because the course between the two was an appointed one and you couldn't do a damn thing to change it and no little bell was going to ring for you.

It certainly didn't ring for Barney, not that way, when he came out of the juke joint and Sabra was waiting for him. She was walking away in the general direction of the car and he was glad of it.

He didn't want to see what that sick green flash of neon would do to her face, for fear it might put it out the way it had the stars.

The taste of bad coffee was still in the back of his throat, a taste like ether smells.

He got Sabra into the car, somehow without looking at her, and swung out of the parking space. He felt funny in a way hard to explain, but as if he had a kind of extra hearing. He could hear things he never noticed before. Maybe that was it, more noticing, and he'd been hearing them all along.

He heard a little ping in the engine that was new to him. He heard the gravel pop under the tires and he'd never listened to that before. When he slowed for the turn into the main road, he heard wind stirring the leaves in the big old maple that had a stop-and-eat sign nailed to its trunk. It sounded nice.

When he finally got straightened away, headed south, he heard her draw in her breath as if she'd been going to say something and had changed her mind.

"What?" Barney looked across at her then for the first time and was surprised and disappointed to find he couldn't make out anything but a kind of shadow there in the seat beside him.

"I was just going to say, you can let me out as soon as we're out of sight of that place."

"Well, that's kind of foolish. If we're both going in the same direction, you might's well ride along as far as you want to. Where you bound, anyhow? You have to live somewhere."

"Port Kezar."

"Oh," he said.

"Why 'oh'?"

"That's where I'm headed, too."

"Why?"

"Why!" He began to feel like an echo. "I live there."

"*I* haven't ever seen you before." The tone of her voice was calling him a liar.

"I been away for a while," Barney said. "I was born and brought up in Port Kezar. And, come right down to it, I've never seen *you* before either. How come? What's your name?"

Suddenly he wanted to know all kinds of little things about her. What her name was, first, because that's the important thing of all. Once you had a name for anything, it got ready to have identity built on it, like a house on a foundation.

"I *wasn't* born there. I haven't lived there all my life. I'm not going to, either. Just until—well—" She stopped and Barney could sense her trying to figure out until what.

If she had been twenty years older and another generation, she would have said "until my ship comes in." But she wasn't and she knew, along with him and the rest of them, that the ship they all waited for had never left the other shore; there wasn't even a loading order for her—her keel was never laid.

"You didn't say what it was," Barney said. "Your name."

"Sabra Baxter. What's yours?"

"Sabra." He tried it over once, out loud. "That's a new one."

It pleased Barney to find that her name was one he had never heard before. It made him think that what was happening to him might never have happened before either.

"Sabra," he said again.

She made an amused sound through her nose.

"Yes. Sabra. You pronounce it right. Would you like to try the sixty-four-dollar question?"

"There's an answer for that, too," he said. "But I'm not ready to tell you what it is. I just never heard that name before."

"I'm used to it, but it usually affects other people the way it did you. Don't ask me what it means, either, or where it came from. I don't know. I don't know where people pick up the names they give their kids sometimes. Maybe my mother read a book."

"I like it."

"I'm so glad." Barney thought she was going to laugh again, but she didn't. Instead, she said, "Now we've had me, how about you?"

"Oh. Well. My name's Barney Cousins." It always made him feel a little silly to have to say his own name aloud.

Now it was her turn. She said, "Oh," in just about the same way he'd said it when she told him where she was going.

So he said, "Why 'oh'?" the way she had.

"Nothing. Only now I believe you live there."

"And didn't believe it before?"

"I thought you were kidding so you could drive me home."

"Now you know better. I probably would have thought of it, though." He put two and two together. "What've you ever heard about me?"

"Nothing," she said again, stubbornly, and he could see whatever it was he wasn't going to find out about it tonight.

"Well, just tell me whether you liked it or not."

"I'll wait till I know you better."

"I'll take that," Barney said. "As long as you plan to know me better."

"I can't very well help but know you about five minutes better —if I want to get home tonight. We're almost there."

They were, too, and he didn't know how they'd got there. It seemed to him they'd just pulled away from the diner a few minutes ago and this was the god-damndest unsatisfactory conversation he'd ever got into. And now there wasn't going to be time tonight to take it any further and there was a lot more he wanted to know.

"What's your father's name? Where do you live? What does he do for a living? What is he?"

"Arthur Kenney. In the old Barlow house. He's a lay preacher."

She'd answered him just the way he'd asked, but the answers left him swirling. He said the important thing first, the one that had really hit.

"Kenney!" he said. And then, "Preacher!"

"You asked me."

"I know! I know! But *Kenney*. You said your name was Baxter."

"It is."

"Adopted?" It sounded foolish, even to him.

"Occasionally people marry."

"Oh."

"And sometimes get divorced."

"Jesus Christ!" Barney said. "Why didn't you say so?"

"I didn't think it mattered."

"Well, it must have, I guess. Now that's settled, let's get back to this preaching."

"I said 'lay preacher.' He's an old man and he's about the only one left who ever thought he was. Except my mother. To eat, he works at the factory."

"Oh."

"For the love of god," she said hotly, and it was like an explosion right there in the seat. "What is this, anyway? A trial or something? Who the hell are you to sit there asking me questions like a machine, and then when I answer them all you say is 'oh.' "

"Don't get mad. It seems I have to know everything there is to know about you."

"You've got a hell of a long way to go."

"I know," he said. "That's why I was in such a hurry. I wanted to get there as soon as I could."

She didn't make any answer to that and he hadn't really expected her to. It was one of the things you say to get it on the record and you don't need, nor want, words back.

"You can stop here," she said. "I get out here."

So Barney stopped the car and sat there waiting, because that wasn't all and he knew it wasn't for her as well as he did for himself. He could hear her moving around, but she wasn't opening the door. He could smell her and it was like coming into the kitchen one morning when Jude was ironing clothes that had been out on the line all night in the fresh wind.

Then he could see her silhouette and she was kneeling on the seat facing him. He put out his hands and found her wrists and pulled her against him hard. For a second every bone in his body felt as if it had grown an inch longer and then he didn't feel anything. There was a minute taken right out of time, and afterward the minute when there wasn't anything was the one you remembered against the minute when there was everything.

A minute only, before she was right there and all there and so was he. Barney couldn't see a thing but he knew what he was looking at. He didn't say anything because there was nothing that needed saying. He found he was still holding her wrists so tightly his own fingers hurt. She made a sound like a laugh or a sigh but actually neither. She was going to say something and he wanted to stop her for fear of what it might be. She surprised him. She said his name.

"Barney Cousins?" It was a question that sounded like every question every woman in the world had ever asked every man.

"Right here," he said. His voice wasn't his. It sounded queer, way back in his throat, and he couldn't seem to get it up where it belonged. "All here."

"That was a short cut, wasn't it."

"Depends," he said. "On where you're going."

Barney was the one who didn't say the right thing. That wasn't the answer and she hauled off and hit him, not with her hand flat the way a woman does, but with her fist and to hurt. She got him under the left eye and he saw stars spattering the dark. Women had hit him before with a lot more reason, and he'd been mad enough to kill them. He wasn't mad at Sabra. She could have done it again and he'd have sat there and taken it and laughed.

"I hope that hurt a lot," she said.

"Well, it did."

"Where? Where?" As fast as she'd lost her temper, she went the other way. Barney could feel her lips against his face, looking for the bruise. He winced when she found it, and felt something else too. She was *crying.*

"My *god,*" he said. "Look. Look. Don't waste all that. Here. Let me—"

"It's cold here." She twisted away and opened the door. "Come in the house."

"In the *house.*" That really startled him. "But what about your folks? Besides—I want—"

"Yes, I know," she said. "It's all right. I'll worry when it's necessary. It's not now."

Barney got out feeling twice as heavy as he was. He knew where each of his bones was and what it was doing because he was telling each separate one what to do.

They went in the back door, into what must have been the kitchen. It was too dark to be sure; but there was a kind of kitchen-stove warmth that made him realize it *had* been cold outside. They went quietly up the back stairs, but not so quietly as he'd thought they'd have to and that was better too.

It was funny to go into a strange house where strangers are sleeping around you like that—you know they're there, but they don't know you are. That night he didn't know how many strangers, either. Halfway up the stairs he got thinking about the old man who, alone, thought he was a preacher. Barney even decided how he'd look if he appeared to them now: tall and skinny and righteous, with thin shanks showing below his nightshirt and some kind of a light, maybe even a candle, held over his head.

Sabra opened a door and shut it again with them on the other side, and turned around and Barney forgot everything else in the world because it simply didn't matter.

Love is a good enough word to cover most of the situations you need it for. It's the word everyone uses. But that's just it. Everyone *has* used it—too often. It comes out as easily as any other word. He never once used it to Sabra and she didn't ask for it, because the word they both wanted should have meant something new. It should have been one word to mean a closed door with the whole world on one side and them on the other, and there wasn't any such word.

It was early, before sunrise, because outside the window everything looked under water, the way it does before sun and true daylight begin to add another dimension to things as flat as the paper cutouts kids make at school and paste on the windows. Inside, the room seemed to be filled with a gray light like fog and all Barney could make out were a few shadowy things that might have been furniture, or might have been things that had been there once but weren't any longer, and he could have reached out and put his hand right through any one of them.

All of a sudden, though, the dream lost reality and he knew where he was and sat up as if somebody had let off a shotgun outside the window. He looked at Sabra to be sure she was there, and while he was still looking she opened her eyes and Barney saw that for her there was sleeping and there was waking, each one clear-cut and with no hangover from one to the other. She was as wide-awake as if she'd never been to sleep at all.

"Good morning," she said.

"Hey," Barney said. "It *is* morning."

"Yes, I know. Only natural."

"Hadn't I better clear out then, before everyone gets up?"

He didn't want that imaginary shotgun to turn into a real one, not by a damn sight.

"Too late."

"What?"

"Father's up already," she said; but she didn't look worried.

"How d'you know?" What he really wanted to say was: What in hell should I do?

"I can smell coffee. Go down and bring me up some."

Barney opened his mouth, once more back in the middle of the same astonishment he'd felt the night before; but there didn't seem to be anything to say. So he got up, hauled on his trousers and went over to open the door and stand for a minute listening. There wasn't so much as a whisper of sound anywhere in that house. It made him feel as if he was the only sane one left in a world full of crazy people. But he could smell coffee, too, out here. So he thought: Well, maybe I'*m* the crazy one. Maybe everything's supposed to be backward anyhow.

He was standing at the head of the stairs they'd come up last night, and they were the steep back stairs you find in old houses where the fellow who built the house didn't think to allow room at the bottom for anyone to stand, so you had to open the door from the last inside step and the next one was right out into the room.

Barney got that far and stood with his hand on the thumb latch listening again, and the room on the other side listened back. That was the quiet he'd sensed before and hadn't recognized. The house was listening to him. That was enough to make anyone nervous; but he couldn't very well turn around and go back up the stairs again. There was no way out in that direction. He even had the feeling that Sabra was listening too, to see what he was going to do next.

He opened the door and stepped down into the room and he'd been right. It was the kitchen. There was a big square extension table in the center of the floor and the stuff they needed for each meal stood in the middle of it—sugar, salt, pepper—and alongside that, folded neatly, the thin cloth that covered it between meals. It had been a long time, not since he was a kid growing up, he'd been in a house where they did that, and seeing it made him feel like a kid again.

He was standing beside the stove—one of those big old black Wood & Bishops with the nickel trimming around it and the big warming oven on top and all the fancy curlecues of ironwork running up the sides. There was a fire going in it that would have fried a boot sole.

All along one side of the room was a sideboard with a sink in the center, black iron sink, and dish cupboards above it. The only light inside came from a kerosene lamp burning in a bracket over the sink and it wasn't much light.

When he'd taken all that in, Barney looked at what he'd been trying to pretend wasn't there. Under the east windows, where the daylight was growing fast, there was a big horsehair sofa. It was a good eight feet long and the head of it went up like the back of a wave, so you could lie down on it and not have to use a pillow.

But the old man wasn't lying down.

People are never the way you picture them and Barney wasn't surprised to find the old man so different, small, with a dry powdery skin that looked as if it would rustle when he moved. He had a clean-shaven, tight face like a bad-tempered snapping turtle. He looked as if he might be going to burst right there and splatter. But Barney found out later, Arthur always looked as if he might burst.

He had been putting on his shoes when he'd heard them beginning to move around overhead. He was halfway through with it. At least Barney thought he was putting on his shoes. One was on. The other dangled from his hand and the hand dangled from a wrist propped across his knee that wasn't any more than a bone covered with skin and cloth.

Arthur didn't say a word. He leaned forward and put the shoe down on the floor in front of him, not making a sound, not even the rustle. There it sat, one of those old, high, laced, black shoes with the elastic sides, all laced. Barney's stomach lurched when he glanced at it because it was a lot more than a shoe. He looked at Arthur again, and this time saw the straps and buckles coming out of the pants leg where there should have been an ankle and wasn't. Arthur had been putting on his whole foot.

It felt to Barney as if all this was going on in slow motion and taking forever, and the old man never once took those two little shining eyes—shining like a cat's so you couldn't even make a guess at what color they were—away from him. It wasn't more than a minute, but a minute can seem like a long time and that one did.

Well, Barney thought, you old devil, I can keep it up as long as you can.

When Arthur spoke, his voice at least sounded the way it should, like a rusty hinge that didn't squeal but just grated.

"Children," he said, but he was still watching Barney. "This is your new uncle."

Barney didn't take in what he said, too surprised to find the two kids in the opposite doorway, staring too. He began to feel like the prize exhibit at the circus. All those eyes! He hadn't heard the children come, but there they were. Maybe seven and four. They had on the nightshirts kids wear that look like long johns, only with feet in them.

And the funny part of it was that Barney had seen them before this morning. He'd only been home a week; but every time he'd gone out on the road he'd seen those two kids, the girl hauling a rough, homemade wagon with the little boy in it. And always in a hurry.

He'd even asked Jude about them, who they were.

"I don't know their names," she'd said. "A couple of youngsters from the factory camps, I guess. Everyone calls them the road runners."

"Where the hell're they *going*?" Even to Barney's casual attention they had been going somewhere, in a hurry and with intent.

Jude shrugged.

"Nowhere. Funny. Poor little mites. They always make me think of Peter Rugg and his thunderstorm. You know: Which way to Boston?"

The baby boy was beautiful. Blond and handsome, his pink and white skin shone as if he carried an incandescent light inside the big nodding head that bloomed like a chrysanthemum over the top of the handcart where he sat staring at anything that captured his vagrant attention.

But his sister's entire face was composed of angles and points, ageless and ugly, like a gargoyle. She walked always in the same way, her shoulders thrust bonily forward against the heavy pull of the cart, her head down and turned a little away from the passing traffic, as if she was thoroughly aware of her brother's shining beauty and the clear contrast between them.

The girl, Barney thought, seeing her closely for the first time, was the ugliest kid he had ever set eyes on. But the boy was another matter. It was awful to see them together like that—her being as homely as a stump fence and that little boy looking like an angel right out of the pictures, until you took a closer look. Because he wasn't right.

He was leaning against the door frame as if it was hard for him to stand up and his head looked too big for his body. It kept moving. Not merely a tremor, but he'd give it a real shake and then push his chin as far forward as he could. Then he'd haul it back and the whole process would start over again and it was obviously something he couldn't help.

Barney could feel his own head beginning to do it too, with no help from him.

"What's the matter with his eye?" the girl said and her voice was a feminine echo of the old man's.

"Nothing that won't be again."

"What's his name?" She hadn't once stopped looking at Barney either, but she was still talking to the old man. Both of them watching Barney and talking to each other as if he'd been deaf and dumb.

"That—" Arthur said, "is something you'll have to ask him."

He took up the shoe with the foot in it and began to strap it on. The boy got down on his hands and knees, crawled across the floor, and started picking at the buckles. Arthur slapped his hand and the kid sat back astonished and made the first decent sound Barney had heard that morning. He let out a roar that nearly lifted the lamp out of the bracket, and the roar kept right on once it started.

The minute the yelling began, Barney heard Sabra coming down the stairs behind him. They all knew apparently what he didn't, that the sound would go on until she stopped it. She didn't look at any of them—went straight to the little boy and down on her knees beside him. She was making a funny humming sound and she took his limp hand and laid it against her throat where the sound was coming from. Barney didn't know either, until later, that was the only way she could get through to the kid when he started screaming. He couldn't hear anything through all the racket he was making himself—he had to feel it—and he could feel the sound in her throat that must have come to mean safety to him, because he stopped yelling.

"What did you do to him?" Sabra looked accusingly at the old man, who was going on about his business as if nothing had happened.

"Nothing."

"He doesn't yell like that for nothing."

"Nothing," Arthur said again.

After the noise was gone, the little girl, still looking at Barney and this time talking to him, said:

"Uncle what?"

"Barney," he said. "I guess."

By that time he wasn't even sure of his name. He was beginning to think there were all sorts of short cuts you could take to knowing people; but you sure as hell missed a lot of the high spots on the way and when you had to go back and check on them, they were kind of surprising. Watching her back curved protectingly over the little boy, Barney was wondering what else he might have missed.

In a minute or two the boy stopped hiccuping and began to play around on the floor and the moment he stopped Sabra appeared to lose all interest in him and her attention came completely back to Barney again. She hadn't even given the girl a glance that he could see. And as for her father, after the first question, he might not have been in the kitchen at all.

"Coffee," she said firmly. She went over to the cupboard and took down a couple of cups and saucers. They looked like the dishes that used to come in packages of rolled oats, but there wasn't one of the four that matched another.

Arthur got up from the sofa and moved, a side and a half to a time, over to the little boy and picked him up, making him walk with his hands under the kid's armpits. Shooing the girl before him, he herded them both into another room and shut the door. He himself turned, without another word, crossed the kitchen to the shed door and went out, closing the door with careful quiet behind him.

When the sound of his steps faded, Sabra put the cups on the table and poured the coffee.

"Here," she said. "We might as well have it here, now *he's* gone."

Barney, feeling as if he'd been hit over the head with a feather pillow, sat down at the table opposite her and drank his coffee and that was all there was to it. He didn't know what he'd been expecting; but certainly something louder than that. And what happened was like walking into a mess of cobwebs across a path in the woods.

There were so many things he had to ask her about he didn't know which one to start on. It was all so damned crazy—and crazier when he looked at her face and saw that, for her, it was simply the beginning of another day, no crazier nor any less crazy than any other day. She smiled at him then, and the smile closed the door that made everything all right again.

"Come again, Barney," she said softly, but he had been going to before she issued the invitation.

Barney and Sam Cousins had lived together off and on for a long time, for twenty-two years. They say, if anything is too familiar you don't really know it, but it didn't work that way, because Barney knew Sam. He was the first to admit that Sam was a good man and mean exactly what other people meant when they said "good man." Sam could be depended upon to do what people expected him to. The unexpected surprised people and they didn't like surprises and with Sam—they could depend on it—there wouldn't be any.

Barney had watched him, trying to figure how in god's name they could be brothers; but it was never quite brothers because Sam was so much older. He seemed to think that gave him the advantage and maybe it would have if Barney had thought so too.

Being older, for one thing, made Sam think he could do things for Barney the way a father would for a son. The kind of things nobody would ever think of asking anyone else to do for him, Sam just went ahead and did before anyone knew what he had in mind.

Routine was the big thing with Sam. When he got up in the morning he wanted to find everything exactly where he'd left it the night before, and if it wasn't there it wasn't because he didn't leave it there. He did. Somebody else came along and moved it when he wasn't looking.

Sam would spend hours fretting about something nobody else would give the time of day to. For instance, there was the night when Barney was fifteen or so and he came home from the movies to find Sam's truck, a brand-new Dodge pick-up, parked in the back yard with the keys in her. So he thought: Well, I'll try her out. He took her out on the main road and it was fun driving and he went a little farther than he'd meant to. He went all the way to Bristol and it didn't occur to him to take off the speedometer cable. He never thought Sam would know exactly what the mileage was. He didn't do the truck any harm. All he did was turn around and come home again, park her back in the yard and go to bed.

The next morning was a Saturday and Barney didn't have to go to school and there wasn't anything to do anyhow, so he slept. When he came downstairs about ten o'clock, that house was spinning! Somebody had taken Sam's truck in the night, put forty miles on her, brought her back, and hadn't even bothered to park her where she'd been before.

Now, who the hell would do a thing like that?

If Sam had come to him first off and said: Did you use her? Barney would probably have said yes. As it was, when Sam finally got down the line to Barney, he was half crazy with not knowing and it had got to be funny, so all Barney was willing to do was look as blank as a fool and say: Who, me?

Sam spent the whole day trying to find out. And for as much as two weeks after that, whenever he'd think of it, he'd stop whatever he was doing and turn this look—as astonished as it had been in the beginning—on whomever he was with and say:

"For chrissake, *who* do you suppose took my truck that night?"

It wasn't the easiest thing in the world for Barney to ask Sam for a job that summer. Before he did, he tried everything else he could think of. But, by July, every job in the factory had had two other guys after it since back in February when things started getting a little snug. In Port Kezar there wasn't much of any other place to try.

That left Sam. So Barney asked him because right then Port Kezar was down the road a piece and he'd found it.

The way Sam looked made Barney feel as if he'd handed him something bright and shiny that he'd been wanting for a long time.

"God, yes!" Sam said. "I sure can use you. I've got a new pulp gang going in to Sisk Mountain up near Chain O' Lakes and there isn't a man I can find to take charge of them."

Barney nearly swallowed his tongue. Sisk Mountain! Chain O' Lakes! That was way to hell and gone north of Rangeley somewhere, so far he didn't even know where.

"No!" he blurted. "I don't want to go way up there, Sam. The idea was, I want to stay in Port Kezar."

"It was only a couple of weeks ago Port Kezar wasn't big enough to hold you," Sam said, and the light had gone out and Barney had taken back the shining present.

"I've changed my mind," Barney said. "It's plenty big enough."

Sam looked at the black eye which was fading but was still a handsome shiner.

"Looks to me as if one night had been enough."

"Well, hell," Barney said. "If you feel that way, forget it. I guess I can pick up something."

"You could always try the boatyard," Sam said.

That was a dirty dig. Barney could have tried the boatyard; but he wasn't going to and Sam knew it and why. He'd worked there for three weeks one summer and got through in a hurry. He *did* do a damn fool thing without stopping to think what it might mean; but how many people stop to think when it's a matter of covering up their mistakes? Barney was using one of those electric drills to make screw holes through the planking into the timbers in this fifty-foot hull. She was an offshore dragger they were building on contract for some out-of-state party. He missed the timbers in a couple of places and it would have been a hell of a job to take those planks out and replace them. He didn't have any idea how to start.

So he'd mixed up some sawdust and Weldwood Glue and stuffed the holes full. Made a good job of it too. It would have been hard to tell where they were until they started taking water. He didn't think about that part of it. All he'd had in mind was holding onto the job.

Paul Hanna was the only guy who could have told about it because he was working on the inside of the hull, the same Paul who worked for Sam now. It had had to be Paul who'd told about those damned holes, and whenever Barney looked at him all he could think of was those screw holes and wonder if Paul was thinking about them too.

"There's other places besides the boatyard," Barney said.

Sam gave a half-disgusted, half-amused snort.

"I know you've tried all over town."

Christ, Barney thought, what it must be to know everything.

"I can try some more."

"It won't do you much good." Already Sam was beginning to walk away from the conversation, showing that he was through no matter whether the other fellow was or not. "No, Barney. There's no other place. I can use you here if you want to help Paul and Cliff around the hen houses this summer. But I thought the other job would really give you a chance to see what you could do."

"A job's a job," Barney said to his back. "The only chance I want is to stay right here."

Sam didn't even bother to answer that. He just shrugged and kept on going. The shrug meant he disagreed with what Barney had just said, but that it wasn't worth arguing about.

The rest of that summer Barney felt as if he existed on two levels. It was one of the queerest times he had ever lived through.

Whatever he was doing, while it was going on, was the only thing there was. If he was cleaning out the dropping boards in the big hen house, there wasn't anything else in the world but Barney and those dropping boards. But when it was past, whatever it might have been that was so sharp and real at the time, it receded into a kind of haze. He'd be looking back on it from another time when things were real, and the first reality would be like a dream of another place and another man. He felt as if he lived inside a big thick glass bubble and only one other thing at a time could get in there with him.

He never worked so hard in all his life before, because that didn't matter either. He didn't get tired. He started out at five-thirty, six o'clock, and at eight-thirty or nine that night he'd be cleaning up to have supper.

Eating was another thing. He didn't seem to get hungry either. Or he would be hungry and sit down at that table with a good appetite and two mouthfuls would go down and the third one wouldn't.

And all the while he would be hurrying through the week as if it was Grand Central Station and Friday night was a train he had to catch and if he didn't start hurrying on Monday morning, he'd get down the ramp to see the last car hauling out and he watching it go.

Even hurrying to catch the train, he wouldn't be thinking about

Sabra or anything to do with her. At five o'clock on Friday night, he wouldn't be thinking of anything else but Sabra. As if she'd been standing there waiting in his mind until he got up to her through all the other things in the way, and there she'd be and there wouldn't be anything else.

He could feel Sam and Jude watching him. That didn't even bother him, because nothing could have. He didn't give two hoots in hell. He had to be kind of amused to himself, though. He could feel this worried watching and it really was damned funny. They always used to watch him like that and worry when he wasn't working. And here, this summer, he was working like a dog and *that* didn't suit them either. They watched as if he'd been a time bomb and they didn't know when he was set to go off.

He could have said to them: It's all right. You haven't anything to worry about. But that was too much trouble. Hell, if he said it they'd just worry all the more because he was able to say it.

Besides, he figured it did them good. If they hadn't worried about that, they'd probably have found something else. And he'd a hell of a lot rather have them worry about his working too hard than about what he was doing from Friday night to Monday morning.

Finally the week would be through and Barney would come alive as if he'd been a zombie all week. He'd go into the house like a hurricane and up over the stairs to get dressed, in such a tearing hurry it would seem as if he couldn't even wait to shave. His hands would be shaking so he'd have to steady his wrist like a drunk with his first shot of the day. It was a good thing he had an electric razor. He thought he might have cut his throat if he'd tried to use a blade.

He'd get himself into a heap somehow and out into the car and the car pointed toward town and then all the hurry would run out of him the way sand runs from one end to the other of one of those egg timers that used to hang on the wall behind the stove at home, the little glass tube with the narrow waist and the bottom full of fine sand that took just so long to run through when you turned it over.

He didn't want the week end to be past too soon and he felt

if he didn't hurry now to get *to* it, he would be able to slow it down and not have to hurry *through* it.

Sometimes he stopped in to Aunt Bessie Howe's to pick up a fifth of rum. If she wasn't feeling too crotchety he might sit there a while, across the kitchen table from her, listening to her talk. They might even open the bottle and have a short one. She didn't drink much. She had to keep her wits about her and she said two drinks were enough to make her forget she'd ever had a wit.

She was an institution, little tiny shriveled-up old girl; nobody knew how old she was, but she'd looked the same ever since Barney had known her and that'd been since before he could remember. When he started to notice, she was already there and had been forever. She had a prim look about her, corners of the mouth tight and pulled in, hair the color of steel and hauled back so straight into a pug she always looked as if she had her eyebrows raised.

If an old-maid schoolteacher ever looked the way she was supposed to, Aunt Bessie could have posed for it. And all crippled up with arthritis. There were times when she could hardly flatten her hand out enough to take the money.

Of course, she wasn't Barney's aunt, nor anybody else's. All alone in the world and older than God. Barney asked her once if she didn't get lonesome and she gave him a look out of those snapping black eyes.

"Lonesome! Hell, yes! Sometimes I get lonesome enough to howl like a timber wolf. But then I think: What're you lonesome *for*, you damned old fool? Never had anything. Never wanted anything. Consider yourself lucky."

She was still cackling over her good luck when Barney went down over the steps, his fifth in his pocket, thinking: Some schoolmarm!

He headed uptown then, and when he stopped the car in front of the house Sabra would come out. He'd never know how she was going to be feeling, but it was always definite, one way or the other, and the minute he got a look at her he'd know. If there were those two little white marks like parentheses, one on either side of her mouth, she'd be mad—really mad—so mad she'd be shaking and hardly able to speak. It was Arthur who did that to her. Barney got to know when she looked like that, she and the old man had been having something over, although she would never tell him what it was.

This night, when she came out, she was all right, looking at him with her eyes light and shining and happy in a way that would have satisfied anyone to have her look. The look said he was there and she was there and nothing else was necessary.

Just then a young fellow Barney had never seen before came out of one of the factory camps and started up the hill to the main road. He was obviously on his way to a fine Friday night—dressed up to the nines in a heavy tweed sport jacket and gabardine slacks, his black hair carefully combed into a high wave. He had the kind of smooth good looks that invariably put another man's hackles up, and Barney turned to Sabra to jerk his head and say something about the dude. But he found her looking after the stranger and she had the exact luminous look with which she had greeted him.

"Who the hell's that?" Barney said sharply, turning to look again himself.

Sabra shrugged.

"I don't know. He just turned up a day or two ago. Nice looking, isn't he?"

"I wouldn't know," Barney said stiffly, but he wasn't thinking about the dressed-up stranger or the way Sabra had looked after him. He was remembering instead something that came back so clearly to him now that he knew he'd been purposely *not* remembering it before, something that he had intentionally stuffed into the back of his mind for over a month, and the intentional forgetting was clear in the force with which he remembered it now. It came jerking out of him the same way he'd remembered it.

"What'd Arthur mean that first morning?" he said, staring at her. "What he said to me."

"I don't know." She turned her head with a slow thoughtfulness Barney recognized by now as a warning signal, and looked at him and the pupils of her eyes went small like a cat's in the light. "I wasn't there. What did he say?"

Barney knew he should never have started this; but having

started, he could only go on with it. Besides, he had to know the answer fast.

"The kids. It was what he said to them really. Not me."

There wasn't much Sabra could say to that; but Barney stopped and waited and while he was waiting he thought suddenly: For god sake, I don't even know their names! A whole month he'd known her and she hadn't even told him what her two kids' names were. But that was the way it was. When they were together there wasn't anyone else in the world important enough to have a name, kids or anyone.

"He said, 'This is your new uncle.' "

"I suppose he *had* to say something."

Her voice was level and tight as a wire and with no more expression in it than one of those recordings people make sometimes when their voices not only don't sound like theirs, but they really don't sound human either.

"Was it their 'old uncle' you were trying to shake that night in the beer joint?"

"You can't ever be satisfied with anything, can you? You can't ever let anything alone!"

"No, I guess not," Barney said. "How long'll it be before they have another new uncle?"

He sat listening to his own voice with a stiff astonishment. He didn't want to know the answers or even ask the questions; but the way she was looking at him and what she was saying, it was as if she were pushing him to see how far she *could* push before he'd do something.

"*That's* up to you," she said.

"Is it?" he said. "When you look at every man who goes by the way you did at him?"

"Barney," Sabra said carefully and with intent. "Neither you, nor anybody else, owns me. And I'll look at anyone I want to any way I like. And if you don't like it, you know what you can do—right now."

What he did surprised him; but the minute before he slapped her, Sabra knew he was going to do it and she was ready for him.

While the sound it made was still so sharp Barney couldn't hear anything else, she reached over and pulled her fingernails down across his cheek. Then she was out of that car so fast it was like a cat moving and across the yard and into the house. Barney was mad enough to move fast too, and he was right behind her when she went in through the shed door. He came up against it with a crash before she had a chance to lock it and all she could do was keep on running. In through the kitchen, through the other door and up over the stairs, with Barney on her heels.

Her mother was standing at the sink when they went through the kitchen—big woman, floppy, and looking as if she didn't have anything as solid as bone to hold her together. She turned and looked, eyes like two raisins in a big doughy gray face. Barney could feel the blood trickling down his cheek and down inside his clean shirt collar. Judging from her expression, he looked like the Devil himself. When he went up over the stairs he could still hear her screaming in the kitchen.

"Arthur! Arthur! Arthur!" Just like a stuck whistle.

He was past caring about Arthur or anyone else, when he got to the head of the stairs and put his hand on the latch of the closed bedroom door and shoved. The door gave a little and then shut to, hard, and he knew the only thing holding it on the other side was Sabra. He stood listening and he could hear blood thundering in his ears and, after a second, he could hear her breathing.

"Open the door," he said, and had to keep his teeth clamped together to hold his voice down.

"You go to hell!"

Barney put his thumb on the latch, set his shoulder against the door, and pushed. At the same instant, on the other side, she let go. The door gave and he went off balance halfway across the room before he could turn. When he did, all he saw was that damned green lamp coming at his head and he ducked just in time. It hit the wall behind him, but it didn't break.

For about five minutes they had it, around and round that room. It was lucky for them both he couldn't catch her at first. He was mad enough to kill her right there. When he *did* catch her, it was bad enough. She was just as mad as he was and she fought like a cat, too, spitting and hissing, and with her eyes shining.

When she quit on him, she quit like a switch turned off. One minute he had his hands full, the next minute, nothing. She just turned around and walked away—went over to the bed and lay down with her arm across her eyes. Her lower lip was beginning to swell up and he could see a black-and-blue place like a shadow along her jaw.

Down in the kitchen her mother was still making some kind of a noise, high and shrill and setting Barney's teeth on edge. But she wasn't hollering for the old man any longer because he was standing in the bedroom door watching. His face looked about as usual, but he kept opening and closing his hands.

"Have you finished?" he said. "Aren't you going to beat her now?"

Barney went over until he was standing toe to toe with him and Arthur had to tip his head back to face him. Barney was still breathing hard and still mad enough to want to hurt somebody, but no longer hurt Sabra.

"Get out of my way, old man," he said. "Or I'll take care of you too."

He didn't know what he might have done to Arthur; but there was no need for either of them to find out. Arthur stepped to one side and Barney went past him and down the stairs. He went out to the car, got the rum and came back into the kitchen. When he went out through he didn't see the old woman; but when he came back she was sitting in a straight chair in the corner with her face in her hands, letting out the same high shrill noise and sounding as if she wasn't even stopping for breath.

She was just a piece of furniture. She didn't even look human to him—so far from it he couldn't even feel sorry for her. He went over to the cupboard and took two jelly glasses from the bottom shelf. When she heard the dishes rattling, she stopped yelling long enough to see what was going on and then she started again, a note or two higher.

Arthur was still at the head of the stairs looking in through the door; but he was flattened against the wall and he looked as if he might slide—if he relaxed for a minute—down into nothing but a pile of old clothes.

Barney didn't glance at him until he was past him and standing in the bedroom doorway. Then he jerked his head toward the stairs and went in and shut the door. Outside there was that kind of silence that tells you somebody's there and not making any noise. Barney waited a minute longer before he opened the door again. Arthur hadn't moved. His shoulders were pushed back against the wall, the palms of his hands flat against the rough unpainted plaster; and his eyes, without his having to change the direction of their stare, met Barney's.

"Beat it," Barney said, and took a step toward him.

The eyes moved then, slid from Barney's face down to the bottle and the two glasses he had in his hand. Arthur turned and started down the stairs one foot at a time the way a child does, with his wooden foot hitting each tread hard. Thud, slither; thud, slither; thud—

Barney went back into the bedroom not knowing what he'd find when he looked at Sabra and so not daring to look. He put the two glasses on the bureau and poured a good shot into each one. Then he picked them up and turned around to hand one to her. She was sitting up with her hands propping her and her arms straightened out, and her face—

When he saw her face and what he'd done, he felt as if somebody had taken his stomach in both hands and twisted it the way you wring water out of a cloth.

"Barney, you don't have to," she said and she tried to smile but it wasn't much. "*You*'re mine. You don't have to worry."

Barney dropped the glasses, liquor and all, right in the middle of the floor and went over and sat down on the edge of the bed. When he put his arms around her, he did it as gently as he could; but even that hurt her.

"Oh, my god," he said. "What was it? I don't— Sabra, listen. Listen to me."

She put her hand over his mouth.

For an hour or more the two voices droned on in the kitchen below and then they stopped and there was the sound of a door slamming and after that nothing but silence in the silent house.

It must have been an hour after that when Barney and Sabra

decided to go down to the kitchen to have a drink because he'd smashed both glasses, and once they were down there it was warm and quiet and shadowy, sitting at the kitchen table with only the one lamp lit, and Barney couldn't make out her face too clearly. He felt horrible and wonderful all in one. He wanted to do everything there was in the world for her, to make it up to her. And he knew he didn't have to.

They were talking a little, mostly though just sitting in peaceful silence, when the back door opened and two people came into the shed. Barney'd thought her mother and father had gone to bed; but when he heard the steps, he knew he'd been mistaken. One of those two people was the old man.

Barney would have known that walk anywhere, the thud and drag as slow and steady as the ticking of a clock. So he knew Arthur was standing in the shed outside the kitchen door now. He glanced at Sabra and she had her head half turned, listening. Somebody spoke in a low voice, a man's voice, and not Arthur's either.

"Who's that?" Barney said loudly.

There was silence in the shed, as if whoever stood out there hadn't expected voices from the kitchen and wasn't quite sure what to do about it.

"Well, go on," Arthur said impatiently and Barney could hear that all right. "He's right there. Didn't you hear him?"

There was an answering mutter. Arthur set his hand on the latch and opened the door so hard it banged against the edge of the stove and swung half shut again. He stood glaring at them and, over his shoulder, like a big pale balloon floating in mid-air, was another face, one Barney had got to know fairly well. He pushed back his chair and stood up.

He couldn't remember when he'd found out that people were more afraid of him than he was of them—it was something you didn't know when you were a kid; but a little later it was something you did, and it happened somewhere in between the two times, maybe when you got tall enough so you could look authority in the eye from its own level, or either make authority look up to you and it's as simple as that.

Linwood Vance had been the deputy around the Port for ten or

fifteen years and he wasn't scared of much. But Barney had discovered Linwood was scared of him. It didn't show on the surface
in anything he said or did—it was more the look in his eye like a
skittish horse, or something like the smell of fear he gave off. The
look was there now; there was a ring of white all the way around
the iris of his eyes.

"Well, there he is, right there!" Arthur said. "Go ahead."

Linwood, set to do his duty, pushed past the old man into the
room. He glanced at Sabra and hesitated as if he hadn't noticed
her before. He looked at the bottle on the table. Then he looked
at Barney.

"You hitting that pretty hard?"

"See for yourself." Barney put his finger against the level in the
bottle. There wasn't much gone, only the two shots he'd spilled on
the bedroom floor and what there was in their glasses right now.

"That the first bottle?"

"Look!" Barney said. "You can haul me in for drunk and dis-
orderly if you want to. Go ahead. I'd like to see you make that one
stick!"

Linwood glanced over his shoulder at Arthur.

"I don't see he's doing anything much," he said.

"Look at my daughter's face!"

Linwood did and then back at Barney; but he was still talking to
the old man.

"All I've got is your word he did it. I haven't seen him do it."

"Do you think—" that voice didn't ever change expression,
just grated along; but expression or not, Arthur was beginning to
sizzle—"she did it herself?"

"Why don't you let her talk?" Linwood said. "You been doing
all the talking. You say she wants to swear out a paper for him.
Okay. Let her tell me about it. If she does, I'll have to take you to
Bristol, Barney."

Sabra hit the table suddenly with the flat of her hand, and
Barney jumped almost as high as Linwood did.

"You get out of here," she said, icy and quiet. "That old man
is crazy! Barney never laid a finger on me!"

Linwood turned as if somebody had pressed a button that started his walking mechanism. When he went past Arthur, he said:

"Next time you get me out of bed in the middle of the night, Arthur, make it good, will you?"

The three of them were alone in the kitchen like three people frozen into something heavier than flesh, listening to the quick relieved sound of his steps going out along the driveway to the road. They heard the sound of his car starting, pulling away, dying into the quiet night.

Arthur was standing half in shadow, the upper part of him in light, and suddenly he tipped back his head and looked at the ceiling. Barney looked too, wondering what he was going to do now. All he saw was the cracked and patched old plaster; but Arthur saw something more. The voice that rolled out of him this time *was* different and one Barney had never heard before.

"Almighty God!" Arthur said and it sounded as if he was calling on a personal and powerful servant. "Almighty God, what have I done? What have I brought into the world? Look at my daughter! The sins of the fathers are visited on the children; but what did I *do?* Where did I sin? You must know, God. I've told You, I did my best for her; but my sins must have been worse than I ever knew. You know best."

For a second Barney almost felt sorry for him. He could look down on Arthur's upturned face and it was wet. Arthur was standing there praying and crying, real tears coming out of those little angry eyes.

"Every penny I ever made, Lord, I spent on her. Me and her mother, both. *And look at her!* I've been her slave. Slave to a Magdalene! I bear the cross You gave me for my sins; but it's a heavy load. You move in a mysterious way."

His voice rose to a howl of protest and Barney wasn't sorry for him any more because he could see what Arthur was doing and it wasn't really praying. Maybe he meant it to be. Maybe it was his kind of praying. But all he was doing was complaining because he'd made an investment and it hadn't paid him back the way he'd thought it was going to. He hadn't got his money back and he wanted it, either from the ravens like Elijah, or from Sabra, or—failing them—then he would accept it from God Himself.

That didn't keep the tears from being as real as if he'd been weeping for his sins.

"Do you want to stay here and listen to this?" Barney said.

"I've heard it all before." Sabra shrugged.

"Well, come on then."

She went over to the door and Barney picked up the bottle and followed her. Arthur didn't move and he was still going strong. Barney didn't bother to listen to what he was saying any longer, now that he knew what Arthur wanted. He *did* look back before he closed the door, and Arthur had swiveled his eyes around so he could see where they were going. The look on his face froze Barney on the bottom step with the door half shut and the two of them staring at each other through the gap.

The feeling Barney had then, he had had before. One Saturday night coming home from a dance, it was late and he'd had three or four drinks, maybe more. He was feeling no pain and when he looked at the speedometer he couldn't believe his eyes. He was doing eighty and it felt as if her tail was dragging.

There's a sharp left turn right after you cross Tatlock's Bridge on the Port Kezar road and when you make a left turn, there's a tendency to sag over on the wrong side of the road.

He hadn't seen any other lights and when two jumped out of the darkness, coming at him, he thought for a second the other guy had been driving without lights and had just that minute turned them on, they came so fast. He didn't have time to think much. There was a hell of a racket, metal on metal, but hardly a jar. Barney was sober enough to know all he'd done was scrape along the side and probably make a complete mess of the fenders. But, if he'd been six inches farther over to the left—

He sat behind the wheel, the car still doing sixty because he hadn't had time to do any more than touch the brakes, and wasn't even scared. He could feel himself thinking, but slowly. Should I stop? Why not keep right on going? That happened so fast he never had any more chance to see who I was than I did who he was. He glanced into the rear-view mirror though, and he could see the lights sweeping in a circle in the middle of the road and coming after him.

Aha, he thought. He's feeling tough. Maybe he wants a good fight.

Barney hauled off to the side of the road and got out to get ready and was standing there when the other car pulled in behind him. The lights were bright and he couldn't see a thing against them. But he heard the other driver getting out and he had to get out on the right side because his driver's door wouldn't open.

Steps came slow and firm around the side of the car and along the road shoulder. Barney still couldn't see him, only a blur moving in the glare of light; but there was something assured about those footsteps that bothered him. A man who's mad—and if anyone ever had a right to be, this guy did—and doesn't know what to do about it except fight, usually comes on the dead run; but the approaching footsteps were slow and steady and absolutely confident.

When the other fellow got out of the glare and grew visible, Barney saw why. He started to laugh. What else was there to do? Here he was, half tight, ready for a good fight, driving on the wrong side of the road, and everything else in the book, and he'd picked the State Cop to wing.

"Hello, Barney," Kermit said.

"Long time no see," Barney said.

"Drinking?"

"Had a couple of beers."

"Funny thing," Kermit said musingly. "I never found one of you boys yet who'd ever had more than a couple of beers. Well, pull your car off the road so she won't get sideswiped."

"Oh, no!"

Kermit thought he'd catch him on that one; but Barney had thought of it too. He wasn't even in the car when Kermit came up to him and as far as Barney was concerned, Kermit wasn't going to see him drive her either.

"That's undoubtedly my car," he said. "But I've been parked right here for a long time. I wouldn't think of starting that engine when I've had a couple of beers. You know better than that."

"Pretty smart cookie, aren't you, Barney?"

Kermit gave up like a gentleman. He got in behind the wheel himself and hauled the car well off the pavement. He left the parking lights on though, and when Barney got back to pick her up a couple of days later, there wasn't even a sneeze left in that battery. Barney always held that against him. He always figured Kermit did it on purpose.

Barney spent that night in a nice private cell. He crawled into the cot and went to sleep as if he'd been hit over the head. In the middle of the night he woke up.

That was when he had the feeling—the same one he got now just looking at Arthur. He woke up and was right in the middle of what had happened, as if it had been going through his mind all along and he'd just caught up with it: My god, six inches more to the left and going that fast! Barney, he thought, it's only pure bull luck you're lying here whole now instead of spattered over that road like hamburger!

Sometimes you don't get scared when a thing is happening and you're right *now* in it. It's only afterward, when you wake up sober and alone in the night and think how close you came to being so you'd never wake up again. Jesus, he couldn't think of anything worse!

So he lay there and began to shake and couldn't stop and pretty soon he had the whole cot going and still he couldn't stop.

When he and Arthur stood looking at each other through the half-closed door, Barney didn't start shaking; but he had a tight feeling in the stomach that told him he could have without trying very hard. He shut the door quietly and went upstairs and somewhere inside his head a thing as definite as a voice was saying: Watch that old man, Barney!

Hell, he thought, I'm a good guy. I don't like it any more than anyone else would, having somebody feel about me the way he does. But I haven't done anything to him. I haven't even said more than half a dozen words to him. If he wants to make my business his and feel the way he does about it, what can I do?

Arthur kept at it down there for as much as an hour. Neither

Barney nor Sabra could hear what he was saying, only the mumble going on and every once in a while, when he thought of something that really touched him up, he'd let out that howl of pure frustration that had first told Barney exactly what was bothering him.

"For god sake!" Barney said finally. "How long will he keep that up? In another five minutes he'll have me crazier than he is."

"He'll wear out pretty soon—with no audience." Sabra apparently hadn't even been hearing it. "Don't listen to him."

"Don't *listen* to him!" he said. "How would you go about that?"

"Have another drink. That might help."

He did. Then he thought of something.

"Hey! What *are* their names?"

"What?"

"The kids. I don't even know what their names are."

Sabra lifted herself on her elbow and lay there looking at him with a queer expression on her face.

"Why do you want to know?"

"Well, I don't know as I do, really. But is there any reason why I shouldn't?"

"I don't know. Is there?"

"Look, it's all the same to me. I just thought, it seems kind of funny, me not knowing."

"Those kids are *mine*, Barney!"

He couldn't figure out what kind of a notion she had in her head now; but it began to sound like a funny one. He'd just asked her what their names were because it *did* seem kind of odd—here they'd been calling him Uncle Barney for a month or more—when they spoke to him. Or the little girl, anyhow. The boy didn't talk at all.

"It's sure as hell they aren't mine," he said, grinning at her. She lay down again and stared at the ceiling.

"The girl's name is Ann," she said.

"How about him?"

"His name is Christopher."

"You ever take him to a doctor?"

"Yes."

"Well, what'd he say?"

Sabra turned over, all in one motion, and burrowed her head into the pillow and Barney couldn't see her face. Her voice came out muffled and tight.

"The doctor said it was inherited."

"Oh," Barney said. "That means there isn't anything you could do about it?"

She gave a jerk of her head that meant: No, nothing.

"It won't get any better?"

"No. Worse as he gets older." She stopped momentarily and then the words started coming fast. "That's why I left him. *He* knew it, too. *He* knew it might happen. His brother was like that and he never told me. There was someone else back in his family too. They all knew it—and they let me marry him and have those kids. And they all watched Chris and knew what was wrong with him—except me. I didn't know. I thought he was just slow, the way some kids are."

Her voice got strangled and stopped and Barney could feel her shaking. He put his hand on her shoulder and the shaking went all the way up his arm.

"I was going to have another when I found out about Chris," Sabra said, and the voice had steadied and sounded like ice. "When I *did* find out what was wrong and why he was the way he was, I saw to it I'd never have another kid of *his*. Not even the one he thought he had. I got rid of it. It nearly killed me. Not him! Me!"

Once getting it out, about the little boy, was like taking the stopper out of a jug full of water. Barney had never bothered to stop and think before how Sabra felt about her children—they hadn't seemed important because she'd never once mentioned them to him or ever seemed to make very much of them when he was around. But tonight he found out why, and it was just the opposite of not caring anything about them.

Sabra had been behaving just like one of those big plovers you scare up out of the grass above the ledges sometimes walking around the shore in the early summer. At that time of year they don't fly. They fluster along the rocks ahead of you making a funny piping sound. If you stop walking they stop too, and stand on some high point right up in front of you where you can't miss seeing them, and teeter up and down.

The first time it happens you wonder what in hell ails them. It's as if they were trying to attract your attention and when you stop coming, they feel they've lost it and have to get it back again. By the time the light dawns on you, you're so far past the place where you first scared them up that you can't remember where it was. And, of course, that's the whole object. You didn't see the plover in the first place until she was well down onto the ledges, well away from the nest with either eggs or young ones in it, and wanted you to see her. By the time you've caught on, you're too far beyond ever to find it and the old bird's not going to lead you back to it.

That was what Sabra'd been doing with the kids; but Barney couldn't see why she'd had to. She must have known from the beginning they didn't make any difference to him. She was all that mattered. Or maybe that was it. Maybe they should have made a difference; but they still didn't.

He wouldn't have cared if she'd had fifteen—all colors.

But all the same, he thought suddenly, it must be kind of hard on her to realize there was something really bad wrong with one of her children—something that was going to mean he'd never be able to lead any kind of a life at all—and maybe something that meant he was going to be the worst thing that ever happened to her. Because there's no way of telling, with a boy like that, when he grows up, what'll happen. He gets big and strong and a man grown; but inside he's never anything but a three- or four-year-old, if that.

Sabra knew all that and she didn't care. All she had to know was that Chris was hers and she had to take care of him and it seemed to Barney she even thought more of him than she did of the little girl.

"The doctor said I ought to have him put in some kind of a home," Sabra said, hesitating, and then adding, "especially later on."

"Well, don't you suppose you ought to do it? You can't tell—" Barney got that far and felt as if he'd put his hand in a bear trap, thinking: Well, it won't shut to on *me*. But one more word and it would have.

"No kid of mine is going to be put in any home as long as I've got anything to say about it!"

After that she lay so long without moving Barney was beginning to think she'd fallen asleep. Suddenly she got up and went over to refill her glass. When she came back, she started talking once more. Not about the kids, now, though.

In the next hour Barney found out more about her than he had in the whole time he'd known her. He found out what the old man had meant when he'd said that about every penny he made going into her. It was one of those setups where the old folks decide they aren't ever going to do anything themselves so whatever gets done, their kids'll have to do. In this case there was only one and that one a girl. That had been the first disappointment for Arthur Kenney and he told her about it pretty often.

Usually those little men, especially the ones with that tight look around their eyes, are the ones that have the big families. One every year or they think they're slipping. Arthur only had Sabra.

When he realized that was going to be it, he decided he had to make the best of it, and she was only about five when Arthur started telling her what he expected of her. She was going to *be* something. He didn't much care what it was as long as she was the best one of them there was.

They never let her play around with other kids. Always told her she was too good, until she began to get the idea she was. It's not hard to make a young kid begin to feel she's a hell of a lot better than anyone else, because most kids want to feel that way anyhow. Most grownups do too; but by the time they've lived long enough to be a grownup, they've discovered it's not so and there's so many others so god-damned much smarter it's kind of a hopeless battle; so you might's well make the most of what you've got.

Arthur used to pray with her too, about the way he had tonight. After she went to bed they'd come in—her mother and father— and stand there at the foot of the bed while he prayed. Or while he stood staring at the ceiling and told God what he expected Him to do and what he expected Sabra to do and how he wanted both of them to go about it.

The mother went along with all this, probably being the way she was now, always hollering Arthur, Arthur, whenever anything went wrong and letting him take care of it.

He did it, all right! After Sabra got through high school—and it was hard to see how she ever managed to get that far without finding out she wasn't any better or any worse than anyone else, but she did, and they never even let her go to the movies without one of them with her—things still weren't going so good around this part of the country. The depression was over everywhere else; but not here. There was work, all right; but not much pay. Good deal the way it is right now when you work as hard as they do anywhere else and get about half the wages; but you still have to pay higher prices for what you buy with your money.

It was all arse-backwards up here and sometimes Barney wondered why any of them with half a breath of life left stayed here. But there was something about the place that got under your hide and you'd give up a lot, once that happened, for the sake of staying.

Arthur practically had to hock his hide to send her to college. Not business school, not teacher's college, but a university! He got mad with her the day he told her what she was going to do, because if she'd been a boy he would have sent her to theological school to learn to be a real minister. But he had to settle for the next best thing, so she was going to a university to learn to teach school.

If he could have fixed it so all three of them could have gone, he would have done that too. He told her how women were all weak vessels and he didn't trust her out of his sight for a minute and he also told her what he'd do if she so much as took a side step. It wasn't pretty.

So, of course, when she got out from under and far enough away from him to realize he couldn't see everything she did and there were quite a few side steps she could take, she took them all.

She was a sophomore at the State University when she met this Baxter guy and two nights after they met, they lit out for upper New York State, where he lived, and as soon as they could after that they got married.

Once that was done, Sabra sat down and wrote a letter to Arthur. Even telling about it, she could make Barney see what the letter must have been like. She said she put everything into it she'd been thinking for two years and it must have blistered the paper.

Arthur couldn't do one damn thing about it, because she was nineteen and Baxter was twenty-one and there they were, married and living with his family and everything aboveboard. Arthur came all the way down and arrived spouting hellfire and brimstone and calling down the curse of hell on them both.

"If you think tonight was anything," Sabra said, "you should have heard him then, heard *that* performance!"

"Well, how come you ever came back? How'd you ever let him get hold of you again?" Barney couldn't figure that part of it.

"Don't make any mistake," she told him. "He hasn't got hold of me again. I'm just here until something else turns up."

It was Barney's turn to lean on his elbow and look at her.

"How long you been waiting?" he said.

"I can see what you're thinking; but it's not so. I could pick up and leave any time I wanted to, and will when I'm ready. But Chris was only a baby then. I want it fixed so anyone else won't have to take care of him till he gets just a little older."

"Oh, I see," Barney said.

"No, damn you, Barney, you *don't* see! You think you do and what you think is that I'm stuck here for good. But I'm not! And when the time comes, I'm going."

"All right," he said. "If you think so."

"I don't think. I know. I'll know when the time is, too. And then I'll go so fast none of them will ever set eyes on me again."

Barney had heard it before. Not from Sabra, but from a lot of other people. He'd heard it from himself, about how far away he was going when he got the chance—so far it'd take a dollar to send a letter to him. Nobody had ever had a better chance than he had and here he was. It didn't take a dollar. All anyone he'd ever known all his life had to do to get in touch with him was stick his head out the window and holler, "Barney." The only one who'd ever said he'd get away and then had done it was Joe Samuels. He'd got away, but good. And maybe his way was the only sure one.

"All right," Barney said again, knowing how far her going would get her. "But don't go so far away I can't find you, will you?"

"That'll be up to you, Barney. Not me."

"Then I won't worry," he told her, and had to listen to her

affirmation all over again because he couldn't keep out of his voice the knowledge that she would not be hard to find because she wasn't going anywhere, not now.

The summer went fast. It seemed to Barney before he had a chance to turn around it was over, and he would come out in the early mornings to find the grass on the north side of the house white with frost in the shadow where the sun hadn't struck yet. Then the sun would get up high enough to hit it and there'd be a sparkle for a minute and the frost would be gone. That was the way the whole summer went—in a minute—in a sparkle.

Early in September, Cliff turned seventeen. He was starting his senior year in high school and for the past month he'd been chewing about it and how he didn't want to go back because what was the use? He'd be in the Army before he could turn around and what the hell good was Latin going to do him in a foxhole?

The morning he was supposed to start, the first thing he did, he got up without having to be called three or four times. When he came down to breakfast he was wearing the same filthy sweat shirt and dungarees he'd been wearing around the place for the last week.

Jude glanced at him casually, then thoughtfully; but she didn't say anything at first. Barney, watching in amusement, could almost see her brain working. Finally, when she poured her second cup of coffee, she leaned back in her chair and looked across at Cliff, who was unnaturally busy with eating, even for him.

"I don't know that I care to have you go out of my house looking like that, Cliff."

Cliff's stare of innocent surprise was a beautiful thing to see.

"For pete sake, I've been looking like this all summer and you never complained. Who's going to want me formal? The hens?"

"All right, Cliff." Sam didn't even glance up from his bacon and eggs. "Jude says you're going to change your clothes, go change them! You'll look like hell, going to school that way."

"Oh, yes." Cliff was elaborately casual. "This *is* the first day of school, isn't it."

There was a minute of dangerous quiet in which nobody moved.

Then Sam put his fork down and swallowed what he had in his mouth and looked thoughtfully at Cliff.

"Yes, it is," he said.

"Well, I've been giving it a good deal of thought," Cliff said.

"I'm glad to hear that." The voice Sam was using was his beginning-to-smolder one. Barney recognized it if Cliff didn't. And Barney was thinking, too, that he'd sat through this discussion that was edging into words before. He could foresee the very arguments, the exact words, the same ones that had been used to him.

"Yes, and I've decided it would be a waste of time for me to go back to school."

"Well," Sam said, still dangerously quiet, "it's god-damn good of you to let us know."

"Sam," Jude said. "It won't do any good to talk like that."

The trouble with Cliff, Barney was thinking, was the same thing that had been with him. When you're seventeen and making thirty-five or forty dollars a week, it looks to you as if you had it made. That's all you want at the moment because it looks like a lot and you can't foresee a time when you'll want much more— either that, or you think you'll go on making more and more just through the natural process of keeping on working.

"Just let me ask him one question," Sam said. "Cliff, the thing is, do you want to go on playing wet nurse to a mess of hens for the rest of your life?"

None of them turned to glance at Barney but they might as well have. Sam had said: There's the horrible example, right in front of you. Because the arguments hadn't worked with Barney and he hadn't gone back to school and here he was, at twenty-two, right where Cliff was at seventeen.

"I won't have a chance," Cliff said. "I'll be in the Army."

"Yeah, but you'll have to get out of the Army sometime and *then* where'll you be?"

"Look, Cliff," Jude said firmly and in her last-word voice. "That diploma doesn't look very important to you right now; but it will someday and it'll look a lot bigger if you haven't got it."

Cliff looked doubtfully from Sam to Jude. He was beginning to waver.

"Come on," Jude said, with the reasonable tone of restraint you use to momentary recalcitrance in the young. "Go upstairs and get cleaned up now."

At seventeen Cliff was younger than Barney had been. That tone of voice still worked with him. He got up reluctantly and headed for the stairs, muttering.

"What'd you say?" Sam called after him.

"I said I didn't see what good Latin was going to do me in a damned old foxhole."

"Cliff!" Jude and Sam lit together that time and before the combined outrage and anger, Cliff vanished up the stairs like a puff of smoke.

That left only Paul and Barney to do the work three had been doing all summer, but it didn't seem to make any difference. Cliff had been pulling his weight all right; but Barney found he could absorb that much more and not even feel it.

They were unloading the feed from the truck to the storeroom one Thursday morning in October when Sam—just back from upstate somewhere, maybe Sisk Mountain—came out of the house with his face wrinkled into that scowl he got when two and two came out five for him.

"Barney, I want to talk to you," he said and was already halfway back to the house by the time Barney jumped out of the truck bed and started after him. That trick of Sam's was maddening, and Barney was touched up a little by the time he caught up and Sam stopped walking away.

"What the hell are you trying to do?" Sam said, and his own shocked surprise at what had come out of him showed in his face. He hadn't intended to say that at all.

"Whatta you mean?"

"You look like the wrath of God." Once he'd started it, Sam apparently thought he might as well carry it along.

"Look, Sam, I work for you and that's all that's any of your business. Are you dissatisfied with the way I'm working?"

"My god, no!" Sam said. "But I never meant you had to work yourself into the ground."

"All right," Barney said. "Was that all you wanted to say?"

"No, wait. That wasn't it. I'm going to take the dogs out to-night. I see where there's some coons been into the corn patch. Come along with me, will you?"

It sounded good to Barney. He always liked to go coon hunting with Sam because it was one of the few things they got along doing and were easy with each other while they were doing it.

"Yeah, sure," he said. "I'd like to."

He glanced back at the hen house and found that the unloading wasn't getting along very fast without him. Paul was standing right where they'd left him in the wide upstairs door to the grain room, and the bag of feed leaning up against his knees was the same one Barney had dragged over to him.

Eyes! Barney thought. If it wasn't for their eyes! My god, some-times he felt like the old boy in the schoolbooks, the one who took the torch and did for the big character who only had one eye to begin with. One eye would be worse. Two's bad enough when whatever they're thinking about and can't get out in words comes out that way instead. It was hard to look a man in the eye when he didn't want you to, and Sam didn't want Barney to now because he wasn't ready to say whatever else it was he'd started out to.

That night when Barney stowed the truck in the garage and started across to the house for supper, he felt hollow all the way to his toes for the first time in months.

There was still some faint light left in the west from the sunset and a streak of cold color over the trees, low down; color that should have been hot but wasn't because it was October and that orange bar under the heavy line of clouds meant frost before morning.

"Hey, old ringtail," he said. "You waiting for us?"

Coming home late the other night, he'd met a coon. First he'd seen the eyes reflected in the car lights, too low down for a deer, and he'd thought it was a dog or a cat until he got up close enough to see the big tail and the black mask. It was old man coon him-self, coming down the middle of the road, sniffing. Barney stopped the car and rolled down the window, but the coon didn't hesitate. He was hunting for something and he made a funny whining noise when he went past the car, almost close enough for Barney to reach out and touch him. He didn't even seem to notice the car was there until Barney spoke to him.

"Hey," he said. "Where you going, brother?"

When the coon heard the human voice it startled him and he scuttled over to the shoulder of the road and, feeling that was far enough away to look the situation over safely, sat up and stared.

He was a cute little devil, sitting up there with his paws dangling and that sharp face with the black streak across the eyes. After a minute he decided the car wasn't going to harm him, so he lowered to all fours again and shuffled off through the dead leaves, still whimpering.

Maybe he'd be the one waiting tonight.

As he passed the kennel, Barney could hear the dogs beginning to stir around too, as if they knew they were due for a run. That old Bruce, that old black devil of Sam's, he probably did know. He was a damned smart dog and sometimes he'd look at you just as if he intended to say something in English and then decided it wasn't important enough to bother. He was muttering now and Barney spoke his name just to hear the sharp high hiccup of response.

The wind was dying with the sunset and in the east the edge of the moon was just showing over the islands. Beginning to rise like that, it looked bigger than the world and the color of fire close to the wood.

No dew had fallen yet and there would be a lot of dead leaves in the woods to make a hell of a racket; but that didn't matter the way it did when you were after deer.

You hunt coon with dogs and the coon knows you're coming and there's a hell of a racket anyhow. A few dead leaves don't make any difference. With deer, though, it pays to wait for a day when there's been a little snow, or the day after a rainstorm, when the crisp and rattle has been soaked out of them. Barney had been in the woods on a frosty November morning, knowing it was useless, and could hear a twig snap half a mile away and one man walking through dead leaves sounded like a troop of cavalry.

He went into the kitchen and his place was set at the table but everything else had been cleared away. And there were the eyes again. He couldn't figure it out tonight—they were watching him as if they were wondering what he was going to do and he couldn't see why it was any different than any other night; but it was.

He ate a lot because it tasted good to him and Jude was one of the few women he'd ever seen who wasn't afraid to make a decent cup of coffee. It came out of the pot the color of mahogany and with a smell that would bring old men from their chimney corners.

Sam was sitting by the stove oiling his pistol. It was a light one, twenty-two, because shooting isn't the important thing about hunting coon with dogs. All you needed was something to stand under a tree with and knock the old man down from where the dogs have put him.

For some reason Jude was nervous as a cat. She couldn't sit still. She'd light in the chair across the table from Barney, talking a blue streak about nothing and that wasn't like her. After a minute, she wouldn't be able to sit there any longer and she'd get up and take a cup from the closet and pour herself some coffee. Then, instead of sitting down to drink it, she'd start wandering around the room, maybe stopping to look out the window into the night where there wasn't a thing to see she hadn't seen a thousand times before and couldn't see now if she'd wanted to.

Barney finished the piece of apple pie she put in front of him, leaned back, lit a cigarette, and realized suddenly that this minute was what they'd been waiting for.

Both Jude and Sam stopped what they happened to be doing and looked at him. As if they expected him to be lighting a fuse with that match, instead of a cigarette, and go up in smoke and a big bang right in front of their eyes.

Christ, he thought, I ought to stand up and take a bow.

Then they realized at the same moment that they *were* staring and the fact hadn't escaped Barney. They looked away so fast it would have been funny if he could only have figured it out.

He opened his mouth to say: Well, Sam, you ready? But they both started to talk at the same time too. In the ensuing and unavoidable silence, Barney prevailed.

"For christ sweet sake," he said. "What *is* the matter with you? You both gone crazy?"

"Just waiting for you, Barney," Sam said. "You ready?"

He leaned down, hauled his larrigans out from under the stove and put them on.

"I guess so," Barney said. "Should I make a will or anything, before we go?"

He hadn't thought how that might sound to Sam until he saw the white bunch of muscle come out against his brown jaw. Oh, christ, Barney thought, now he thinks I've said he shot Pa and I was just trying in my feeble way to be funny. Sam went into the entry and they could hear him scrabbling into his leather jacket.

God preserve me anyhow, Barney thought, from people who carry their innards on the outside. And you wouldn't ever think Sam did, either, to look at him. It was only when you said one of those half-baked things you *do* say sometimes without thinking, and watched it flick him, that you realized he didn't have as thick a skin as most, and, in some places, maybe no skin at all.

The outside door opened and closed; the three dogs began to bellow immediately and Sam's voice sounded almost as loud. By the time Barney got down to the kennel, Sam had the dogs on leash. Old Bruce was quiet, but the two young ones were right on their toes and bragging about being ready for it. Sam was too busy to say anything and Barney figured that was partly on purpose. He handed Barney a flashlight and one of the leashes and they started down past the hen houses into the dark fields and the secret woods.

Barney wasn't sure which dog he had until they got into clear going and he got the feel of him against the leash. The dog would go along at a good jog and then, suddenly, he'd give a leap that would take all four feet off the ground, come up against the lead, snatch Barney's arm half out of the shoulder socket, and settle back into his jog again. The first time he did it, Barney knew he had Bray, the youngest one of the three, hardly more than a pup, given that name because of his sound that really wasn't either bark or bell but just exactly what Sam called him, a bray. Out in the woods, once he got scent of anything, he sounded like a lost calf.

Sam, with Bruce and Spade, was well ahead, nearly down to the corn patch already and Bray was having a fit at the idea of being left behind. So Barney stepped on it and they caught the others at the edge of the garden. The coons had made a mess of it too, pulling down stalks that had been over six feet tall, stripping off the ears and eating them right there. The paths between the rows were strewn with cobs and Bruce was snuffling along, his paws scrabbling with impatience. Spade was whining. But Bray, he put back his head and bellowed.

"Christ almighty," Sam muttered. "I'm going to muzzle that pup. Keep him back, will you? He'll get wound up with Bruce if you don't."

He was a little too late with his warning. Bray had already got up a little too close and he must have weaseled in between Bruce and whatever scent he was getting. There was a snarl and a snap and Bray let out a high startled yawp and came back fast. Barney switched on the light to look at him and there was a gash two inches long on his shoulder as clean as if it had been done with a razor.

"Serves him right," Sam said. "Maybe he'll learn."

"Well, why not let them go? Let him run a little of it off. He's going to have my arm from the shoulder down, if we don't."

"Might's well."

Sam leaned down and snapped the swivel off Bruce's collar. That old dog gave tongue and no matter how many times he heard it, it always gave Barney the same feeling—an icy trickle down his spine. There's no other sound like it so you can't say it reminds you of anything. It's a dog running in cold October woods on a moonlight night. It's death on four feet scudding under the leafless trees, in and out of the shadows of the spruces, in and out of the moonlight, just where and how you might expect to find and maybe even hope to find death if you went looking for it.

Everything is clean and cold and decent—even for the coon, because he has his chance too. He can run. He can lose the dog if he's smart enough and if he isn't that smart then it catches up with him.

Sam waited a second before he let the other two go and they went out from under his hand like shadows and so fast Barney was ready to swear they'd never been there.

It was a handsome night, with that moon—silver now and high

up and cold—casting shadows where there didn't seem to be anything to cause a shadow. The dogs were too busy to make much
noise. There was a conversational greeting when the youngsters
caught up with Bruce and then silence again, except for an occa-
sional reassuring bay. They heard the dogs hit the little creek that
flows down from the marsh below Mount Hagar across Sam's
back field and on to the ocean. The young dogs lost the scent
there and screamed about it; but there still wasn't much sound
from Bruce.

"*He* hasn't lost it," Sam said.

Barney could see his face in the moonlight and his eyes were
wide open and looked solid black. Bruce, up the creek, told the
other two to shut up and come along. It was up this way.

"We'd better get started," Sam said, when all three voices rose
into a song of triumph. "That old devil's not very far ahead of
them now. He won't take long."

They lit out down across the field for the woods. There wasn't
a breath of wind and Barney thought he could hear the sound of
pads through the underbrush. He couldn't, but it was that kind
of a night. What he was hearing might have been the sound of
paws passing a long time ago that the silence and the secret had
held until he was here and now.

He felt good.

Sam seemed to think the dogs would tree pretty soon, but Sam
was wrong. Up ahead the roar was tracking sound and it didn't
change to treeing sound.

They led straight across an old pulp clearing, about five years
old and growing up to poverty birch and bull briars, and the moonlight only gave solid ground where there wasn't any. Once there,
Barney was in a pile of slash to his waist and he thought to god
he'd have to get down on his hands and knees and crawl to get
out of it. He could hear Sam on ahead and see him, floundering
around in the slash and swearing like a trooper. He got out of
that and started across a cleared space and caught his foot in one
of those running blackberries that roots its top too, and went
down. There was a splash when he hit water. His flashlight rolled
out of his hand and lay there still burning. For a second he stayed

on his hands and knees, not moving, just swearing. Barney didn't want to laugh and didn't have the wind to spare, so the sound he made was more as if somebody had hit him in the stomach. Sam glanced back and Barney could see his teeth flash when he grinned.

"Some fun!" he said. "God, that water's cold!"

Then he was up and gone again. For a big man he could move fast. Barney didn't set eyes on him until they got across the clearing and into the edge of the woods. Sam was standing there listening as Bruce's voice got fainter and fainter down to the southard until it finally passed out of hearing, as if he'd gone right off over the edge of the world.

"Funny," Sam said, puzzled. "I thought, the way they sounded, they'd tree in five minutes."

It had already been over half an hour. There wasn't anything to do but keep after them, or at least in the direction they'd last bayed.

The only sound now was what they made themselves, crashing around through the woods. Every once in a while they had to stop to breathe and Sam would give out with that high sharp yell that doesn't sound really loud but will carry a lot farther than a louder noise will.

They stopped again, both of them blowing hard. Sam heard the dogs first, barely audible and sounding sweeter than bells ringing. Somewhere down there, well out of hearing, the old coon had foxed them a little; but not enough. He'd either managed to lie doggo and let them get by or he'd doubled and was coming back as fast as he'd gone in the first place.

"Judas," Sam said. "That's a smart old bugger and he sure can travel. But why do you suppose he doesn't find a tree?"

"Maybe he can't get far enough ahead of them. We might as well wait right here till we see where they're going."

It was in the middle of a little grove of gray birch, the way they'll grow sometimes in the heart of a spruce woods where you'd never expect to find them. Underfoot, where most of the leaves were, it looked like gold in the moonlight; and the few leaves left on the highest branches made a dappled shade on the gold.

The dogs got closer and closer and after a while it began to make Barney nervous, that yelling coming at him out of the dark and not being able to see what made it. His feet wanted to run, as if whatever was making the noise might be after him.

Every once in a while Sam would shake his head, puzzled, and say, "Why don't they tree?"

They never did. That coon never gave up. And he couldn't have been more than a hundred yards away when the dogs caught him on the ground.

He screamed twice and then there was nothing but the sound of the dogs, not like bells now.

"Well," Sam said. "There's one hide that won't amount to much."

Barney found he'd dropped his cigarette into the dry leaves and when he bent down to pick it up, his fingers wouldn't close enough to feel it. So he stood up and scrubbed it out with his toe and waited, because there wasn't anything else to do.

Finally the snarling and the worrying slowed down a little and Sam called the dogs in. Bruce and Spade came, but Bray was still interested in whatever they had left.

"Here, hold them," Sam said. "I'll go get him."

"No. You hold them. I'll do it."

He had to. He knew there wouldn't be anything left of that coon; but just in case there was, he wanted to be sure it wasn't alive.

"Let me have the gun, will you?"

"Hell, Barney, he's dead. He was dead the minute he stopped yelling."

"All right," Barney said. "But just let me have it."

Sam took the pistol out of his pocket and passed it over and Barney went off through the woods toward the place where Bray was still snarling. When he came out of the shadows, the dog lifted his head from the unidentifiable mess he was worrying, and for a minute Barney wanted to kill him. Not with the gun but some way that would take time and would hurt. Before he thought, hell, it wasn't Bray's fault. He was only doing what they'd trained him to do all his life.

When you drill all mercy out of an animal, you can't expect it to show any when the time comes. It's like people—from the time a kid learns to talk, he hears the same thing over and over. Devil take the hindmost. Get what you can. Any way you can. Dog eat dog. And then, when he puts what's been drilled into him into practice, there's hell to pay.

Barney put his hand out to Bray's collar and the dog snapped and growled. When he heard the familiar voice, though, he let himself be leashed; but he was shaking and looking back over his shoulder as Barney tried to get him away from his kill.

It wasn't possible for what the dogs had left to be alive. But just to be sure Barney put two shots into what had been the head and came away, hauling Bray. Bray didn't want to leave at all, and Barney hauled a little harder than he really had to.

Sam was standing tall and still, waiting for them, Bruce and Spade sitting at his feet.

"Well, Barney," he said. "What do you think?"

"I think I've had enough for one night."

Barney was remembering the one other time he'd heard this same thing happen. That time it hadn't been so near. The sounds, sifted down through trees and muted with distance, had been bad enough.

"Okay."

Sam didn't argue and they started back through the woods toward the house, Sam on ahead with the two older dogs, Barney and Bray behind. They didn't go back past the corn patch, but cut straight across to the road. Down behind the house there was an alder swamp and then the field. They came into the swamp and were nearly into the open when Bruce, still excited, still not run out, caught a scent and snatched his lead out of Sam's hand and was gone. Naturally Spade went with him, he couldn't help himself.

They plunged down along the edge of the alders, two black shapes going like bats out of hell and the rest after them, Sam swearing, Bray and Barney too busy, Barney trying to hold Bray and Bray trying to get away from him.

"God dammit," Sam was yelling. "God dammit, that's no coon! God damn you damned hounds, come back here! Bruce! Spade! Damn a half-witted dog, anyhow."

He was right. It wasn't a coon. It wasn't in a hurry either, and the dogs came up with it in a matter of seconds. One of them let out an anguished yell and the other started to prance around him barking. The one who'd yelled had his stern high in the air now and was rubbing his head along the ground. Every once in a while he'd turn completely over. Then he'd scrub again.

"God, I hope that's not Bruce," Sam said.

It was, though. His excitement had carried him well beyond his wisdom. Bray, horrified at the exhibition, squatted quivering against Barney's leg.

Bruce had caught the porcupine out in the grass where he could get a good nip at it and he should have known better.

"For god sake," Sam said. "Moor those two somewhere, will you? We've got to go to work on him."

Spade let Barney pick up his leash and he took the two of them over and lashed them to an alder he took care to see was as thick through as his leg.

"That'll hold you boys," he said. But they'd lost their excitement too. They didn't like what was happening to Bruce one little bit. They both sat down and watched, panting, tongues out.

Barney got Bruce down on his haunches and he wasn't howling or making any noise now, just fighting as hard as he could and that was almost hard enough. Those black hides cover concentrated muscle that doesn't wait to be told what to do. Bruce's whole body was shaking with a deep tremor that started somewhere in his belly and came out in waves. When Barney got him down and was sitting astride him, back of his shoulders, he reached around gingerly and got one arm across Bruce's throat and shut to until it cut his wind. He had to let go long enough to grab the dog's muzzle in both hands and haul his head back. Bruce had a second before Barney got him and it was long enough for him to snap. Barney got a closer look at those white teeth than he cared for, and all he could think of was what was lying back there near the birch grove that had been running and free half an hour before.

"Hurry up!" Sam said. He was standing in front of them, pliers in one hand, light in the other, and Barney had only time to see his feet and the cuffs of his pants.

He had to jerk to get the jaws open again, but once open he could hold them that way. The poor old devil! Sam shone the light down his throat, and from the look of his tongue and the roof of his mouth the porcupine must have been damned near bald when he got away.

The next fifteen minutes were bloody. Sam was down on his knees peering into Bruce's mouth. He'd get the pliers shut on a quill, give a yank, and a dark spurt of blood would follow it out. Between Barney's knees, Bruce would jump and moan. Toward the last of it, the fight went out of him and he lay there and shook like a bowl of Jello.

"There, damn you!" Sam said at last, getting to his feet, breathing hard through his nose the way he did when he was mad or excited. "Let's see you do it again in a hurry! I've got everything I can see, Barney. Let him up."

Barney got off fast because he wasn't sure what Bruce would do, but he needn't have hurried. The dog was too far beyond knowing what had hit him to realize he wasn't pinned down any more. When it did get through to him, he got to his feet, slow and dazed, one bone at a time, and stood shaking his head. He was a living sight. That old black head in the dim light with blood and foam hiding the gray on his muzzle and his eyes looking like a man who's been on a four-day drunk, half shut and swollen.

"Darned if I know what got into him." Sam took his leash and started toward the house. "Maybe that'll hold him for another five years."

Barney went to get Spade and Bray and they came as docilely as Bruce had. When they were putting the dogs back in the kennel, Sam said:

"He may have a few more, the way he's moving his head. I'll have to take another look by daylight. The old fool!"

He couldn't have been any more put out with that dog if he'd been a human being who'd done such a damnfool thing. He really felt Bruce was human, and expected the same kind of behavior of him you would of a human being. And then, of course, when he got it—because what could have been any closer to human than this performance tonight—he'd get mad as a hatter.

He'd cooled down a little by the time they got into the house. Jude was still in the kitchen. She'd made a fresh pot of coffee and it smelled like heaven. Sam went over to the pantry and came back with a pint of Four Roses and set it down in the middle of the table.

"How about it, Barney?" he said. "I could use it, couldn't you?"

Barney looked at the bottle, then at Sam, then Jude. She was back to, but she hadn't been a minute before. He couldn't recall when he'd last seen Sam take a drink. Sam didn't really like the stuff and he certainly hadn't offered Barney one since the time he'd had to bail him out on that drunk-driving complaint when he'd sideswiped the State Cop.

"Have any luck?" Jude said into the silence, and that reminded Sam of what he'd just had to do and he was mad with Bruce all over again. He started telling her about it, his voice tight with rage.

Barney picked up the bottle and the seal hadn't even been broken. Jude poured their coffee and they sat down at the table while Barney opened the whisky. He drank about a third of his coffee and poured a good slug into what was left. They were still talking about Bruce but their attention had wandered a little and they knew exactly what he put into his cup. He passed the bottle to Sam and you'd have thought he was measuring it with a medicine dropper. He must have got all of half an ounce. He glanced questioningly at Jude and she started to shake her head "no" and then thought better of it. She waved the bottle over her own cup and set it down on the table again.

Then they sat. They sat and the silence got silenter. And Barney thought: I don't know what's coming, but they've got to start it. Because something *was* coming. They weren't exactly exchanging glances, but he could feel them wanting to.

He had to grin a little, now that he could see the elaborate way they'd gone about softening him up for it. Whatever it was, they both felt it was pretty important, judging from the trouble they'd taken. Always before, when they started uphill into one of these talks they seemed to think were so important, they'd just gone: Whiz. Boom. This time, though, the stage had been set so well he'd walked right onto it before he even realized it was a stage and there he was with the spotlight on him. They'd made one mistake, though. They'd given him time to see what was going on and get his feet braced.

"Barney," Sam said loudly. It sounded as if somebody had jabbed a pin into him and he'd said "Ouch!"—it came out that way. "Barney, you satisfied with what you're doing?"

"What?"

"This job. You satisfied with it?"

"If I wasn't, I wouldn't be here."

"Not much future to it."

"What's the matter? You want me to quit or something?"

"No-o. But I hate to see brains going to waste."

"Brains?" Barney sounded stupid because that surprised him. Sam had never admitted he had any brains before and now he was saying they were being wasted. "Look," Barney said. "What's that red-headed son of a bitch been telling you?"

"If you mean Paul—" Sam hesitated, looking down at his hands, finding, apparently to his surprise, that he'd taken the spoon out of his cup and was puddling coffee around on the oilcloth. "Paul hasn't said anything to me. Should he?"

"Not because of anything *I've* done," Barney said. "If you aren't satisfied with the way I'm working, Sam, will you for god sake say so?"

"It hasn't got anything to do with what you're *not* doing."

"Well, then—" Barney was beginning to get really hot. "Will you tell me what the hell I *am* doing you don't like?"

"Sam, for heaven sake!" Jude said, unable to stand it any longer. "Why on earth don't you say what you're trying to? I don't blame Barney for getting mad."

"I'm not mad," Barney said; but he was. "I'm just wondering what gives."

"*You* tell him," Sam said, looking at her. "You can talk better than I can."

"Well, all right." Jude looked at Barney as if she was hoping he'd say something to make it easier for her; but he was really up in the air. He didn't yet have any more idea what they were coming at than the man in the moon. "What he's trying to say, Barney, is that you're just going to waste, doing what you're doing now."

"I got that much," Barney said. "He's already said that."

"If you're willing to work the way you have this summer on a job that doesn't matter, Sam's trying to say there's a bigger one you could have that would help him more and pay you more."

"Virtue rewarded," Barney said, and Jude got that look on her face that made him feel as if he'd slapped her. "What if I don't want a bigger job? Money's not everything, is it? What if I'm satisfied with what I'm getting now?"

"Are you?" Sam said. "That's what I'm trying to find out."

"Well, I don't know. It depends on what's coming."

He thought he might as well find out just how far Sam would be willing to go. He'd said money wasn't everything; but it came pretty close to being. Anyway, he could always use a little more.

"Well, something's sure chewing on you," Sam said quickly, half-ashamed at having to say it. "You can't be satisfied with everything and look the way *you* look. Christ almighty," he warmed up to it fast, "you look as if you'd been dragged through forty-seven cities and the last one was a—"

"Sam!" Jude said sharply.

He gave her a sheepish grin.

"Well, hell, all right. But he does."

"You know—" Barney said, "that's one thing I can't do a lot about. The way I look. You want me to get a permanent wave or a manicure or something? My face is something I can't change for you, Sammy, new job or no new job."

"It's more than the job, Barney," Jude said, and at the sound of her voice he thought: Here it comes.

For a minute he was still back out there in the shifting shadows of the trees, listening for the dogs, still his own man, still feeling good. Then he wasn't, because they'd got down to what was bothering them and it wasn't the job and nobody had said what it was yet, but all of them knew. They'd been talking about the same thing right from the beginning—and now they were getting ready to call it by name.

My god, Barney thought, you must have to be damned sure you were right if you're willing—it was more than willing, it was feeling

like you had a god-given right the way they did—to tell somebody
else how to live his life! There they sat, looking at him, as sure as
they were of their own names that they knew what was the best
thing for him to do and that he wasn't doing it.

"Barney," Jude said.

She put her hand halfway across the table toward where his
was lying beside his cup—she wanted him to meet her, but he was
damned if he would. She wanted him to be a child again and he
wasn't. She wanted to be his mother and she wasn't.

"A door's got to open on tomorrow," she said slowly, "or it's no
use even tripping the latch, Barney. Nobody every got a round-trip
ticket down an elevator shaft."

"What in hell are you talking about?" he asked, for time, because
he didn't need the answer now.

"*You* know."

That was just like her, too, and it bothered him. Saying something like that and leaving you to put whatever you wanted to
behind it—going away from it herself and leaving you to think
perhaps she knew more than she did, or leaving you trying to hold
onto what she *did* mean.

"We talked it over," Sam said suddenly, and before Barney had
time to say, you talked *what* over, went on. "We decided we
wouldn't say anything to you if you didn't go with me tonight,
you see. If you didn't go with the dogs. Because we figured that'd
mean it was too late already, Barney. That she had you and you
couldn't— Well, anyhow, you went. It isn't so bad. We could
help you if you let us. You could get out of Port Kezar for a while.
You could take this job—and—"

He ran down and stopped and it must have been the look on
Barney's face that had done it. Sam sat there with his mouth open,
ready for the next word, the one he no longer needed.

"What?" Barney said. "What about tonight?"

"Friday night," Sam said. "You always—it's Friday night."

Barney saw then what they'd done to him and what they thought
it proved. He saw what he'd let them do. He'd lost a whole day
and he'd thought it was Thursday. He'd let them drive her right
out of his head, and she'd been waiting for him since six o'clock.
It was ten o'clock now.

He got up so fast he knocked the chair over backward. He didn't even hear the noise it made when it hit the floor. He reached over and took the pint and shoved it into his pocket.

"Thanks for everything, Sammy," he said.

The only thought in his head all the way uptown was: So that was why they were watching me! *That* was it! Twice he took Sam's pint out of his pocket and, holding the bottle between his knees, managed to get the cap off and pour some of the whisky down his throat. He couldn't feel it on the way. He was that mad. Not with Sam and Jude—with himself. *He'd* let them do it.

The house looked dark when he turned in the driveway; but then he saw that little bug-in-a-bottle lamp in the kitchen was burning and that was all. He wanted to get out of the car and didn't want to at the same time. His hands were cold; but there was a hard hot knot right about where that whisky sat in his stomach.

He got out finally and went over to the door and didn't even see, until he put his hand out to the latch, that it wasn't necessary. The door was open and the old bundle of bones done up in cloth that called itself a man was standing there grinning at him. It was the first time Barney had ever seen any expression on Arthur's face but the first and all-the-time one. Tonight Arthur was grinning and it was worse than the constant look of steady and bursting rage. The grin took his face right out of the human race and made a skull of it before his time.

"You're too late, Uncle Barney," he said.

"Hey?" Something, maybe the whisky, had made Barney so stupid that what Arthur said didn't penetrate.

"Too late," he repeated triumphantly. "They couldn't wait for you. They went off out somewhere."

"Well, where? Who?"

"I wouldn't tell you if I could. I don't know who, either. They didn't say."

He tipped his head back to look up at Barney's face and in the moonlight he looked like a blind man. His eyes were flat silver spaces between the lids, and for a second they were all there was to his face.

"Someday—" Barney said and even to himself his voice sounded slow and working against odds, "probably I'll kill you, old man!"

It wasn't a threat. He was simply saying what there was in his mind to say. It was there and it came out and he heard it himself without surprise, knowing it for something that had been there long enough for him to get used to it. It was the first time Arthur had heard it, though. He took a step backward, dragging his foot after him, and put up his hand across those god-awful silver eyes.

"No," Barney said. "You've got a while longer. I've got other things more important to do tonight."

He knew where Sabra was as well as if she'd left a map drawn out with arrows, saying: Here's where I am. So he went to get her. He headed for the beer joint where he'd met her last July and where he knew she was now and when he got there, whatever would happen would happen without his having anything to do with it.

On the way he finished the pint, and the whisky had only one effect. There were two of him driving the car. Two of him got out and went over to the door under the sick green flashing sign. Two Barneys looked in through the glass, their hands on the latch, watching her.

Sure, she was there. She was sitting up at the counter and all he could see of her past the back of the guy with her was part of a shoulder; but he didn't need that much to know her.

He opened the door quietly and went in and it seemed to him that every sound in the place stopped as if it had been cut off with a knife. Of course it didn't. It just stopped for him. He went in and walked—in silence that felt deep and solid like water—down along the counter and put his hand on the guy's shoulder to turn him around.

He was big. Under his hand Barney felt solid muscle get tight with surprise. Barney'd thought first it might be somebody he'd seen before, somebody from the Port; but the square hard face and the pale cold blue eyes belonged to a stranger. His dark hair was cut short like a college boy's and the forelock was waxed to stand up and looked like a dark picket fence.

"Git," Barney said, his tongue feeling heavy and stiff. He didn't have any quarrel with this guy, but he was in the way. "While you're still able."

For a minute the stranger's eyes flickered while he debated whether to git or to fight. He glanced at Sabra but she was watching with that funny half-smile she got when she was excited, and she was no help to him. She was liking this.

The stranger got off the stool with a shrug.

"Am I intruding?" he said nastily. "Or are you?"

"Believe me, brother," Barney said. "*You*'re the one."

Forgetting him, once he was out of the line of fire, Barney found watching, from the far end of the counter, his old friend the waitress with the streaky copper hair—it looked the way it always did, not like hair. Her mouth was a perfectly round "O" in the dead center of her face. Her right hand was groping for the telephone. There was a half-empty beer bottle on the counter in front of Sabra, and Barney saw his own hand reach out and grab it, haul it back for momentum, and send it skating down the full length of the bar.

All hell broke loose. Coffee cups and beer glasses, and everything else breakable and full, shot right and left with a terrific clatter. The beer bottle was really traveling. There had been eight or ten people sitting along the bar and Barney hadn't missed one of them. By the time the bottle hit the telephone, the waitress had the phone out of the cradle, so that was all that went onto the floor. She hung onto the phone, talking into it fast, and she hadn't taken her eyes off Barney for a second.

Only one of the two of him who'd come in through the door and walked down along the counter was doing all this. The other one was still standing behind him looking over his shoulder to see what was going to happen next.

The guys who have time enough left out of their days to sit in a joint like that nursing a couple of beers just to make the time go by before they have to go home are usually ready for anything that comes along and hoping it will. So now he had half a dozen of them, all madder than a nest of white-tail hornets. That looked about right for the way he felt. There'd be two or three who'd go through the motions; but really they'd only be in there making a noise and letting the others carry it to him.

He looked over his shoulder to see if there wasn't something he could get his back up against, and the only thing handy was the public phone booth inside the door. There wasn't a piece of wall big enough that was clear of impediments. With his back against the glass folding door, he knew it wasn't a good spot. They could get at him from three sides; but he didn't give a good god damn if they could.

He was beginning to see everything double now, not himself alone. There he was, facing up to what looked like six sets of identical twins, all of them mad. But none of them would make the first move, all waiting for somebody else.

Barney remembered once when he came out into a clearing after a heavy snow and found a place where a pack of dogs had got a deer and the way the sorry sneaking story had been written out for him, the dogs sitting in a circle and waiting for the buck to turn his back on one of them.

He looked blearily around at his pack of dogs.

"All right. Step on it," he said. "If you want any fun. She's not calling the humane society."

Then one of them, one he wasn't watching, hit him and it hurt like hell. Right behind the ear. Whisky always made him crazy anyhow and that flipped the switch. He didn't go for the guy who hit him. He put his head down and butted the one right in front, got him under the ribs and heard his wind go out with a whoosh when he doubled over, just before they fell. Then he was down, with Barney on top of him and all the rest of them on top of Barney.

It was fine while it lasted. He didn't have to worry about hitting the wrong guy. He didn't have to worry about one damn thing. Anything he had to fight with he used.

He used his knee good and proper on one of them and heard his high hurt yelp. By god, Barney thought, there's *one* won't stand up straight for an hour or two. Once he was out from under and the only one on his feet. He looked around for something loose to use; but he really didn't have time enough and what he wanted was a length of two-by-four and it wasn't handy.

He backed up enough to get a running start and jumped to land feet first in the middle of the thrashing mass and went down under as if he'd jumped into a quicksand.

After that it got all mixed up. There was a steady accompaniment of breaking glass and screaming women. Every woman in the place was screeching like a steam whistle, except Sabra. He came up long enough to catch a quick glimpse of her, like the snatches you get of people through the windows of those crummy hotels between the 125th Street Station and where the train goes into the tunnel, going into New York. She was sitting right where he'd left her and she was still smiling.

That was the last clear thing. He went down once more and out like the lights.

When he came to he was colder than a dead mackerel and lying on something rough and hard. He thought he might be still out because it was darker than the inside of a pocket and his head was attached to him only by a string and floating two feet above his body. Then the green neon sign flashed and there he was, lying out on the tarred parking space and it felt like right in the middle of a mud puddle. He was patting the tar with one hand, which was all he could move, saying: "Where? Where?"

He pulled his head down where it belonged, and when it grew back on his neck he turned it to look and all he could see were these shiny black shoes and the cuffs of a pair of powder-blue pants. He shut his eyes and turned the other way to get away from them. When he opened up again, he thought he'd just imagined turning away, because there were the shiny black shoes, there were the cuffs of the blue pants.

"My god," he said. "*He's* twins, too!"

When he finally looked straight up, he saw there were really two of them and that was a slight relief. The young fellow was training his face to have that square hard look all the State Cops get. Kermit was leaning over, hands on his knees, and Barney saw his face upside down and it looked so funny all he could do was lie there and laugh. There was that big, slab-cheeked face with no more expression on it than if Kermit had just squashed a bug. Nothing could surprise that guy any longer and if it managed to, he'd split a gut to keep you from finding it out. And no matter how well you know a face, seeing it upside down makes it altogether different and funny. So Barney laughed and then wished he hadn't because even moving his face that much hurt.

Kermit said: "Get up, Barney."

"I like it here," Barney said. "You want me up, you've got to pick me up."

Damned if he was going to say he couldn't move anything but his little finger. Kermit knew it, though. Barney was coming to enough to see the two policemen exchange a thoughtful glance. They didn't have to say anything, everyone was aware of the subject of the discussion. Each of them got hold of one of Barney's arms, high up, with a fist in his armpit, and hauled until his head was level with theirs. Barney wouldn't have said they had him on his feet. His feet wouldn't move, just hung and dangled. And if either one of the cops had let go, he would have melted back into his comfortable mud puddle. It was that whisky! He'd never had anything hit him the way that did. He was going around like a merry-go-round and the steam organ was playing *Waltz Me Around Again, Willie.*

They loaded him into the car about the way you would a sack of potatoes. He was trying hard but he wasn't much help to them. That crew of punks must have done quite a job on him after he passed out. The way he felt, every square inch of surface had had a currycombing with a hobnailed boot. He leaned back in the seat and it felt like a feather bed.

Barney didn't even flicker again until somebody started shaking him roughly and he came to thinking his head was going to roll on the floor. A minute later, when he opened his eyes and a streak of sunlight coming in through the bars got him dead center, he wished it had.

It took a couple minutes more for him to focus on the face that leaned above him this time. It was another familiar one, but a few years older than when he'd last seen it. The keeper at the county jail was one of those lazy-looking fat men with a stomach that made you wonder if he'd stuffed a couple of pillows into his front, so big it was like the addition on a house. But he wasn't as lazy as

he looked and there was something more than plain stupidity in
the little bright blue eyes that were about an inch deeper in fat
than when Barney had seen them last, but as bright as ever.

"Up you get, Barney," he said. "You're keeping the wheels of
justice from turning. Or will be, if you don't get over to the courthouse on the double."

"Double!" Barney repeated. Man, what an optimist!

He picked up the pieces with the help of a quart of coffee that
tasted as if it had been brewing on the back of the stove for a
week. If that stayed down, he could do anything else he had to.

He thought they'd head for Municipal Court; but that door was
closed and they went on past it to another one marked Private. It
was a little room with a desk and a couple of chairs in it and the
walls lined with those leather-back books that have REV. STAT.
and a number on them and don't mean anything to you until you
stop to think that whatever you're here for is probably written
down in one of them somewhere, and right after it in the small
print will be written what they can do to you for it.

There was a young man sitting at the desk, dressed up in one
of those nubby tweed suits, leaning back in his chair playing with
a paper knife, and he looked comfortable and easy. As for Barney,
he felt like one of those clown dolls with the round weighted bottom, and when you pushed it it'd go around in a circle and bob up
again. As soon as he thought of that, though, he could see it was
a terrible mistake. He shouldn't think of either circles or bobbing.

He closed his eyes a minute and when he opened them, saw Sam
sitting in one of the chairs near the door and he must have been
there when they'd come in but Barney had only been able to take
in one thing at a time.

Sam was all dressed up too, had on a suit and a white shirt with
a necktie. The tie wasn't straight. Or maybe that was Barney.
Anyhow, the tie didn't *look* straight. Sam's face didn't either. It
looked as if he'd put it on when he got up this morning, like the
tie, and hadn't been quite able to manage the knot. He was looking the way Barney should have been, as if *he'd* done whatever it
was. But he hadn't, Barney thought. Hell, he was just the innocent
bystander.

Barney wanted to say to him: Why don't you give up? Why don't you get to hell out of here and let them go ahead and have their fun? The trouble was, Sam wouldn't have gone. And it would have made him feel that much worse because Barney wasn't appreciating what was being done for him. Because something was. They were both looking at him with that considering expression that makes you feel like a side-show freak.

"Well?" Barney said.

"Don't *feel* very well, do you?" The young guy at the desk gave him a dirty grin.

"I've felt worse," Barney said; but he couldn't think when he had. He felt like death warmed over and he couldn't even dredge up a grin to answer with. His whole face was one solid piece and none of it would move.

"That's difficult to believe."

The young guy leaned forward and threw the paper knife on the desk. It didn't make much noise landing but what it did make sounded like a pistol shot to Barney. The swivel chair squeaked, too.

"Well," he said, and Barney saw that the fun was over. "You're charged with disturbing the peace, assault and battery, and several other items that could cool you off for quite a while. But I've been talking with your brother here."

"Oh?"

"You've never happened to come up before me, Barney, but I find this is not your initial brush with this Court."

That meant this was the judge. Barney took another look at him and didn't like it any better this time. He'd stopped talking as if he expected Barney to say something; but when there's not much to say it's just as well to keep your mouth shut until you find out what the boys have dreamed up for you this time.

"He says he's got a job for you that will take you out of Port Kezar for the winter. And also out of circulation."

Chain O' Lakes, Barney thought, here I come.

"I am inclined to agree with him that it's a better solution than having you spend the winter at the County's expense. You know—" He was chewing the words now as if they tasted good to

him. "We don't enjoy sometimes the things it's necessary to do
to protect other people from people like you. If there's another
solution, I'd be tempted to take it. How about you?"

Barney thought about the long winter evenings and, at the moment, he didn't care whether he spent them in jail or up back of
Rangeley. He couldn't see much choice; but he had sense enough
to know that was mostly hangover. If they gave him six months,
he'd be talking to the birds by the time he got out.

"Anything," he said.

"All right."

The judge got up, brisk now and businesslike, all the fun over.
He went out through a door Barney hadn't noticed before and
Barney went back through the door to the corridor and approached
the court in the proper way, accompanied by his keeper.

It went fast. The first thing Barney knew, he was standing in
front of the judge again and the clerk was reading the charge.
Barney couldn't even follow his mumblings, and after a minute
he didn't try. This desk was higher and more impressive-looking
and he'd faced it before. The judge looked a good deal more important behind it than he had in the room they'd just left and it
doesn't take a hell of a lot, does it, to make one man more important than another, if all he has to do is be sitting behind a big desk
and the other guy standing in front of him waiting to see what he's
going to say.

He looked at Barney with a face that said: I've never set eyes on
you before.

"How do you plead?"

"Guilty."

"Six months in jail," he said. "Or two hundred dollars and
costs."

That jolted Barney. *He* certainly didn't have it; but he looked
sideways at Sam and they must have talked that over too. The
judge was saying, when Barney finally got over the two-hundred-
dollar hump and back to him, "Probation for six months. I want
the probation officer to see you once a month until he tells you
differently. Next."

Tough guy, he was, real hanging judge.

And it was over and Barney was outside and easing himself down over the wide granite steps, and Sam's truck, parked at the curb below, looked fifteen miles away. He made it, only just, crawled into the front seat and they started for home. Exactly like that. Sam didn't look at him and he didn't speak.

Well, Barney thought, I've kicked the bucket over this time, good and proper!

He still couldn't make himself give a damn about anything but the way his head felt. He should have been telling himself he was forty-seven kinds of a cussed fool. As for ungrateful—that didn't even enter into it. He'd been told that so often and for so long he'd have felt lonesome without it. He hadn't asked Sam for anything, he'd never asked him for anything except just to leave him alone. And Sam couldn't do it because he had it all figured out that Barney belonged to him the way his truck or his house or anything else like that belonged to him.

This time, though, Sam was really mad.

They rode all the way from Bristol to Port Kezar in silence as thick as a pea-soup fog. It suited Barney. He couldn't have talked if he'd wanted to, much less have listened to Sam talk. But Sam sure as hell spent all that time telling him again how ungrateful he was, even if he didn't once open his yawp.

They went through town as if there wasn't any other car on the street. When they pulled in to the house, Sam cut the engine and turned to Barney, his eyes as hard as his jaw.

"Pack what you need," he said.

"You mean right now?" Barney said stupidly. He wasn't even going to have a chance to see her! And here he was as weak as a damned kitten and in no shape to argue.

"It'll take you an hour," Sam said steadily. "At least, that's what you've got. And don't forget, it's going to be a long cold winter."

That was just what Barney was thinking.

PART TWO

THERE were times in your life when you reached a point where you were incapable of saying anything even if there had been anything to say and usually there wasn't. Jude had reached that point. This was her day.

It had begun late last night, the same way the others like it had begun, for the same reason, with the telephone ringing to bring her awake, startled, because the sound of the telephone in a sleeping house always seems to be the prelude to something wrong. Before she was fully awake, she'd known what it would be.

Groping down over the stairs, barefooted, her eyes still sticky with sleep and hard to focus, she found herself saying softly: "Oh, Barney!"

Not angrily yet, because sometime it would ring to say he'd had his last accident, or been in his last fight, and until she knew this wasn't the time she couldn't be angry.

Dragged out of greater depths of unconsciousness than hers, Sam took longer to wake and she was halfway down the stairs toward the jangling bell when he called after her.

"Better let me, Jude."

"I'm there," she called back to him and the jangling stopped as she picked up the receiver and said "Yes?" into it. Not "Hello," because the dangerous summons in the night meant something wrong and she couldn't be that receptive to disaster.

"Sorry to get you out of bed at this hour of the night, Mrs. Cousins."

Jude knew the voice well enough to know with the first few words that this was no worse than ever, that the familiar pattern was beginning all over again with this call, not coming to an end as she always had to think it might be until she answered.

"It's all right, Kermit," she said, still too close to sleep to be quite civilized, and, not being civilized, not too sure that what she was feeling was relief. "I've been expecting you. Has he done—" Then she stopped that question in the middle. It was unnecessary because Barney *had* done something or Kermit wouldn't be calling. Going on smoothly to the next: "Is he hurt?"

"*Hurt!* Hell, no." Hearing pity in that voice that had been trained to exclude pity, Jude winced. At night, when you slept, your armor wasn't ready for the sudden awakening. "He's too drunk to be hurt. But they've set his hearing for tomorrow morning and that new judge, that young Hardesty, he's still new enough to be tough. If Sam could talk to him before the hearing—"

He paused and Jude thought he had been going to say, "It might be easier for Barney," and then hadn't said it because they'd all been making it easier for Barney for a long time now and maybe they were all wrong.

"Thanks a lot," she said, her lips stiff. "I'll tell Sam. Thanks, Kermit." She hung up in the face of his going-to-say-something-more silence, before he could say whatever it was, knowing he wouldn't be offended.

Going back up the stairs she was deep in trying to think how she could tell Sam something he already knew, and Cliff met her at the head of the stairs, shivering with excitement.

"What is it? What is it?" He was like an overgrown puppy at the advent of anything unusual, dancing with curiosity and interest, forgetting in his excitement that he was cold and nearly naked. He had on nothing but a pair of shorts and Jude found herself wondering first how many times she'd have to get after him before he'd wear his pajamas, and second, there he was, there he was, and was it all going to start over again with him? Would there be any way to keep the contagion from touching him?

"You get back to bed before you get pneumonia," she said roughly. "It wasn't anything to do with you."

Cliff, suddenly conscious of what he didn't have on, thudded rapidly down the hall to his bedroom.

"It's Barney," he said over his shoulder. "Isn't it?"

Jude didn't answer him. She went into her own room and shut the door carefully. Sam was sitting up in the other bed and he'd turned on the small light on the night table. His face looked drugged with sleep and his straw-colored hair was standing on end.

"I'm glad we haven't got any kids of our own," Jude said savagely into his waiting silence. "I'm glad. I'm glad. This is bad enough."

"What?"

"Maybe, if they're not our own, we don't feel so bad. I'm glad we won't ever have to find out if we'd feel worse. I wouldn't want to feel any worse, Sam."

"Honey, for christ sake—"

"He's not hurt. He's drunk. He's in Bristol. Kermit said the hearing was set for tomorrow morning and there's a new judge who might make it tough for him if you weren't there and wouldn't that be too bad! Wouldn't it be a shame if Barney just once had to get himself out of one of these hassles!"

"I spose I ought to let him," Sam said slowly.

"I suppose you should. But you aren't going to, are you?" Already she could see him beginning to think: I'd better be there early, have a chance to talk to the judge.

"Jude, you know I can't do it. He's my brother."

"Yes."

"We've taught him to think he can rely on us and you can't take that away from a kid once you've given it to him."

"When does he stop being a kid?"

"Jude, for god sake—"

"I'm not helping you, am I, Sam? I'm making things harder. And that's just exactly what I want to do."

"It's not very pleasant, I admit." His voice was almost pleading. "There's a lot of things happen that aren't, Jude. You have to learn to take them in your stride."

"It would be fine," she said in a purposely hurting voice, "to be able to find a platitude to fit every situation. It would be comfortable."

"Platitudes, maybe," Sam admitted. "But if a lot of folks before me hadn't found they fitted, they'd never have got enough use so's you could call them that."

"Sam." She had been standing by the door, but now she went over and sat down on the edge of his bed and put her arms around him. Sam let his forehead rest on her shoulder and for a minute he was like a child, but a child that must not be treated as one, must be treated as a man. "It's not Barney, any longer," she said. "It's you. And Cliff. Cliff's right at the age where he might think Barney was smart. We've got a responsibility to him too, Sam. You know I love Barney, because he's part of you and I know how you feel about him. But if we keep on taking care of him, telling him it's not his fault, this is going to go on for the rest of our lives. This being waked up at night, or meeting the sheriff at the door in the morning. Until one of these calls turns out to be the last one."

But Sam had thought of that too.

"We'll get the last one anyhow," he said. "You know that, don't you? Whether there're any more in between or not. We'll get the last one. But I keep thinking," his voice rose suddenly into a protesting roar. "If he only had one more chance."

"He's *had* one more out of all reason. Nobody ever had so many."

"I know it."

Jude let him go and went back to her own bed.

"You might as well stop hunting for him, Sam. We lost him for good and all a long time ago."

She lay listening to him get up and start dressing.

"I got to try this once more, Jude. I've got a feeling. I've got an idea. This time he won't go scot-free. But, by the jesus christ, it's the last time!"

His tone was the defensive one of a man who knows that what he is saying doesn't amount to a hoot in the hollow of hell. It wasn't the last time and it wouldn't ever be.

It was only two o'clock; but she heard him stumbling around in the kitchen and presently the smell of coffee came up to her and, just as she fell asleep, the smell of bacon.

Sam was gone when she came down in the morning, and the depth of his disquiet was evident in the state he'd left the kitchen in. Jude felt slightly ashamed that she had been able to sleep while he had not, because nothing ever disturbed Sam's sleep. Until now he had found something that could and she had let him go it alone.

The first thing she looked for when Sam's truck drove back into the yard was to see if Barney was with him. When she found the young dark face through the glass and felt the instantaneous flood of relief that one crisis was over, or, if not over, then at least surmounted, because there he was, the relief was all the deeper for her knowledge that the next crisis would start building immediately, and would reach the same pitch, or a higher one, until they all came up to the pitch that would be so high none of them would be able to bear it.

I might just as well be his mother, she thought. It's been so long now, I wouldn't feel any differently about him if I were. And the only kind of relief you could get with kids was when one crisis was past and another hadn't had time to begin.

It was Barney's day too; his day to stand up on his hind legs and howl if he was ever going to do it and there wasn't a good howl left in him. His chest felt as if it had been hollowed out with a nutmeg grater and the hole filled with Portland Cement. His head felt as if it had been hollowed out with the same thing and then blown full of that gas they put in the balloons you see at a carnival.

After Barney got upstairs and sat down on his bed, his hands and feet were too heavy to move. He wasn't doing anything, just sitting there with his eyes shut, when Jude came in with a suitcase. Barney opened his eyes long enough to see it and know that Sam had told her what he was going to do.

"I didn't think you had a suitcase," Jude said and Barney waited a minute to see if there was any more coming, any of the "after all we've done for you" business; but nothing came.

"Duffle bag better," he said through a mouthful of cotton. "In the closet, on shelf."

He could just see himself arriving in style upcountry somewhere with a piece of Jude's Amelia Earhart luggage or whatever it was. He was going to have to work down being the boss's brother anyhow, he didn't want to have to work down the idea he was kind of nancy too, not in one of those pulp camps.

She got it down and started packing.

"I'll do it," Barney said.

At that she did give him a look and didn't stop what she was doing. It must have been obvious, even to Jude, that he was beyond doing anything right at the moment. So he sat there and listened to his heart—wondering if she could hear it too, banging around in its concrete casing. Every time it beat, there was a two-inch square of skull bone on the top of his head that felt as if it flipped up like a trap door and shut to again.

"You hear that banging?" he asked her suddenly.

"That's Paul out in the barn. He's changing one of the back tires on the truck."

By god, Barney thought, it really *is* making a racket if it sounds like that to her. He knew it wasn't Paul changing any tire.

He sat there watching her and if he could have found something to say to make her feel better, he might have done it. But he couldn't think of anything, so he'd never know whether he would have or not. Because she was really feeling bad. With Jude, he knew, when she couldn't find anything to say herself she was in a bad way. She kept her back turned very carefully, only once or twice she slipped and her eyes, making a circuit to see what she'd forgotten to pack, would meet Barney's and before they could skid away again, he would see it all right there on the surface. She might as well have said it out loud.

The duffle bag was one of those that open on the side and when she zipped it shut the noise sounded as if she'd been tearing heavy canvas.

"I guess that's it."

Jude looked around the room again, half as if she thought of putting in the bureau or something. Then she looked right at

Barney and didn't look away. For a minute they stared at each other and Barney could see her eyes get bright. He knew she wouldn't cry; but the tears were there and he felt as if the bottom had dropped out of his stomach.

She came over to stand in front of him.

"Barney," she said. "I am sorry."

"Yeah. Me too."

"If you could talk to Sam. Maybe he'd change his mind." That meant she didn't think Sam was doing the right thing, that she could see a mistake being made; but that she couldn't do anything about it herself. He wondered vaguely if she'd tried.

"I guess we aren't sorry about the same thing, Jude. I haven't got one damn thing I want to say to him."

"I see."

"You should have told me." He could hear his voice getting high and tight, so he hurried. "I thought it was Thursday, see? You should have told me it was Friday night!"

His throat closed and if he tried to talk any more he'd be sick. He got up and picked up the bag and it felt as if she'd stored half the house inside it. He had been going to hoist it onto his shoulder; but if he got that much weight up there that fast it would tip him right over backward. He wrestled it out to the head of the stairs and gave it a kick and it slumped down into the front hall and Barney stood looking carefully away from it until it stopped moving.

Sam came out of the little room he used for an office, across the hall from the living room and picked it up. He slung it over his shoulder without glancing up and disappeared in the direction of the back door.

Without having to think about anything, Barney went down through the hall, through the quiet kitchen with the teakettle singing on the stove, out the back door. He climbed into the waiting truck, leaned back, and said:

"Let her go, bub."

But by that time they were already out of the driveway and headed north, so that hadn't been necessary either. It was all taken care of for him.

The clouds were low and gray, and about half an hour after they started it began to rain. Not even a good downpour. Just one of those mizzling rains where you can't decide whether the windshield wiper's more of a nuisance than the water. Barney closed his eyes and let himself go along with the motion of the truck and he must have fallen asleep. When he woke up it was really raining and they had reached territory that was new to him. He'd never been much for the country inland, away from the coast. It was all right for hunting, but nothing else as far as he could see.

"Where the hell we going?"

He looked out the window, trying to get his bearings. All he could see was scrub-growth birches and every once in a while what looked like a pasture that hadn't known anything about a cow for years, or a house back off the road that needed a coat of paint badly but had a shiny television aerial right up alongside the chimney that hadn't been pointed up for so long more smoke came out through the sides than through the top. If there was a barn, it'd be broken-backed, and you could look right through it and see sky on the other side.

"Good god almighty, Sam," he said. "Where's this?"

"We went through Dover-Foxcroft about ten minutes ago," Sam said. His face was still looking kind of chiseled out; but his voice was beginning to sound more like him.

Barney sat up with a jerk and stared at him.

"Kind of out of our way, aren't we?"

If they'd been going where he'd got it into his head they were, it should have been Anson or North New Portland or one of those towns. Dover-Foxcroft was way out of line.

Sam shook his head.

"*I'm* not lost," he said.

All right, you stubborn bastard, Barney thought, be damned to you if I'll ask you again. It didn't make any difference to him, anyway, wherever they were. They stopped to eat in Monson. Barney wouldn't have thought, three hours before, he'd ever want to see food again; but by that time he was ready.

Along toward the middle of the afternoon, they were way to hell and gone up into the lake country back of Moosehead, where every puddle as big over as the palm of your hand had a name longer than your arm. There was Seboomook and Caucomgomac and Curabexis and Umsaskis, and Chemguasabamticook. And if they'd gone much farther they'd have had to start speaking French. But the road played out. By that time Barney was beginning to wonder if Sam really *did* know where he was going because it stopped right at the edge of another one of those damned lakes and then there wasn't anything. Only this big silver-colored lake under a low gray sky with the trees coming down to it looking like black wrought iron, until it was just by the grace of God they weren't growing in the water.

Oh my god, he thought, I should have taken my six months in Bristol. Here there weren't even the birds to talk to if he'd felt inclined.

Sam leaned on the truck horn and then sat back and waited. He didn't look at anything, just waited. But Barney didn't know what was coming, so he was watching and in a few minutes he saw a boat put off from the opposite shore.

It was one of those lake launches that look like the last thing ever invented to go on the water in, if you've been brought up with lobster boats. A good lobster boat is a handsome sight to see, the way she takes to the water. It's her natural element and she knows it. But these slab-sided, misbegotten, dories-gone-wrong they use on most lakes scared hell out of him just to look at them. They pounded and thrashed and fought the water and most of their weight seemed to be well up above the water line so the least little breeze or ripple was enough to start them acting like a girl trying out for the Rockettes.

This boat, he could see when she got in close enough, was one of the finest examples. The hull was an old lapstreak affair that looked as if for the last fifty years, whenever it sprung a leak, they'd slapped on another coat of brindle paint instead of using a little calking.

She had a hump-backed sprayhood and she needed it. There wasn't much more than a dimple on that lake; but she was spanking into what there was and sending the old spray flying with each swat. She was powered by what sounded suspiciously like one of those old make-and-break engines. When she got closer in, all Barney could think of was a guy under an oil drum with a ball-peen hammer. She'd go CLANG. Then there'd be a long dying wheeze and you'd swear she'd never CLANG again; but she managed it somehow, just when you thought it was too late. CLANG. And the shattering echoes would clang back at her from the trees like a solid wall along the shore.

Barney could make out something that looked like a weathered basketball sticking out above the sprayhood. The only way he knew it was alive, whenever she'd send a bucketful of water back over the bow, the basketball would disappear and then bounce back up again.

It was still raining, but it had settled back into the same old drizzle.

"That's Ellick," Sam said, and it came to Barney that he was giving a name to the basketball and it was a human being.

"That's good."

He thought Alec was going to bring the boat right ashore and drive her into the truck. But Alec killed the engine altogether, which was the only way to slow her down, and put her nose in against the pebbly shore. Only then one of the seams of the basketball split and Barney saw a few brown teeth and realized that Alec, whatever it was, was grinning.

His first impression of Alec underwent some drastic changes before he got his last one. Alec was a Micmac Indian and as big and clumsy and about as talkative as a bear. He didn't have a visible spear of hair on his body. His head was big, round, leathery-looking, with the eyes and nose jammed up together, right in the center and too small; but he had a mouth that bisected his entire face. He could take a horseshoe in his hands and straighten it out until you'd think it had never been intended to be anything but straight.

He wasn't much on English. He could understand it all right, but his own language was a mixture of English and bastard French and something else that nobody could identify or hardly understand—maybe just Alec. The only thing he ever talked about was his wife and she was dead.

Evenings he used to sit beside the drum stove in the bunk-house telling about her last illness and you could understand only every third word or so until he got to the big scene where she nearly recovered.

"I come in a door!" Alec would sit right up straight and his little black eyes would bug out until you could have knocked them off the surface of his face with a stick. His mouth would open in a round "O" of astonishment, always as great as the day he came through the door into the room where he'd thought his wife lay dying.

"I come in a door, n there she was! Sit up in bed, drink cup of tea, quite plain!"

That was Alec's big minute and the cup of tea must have been his wife's, because right after that she died. He told about it on the average of once a week all winter long. Barney asked him once how long ago she'd died, thinking probably it was last fall. Alec figured it out on his fingers until he ran out of them.

"More than ten years now," he said.

That cup of tea had been the most exciting thing that had happened to him in more than ten years!

But all that came later. When Barney first saw him, he nodded to see if Alec would nod back at him, and he did. Barney didn't say anything to him for fear he might not be able to talk at all. Looking at the split that passed for a mouth, he really didn't see how anything like a language could come out of it. It wasn't shaped right to make words.

"This is my brother, Ellick," Sam said and Alec looked at Barney again, differently this time, and that was when Barney began revising his opinion about whatever there might be for intelligence behind the awful mistake Alec had to call a face. There was no change of expression on it; but his little eyes were considering and thoughtful and not particularly pleased, and Barney knew exactly how he felt. It was the way he would have felt himself, starting out on a nice long winter's job, thinking things were going to go just about the way he wanted them to, and finding at the last minute, and when it's too late to do anything about it but quit, that the boss was planting—not a spy, maybe, because that's something you don't get introduced to—but a source of information. Of course, Alec had no way of knowing that the information Barney would pass on to Sam, Sam could put in his eye.

Barney was going to get that look all winter, so he thought he might as well learn to take it now. He couldn't blame Alec, and if he got mad every time he met the look, he'd spend the next six months in a sweat and he couldn't be bothered.

"You have to boat everything in here?" he asked Sam. They were halfway across the lake by that time.

"Until freeze-up. Then I'll get an old truck and freight it over the ice." Sam must have been thinking along the same lines Barney was. "She'll have temporary plates when I bring her up," he added. "And I won't bother to register her. No need. We won't be using her on the roads."

That took care of that.

"I got to go to Bristol once a month," Barney said; but he knew it was hopeless.

"Don't worry your head about it," Sam said. "I'll see you do."

They were standing back in the stern where Alec couldn't hear them over the jangle and hoot of the engine.

"Sam, what's the good of it?"

Barney really wanted to know what Sam thought he was doing this time. He wasn't even mad when he asked, just wondering in a stunned kind of way if Sam really thought he was God. For the time being, he might have qualified; but the only thing you can be sure of is that time will pass and it seemed to Barney Sam had forgotten that.

He hadn't, though, and when his eyes met Barney's, they were both thinking the same thing. That time never stood still for anyone. But Sam was wishing it would and Barney was wishing it wouldn't, and they both knew the cards were stacked on Barney's side.

"Jesus Christ, Barney," Sam said. "I don't know. I don't know. All I know is, for the next six months I'll sleep easy nights for a change. See? I'm past thinking about you. It's me, from now on out!"

Alec put the boat's bow ashore on this side and they climbed out into a jungle of pucker brush and alders that grew thickly

down to the shore. There was only one break, a narrow path leading up the bank away from the water. But when they'd slipped
and sweated up over that, Barney with the duffle bag over his
shoulder and the alders snatching at it and twisting him off balance, they came out into a clearing full of tarpaper shacks.

This lake shore might have been a pretty place once. Not now.
There was nothing like a lath-battened tarpaper shack with a stovepipe angling either out through a hole in the side or up through
a hole in the roof, to make any place look like the town dump.
There were six shacks here, three side by side with only enough
space between them for a man to walk through, a bigger one set
at right angles to them and with more windows. You could see
enough to tell that was the cook shack. There was the corner of a
big black-iron stove, hotel size, showing at one window and a sink
spout sticking out of the wall, low down, near the door. The fifth
shack was the biggest of all and set well to leeward of the others;
but it was warm under the trees, even for October, and with no
wind and you could smell the stable smell. A restless muffled
thudding came from the wide door, the noise horses make when
they're not doing anything much else.

The last palace was the smallest and newest of the lot; the
ground around it wasn't mashed down and powdered as much as
it was around the others. It sat off in the edge of the alders, as far
away from the others as it could be and still be in the same clearing.

Sam glanced at it and then looked at Alec; but Alec had never
seen that shack before, apparently, and couldn't see it now. He
was standing with his arms folded behind his back the way most
men fold them in front. It sounds hard to do, but he was doing it,
and he wasn't meeting any glances, intent or otherwise, and didn't
plan to until it became absolutely necessary.

"I don't know where the hell you'll sleep, Barney. The bunkhouses are full, aren't they, Ellick?"

"Spare bunk this one." Alec gestured at one of the three in a
row. "Put him there."

"How come?" Sam glared and this time he caught and held
Alec's wandering glance the way a snake will a bird's.

Alec probably swallowed. There was no throat motion to tell

you he had; but he had the look of a man sparring desperately for time.

"*How come, Ellick?*" This time it was dangerous enough to get an answer.

"Well, you know that Michel?" Alec looked hopefully at Sam as if he expected him to say: No, he didn't know that Michel. And that would give Alec the opportunity to go into a long song and dance about who Michel was and probably who his father and mother along back were, until Sam might have forgotten about why there was a spare bunk when apparently there shouldn't have been.

"Yes," Sam said coldly.

"Oh." Alec had his breath all drawn in to tell Sam who Michel was, and it came out in a frustrated puff. "Built shack." He gestured hopelessly at the little building. "Brought woman, kids." In unnecessary verification, from the shack came the long-drawn wail with that "nganh" sound that only a very young baby can make.

"Joseph henry christ!" Sam said. "I told him if he brought that woman in here this winter, I'd harslit him."

"Not worry," Alec grinned foolishly. "*He* thinks she's a looker. Nobody else. You ought to see! There! *There!*"

His small eyes had gone past Sam's furious face and found the proof that there was nothing to worry about. Sam and Barney swung around to look. Coming up the path from the spring with a bucket of water in each hand was a woman, sure enough; but she looked exactly like a pear, narrow end up, set on legs. Barney had never in his life seen anything quite like it. She wore dungarees, so there was no possibility of making a mistake. Her legs were all right and, for all he could see, her top might have been; but the rest of her looked like the back end of the old Boston Boat.

Alec was right. She might have looked good to Michel, whoever he was. But Sam was still furious.

"With this crowd of hooligans—" he said, "that's going to look just like Marilyn Monroe by December. And you'll be right in the lead, you old—"

"Not me!" Alec raised both his big hands in horror. "Find me a lady black bear first."

"See you do," Sam said. He went over and pushed open the door to the bunkhouse. "Here's your boudoir, Barney."

Barney passed him, got one foot over the sill, and stopped dead. It was like running into a wall, that smell. It was so bad after you'd been in there a while and came back out again, fresh air made you dizzy. There were bunks lining both walls, double tier, and an aisle between them. Way down at the back, at the end of the aisle, there was a stove made from an old oil drum, and behind it was one window, right where half the heat from the stove would be sucked out in winter and where no air could get in any other time.

"You supply gas masks?" Barney asked.

Sam grinned unpleasantly.

"You'll get used to it," he said. "Hell, you'll even get to like it before you're through."

He couldn't have been any more wrong. Barney never got used to it. After supper sometimes, even on nights when it was ten below zero, he walked up and down outside that shack breathing deep to see if he could seat what he'd eaten solidly enough so it wouldn't threaten to come up when he stepped into the shack. Breathing deep to see if he could stun into inactivity with the cold whatever part of his apparatus he smelled with. When the cold weather came and there was a fire going in that stove hot enough to turn its sides bright red, there weren't any words in the book to say what it was like.

He stowed his duffle bag in the empty bunk and got out again as fast as he could. Sam was waiting outside the door. He hadn't come in.

Thick smoke was rolling up out of the stovepipe on the cook shack. Out in the woods, not far away, a power saw had been snoring ever since they landed. That's an ugly noise. Now it stopped and the silence hit against the ears the same way the noise had.

"Well, Barney, you're on your own now," Sam said. "I'll see you in a month."

"What am I supposed to do?"

"Anything you're told. And if you think this job is the one I offered you the other night, you've got another think coming. From now on you're the original whistle-punk." He started down the path, had another thought, and came back—still with that nasty grin on his face. "One more thing," he said. "The boss here is a Canuck from up around Chicoutimi. If you get any ideas, they grow them tough up there and he's the toughest one of the lot. You might take a good look at him when they come in to eat. You won't have any trouble picking him out."

Barney stood watching Sam until his back went out of sight in the alders and the old boat started banging back across the lake. He was simply there and not too sure of that. He might have been a deer hide nailed on the bunkhouse wall, for all he was thinking or feeling.

Then, for the first time, it really hit him and he knew he wasn't going to see Sabra for six months and he thought to god he was going to die. Standing in front of that stinking shack, listening to the banging of the engine, smelling the smoke and the stable, finally completely aware of everything there was to hear and feel, he thought he was dying, but wasn't.

He started to run for the shore, his feet working without thought from him to drive them. He slipped and slid down through the slimy path in the alders and came shooting out onto the gravel and the boat was halfway across with the wake spreading out smoothly over water that was beginning to look black now. And he knew they had him. He was here. If he didn't stay, if he showed his nose outside, they'd slap him in jail before he could spit.

He put his head back and howled like a dog.

Then he began to call Sam every name he could think of you might call a man and some things most people never would have thought of. Maybe Sam didn't hear, but he saw. He came back to the stern of the boat and stood watching. Barney stopped yelling and Sam put one arm up straight in the air. He wasn't waving. His fingers were spread out like a man grabbing at the sky.

"You go to hell, you son of a bitch," Barney shouted.

He turned away and then he saw he was standing in the water. He was into that lake right up to his knees and the water was

colder than the hinges of hell. So he waded out of it and went
back up the path to the clearing ringed around with shacks on the
edge of nothing.

While he had been down at the shore telling Sam what he
couldn't hear but must know pretty well, the crew had come in out
of the woods and all they were thinking about was food. Barney
could see a melee of shoulders around the cookhouse door—it
looked as if they were all trying to get in at once. Some of them
were inside and eating already. One guy sitting beside the window
slid his knife under a pile of food on his plate, mashed it down
solidly with his fork, and shoved it into his mouth. It looked as if
the knife went in forever. Barney's mind was a hundred and fifty
miles away and he wasn't any more thinking about that little guy
than he was about the man in the moon; but his eyes must have
been thinking independently. He could never look at him again,
no matter what he was doing, that he didn't see that knife load
packed and delivered.

Barney hadn't heard the boat come back, or anything at all except what was going on inside his own head. Alec came up behind
him and laid his hand on Barney's shoulder. It felt like being hit
with a plank. Barney found out later there was a good excuse for
his not having heard Alec. Alec, when he wanted to, could move
through a blowdown and make less noise than most men would
crossing a room with a thick carpet; other times he could make
himself sound like a moose in a hurry.

After Alec touched him and Barney had taken three gulps to
get his heart back down where it belonged, Alec jerked his head
toward the cookhouse.

"Better eat. Better now, too. It don't last long with them wol-
verines."

He started for the door at a shambling run, and for want of
anything better to do Barney followed along, thinking that the
paper Alec was holding looked like an envelope. Barney wasn't
hungry but if he was going to work the way Sam seemed to think
he was, he decided it would be a good idea to start stoking for it.

In a setup where eating takes the place of every other kind of
excitement, it pays the boss to see to it he gets a good cook, and

the minute they stepped into that shack Barney knew Sam had. All you had to do was smell it. He'd thought he wasn't hungry, but when he got inside the door he was ready to eat one of the horses, if that's what had been cooking.

Alec, not waiting for anything, grabbed a couple of tin plates, handed one to Barney, and stepped up to the stove. The cookee was a little skinny spidery-looking guy, dark, and all he wore in that steam bath was a pair of khaki pants and a dirty T-shirt. He didn't need any more. He had enough hair on him to keep him warm and spare some for Alec. It was like a pelt on his arms and chest, visible through the thin shirt. Even his back between the shoulders was covered with short black hair. There was a lot on his head too; but it was slicked down with some kind of grease. He had a sallow scooped-in face and he needed a shave a lot worse now than he had needed it a week ago when he must have had his last one.

After a while Barney came to know that the cigarette stuck in his mouth was a part of him. Today it was smoked down to an inch of paper and the ash on it was all the rest of the cigarette; but his face was so dished in that you could have stretched a line from his forehead to his chin and it wouldn't have ticked the cigarette ash.

He filled Alec's plate and turned to Barney. By the time he'd finished with his, the ash was gone and Barney hadn't seen it fall; he couldn't find it on his own plate so he hoped Alec was the lucky one. It was difficult to decide what else was on the plate. The cook might have been a jim dandy, but he didn't let consideration for good food stand between him and filling a plate. Meat on the bottom and everything else piled on top of it.

It looked at first as if Barney wasn't going to find any place to sit. He went over to one of the trestle tables and shoved his foot across the bench, in between two men who looked a little skinnier than the rest. They didn't stop eating, just hauled in enough to let him get the other foot across and sit down. Then they each gave him the same sideways glance, considering. He could see himself being filed for future reference—as soon as the important thing was done, they'd tend to him.

He glanced up to see where Alec had managed to squat himself in and found that he'd gone along to the next table and handed the envelope he'd been clutching to a big guy Barney thought was standing up until he took another look. Sam had been right about the Canuck who bossed this layout being an easy man to pick out of a crowd. He was sitting on the same bench with the others; but his head—a little head way out of proportion to the rest of him and looking like the funny lump you find sometimes on a potato—was about two feet above every other head in the row. Barney himself was tall—six-foot-two. And most of the men in that shack were tall. But all of them could have walked under this guy's outstretched arm without bending their necks.

He sat with the piece of paper looking like a postage stamp on the end of a ham, reading carefully. His lips moved for each word. Then he stuffed the paper into his shirt pocket and waited a second before he looked at Barney. Barney had a fair idea the letter had to do with him and he knew he was bound to be looked at sooner or later. He outwaited the Frenchman and when the look came he met it head on.

Barney could hardly believe that face either—on a little blonde it might have looked good, on the big Frenchman it was God's original mistake. What a bunch of characters! The three, Michel's woman excepted, he'd stopped long enough to look at were all of them candidates for a gallery of horrors. Alec with his basketball; the cook and his soup plate; now this big Canuck with a face like a picture you'd expect to see on the wall in a beauty parlor—round pink cheeks, round china-blue eyes, little pouty mouth like a kid's, with no more strength to it, snub nose. Oh, he was a beauty! It gave Barney a cold chill to look at him because that face was a lie and behind the soft blue of those eyes was something as hard and cold as broken glass.

He knew it. He didn't have to worry about any mistakes anyone would make about his face. After they took the second look, the mistake was corrected. He was one tough guy and he didn't have to turn his hand over to make it stick.

Barney shrugged mentally and started eating. Before he was half through, he was sitting alone at the table. Whenever one of the other men finished he got up, took his plate and cup over and dumped it into the sink, and went out. Within ten minutes there were only a few left, none at the same table; but Barney still had a way to go and he was still hungry.

He didn't realize this boy was standing behind him until he sensed more of a silence than there should have been while there was still somebody else in the shack. He looked up, about to the level where you'd expect to find a face to go with the rest of what was right behind him. No face. So he looked two feet higher and found it.

The Canuck put a foot as big as a bear-paw snowshoe across the bench and sat down astride. For long enough to make Barney good and itchy, he sat without speaking. When he did speak, his voice went with his body, not his face. It sounded more like a growl than a human voice.

"Do you work as slow as you eat?"

"Sometimes," Barney said. "Depends."

"I do not like to see anyone dragging his arse around here."

"Why don't you wait till you see me doing it?"

Barney wasn't trying to pick a fight. He wasn't that foolish. But he couldn't sit there and let himself be needled without a kick or two.

"Your *brother*—" The Frenchman bore down on that word and in it was everything Alec had been thinking and a lot more. "He say you're a pretty tough guy. Think you're pretty good, hanh?"

Barney made his stare as steady as he could, hoping it might be dangerous too.

"I know my limitations."

"You want to see if I'm it?"

Barney shook his head.

"Not particularly. I'll take your word for it."

"That's good. Most of these boys will take my word. I am glad to see you can understand why."

The itch was beginning to get worse. If he kept at it much longer, Barney knew he'd make a complete fool of himself. Nobody likes to go into a fight knowing damn well he'll get beaten to a bloody pulp, but much more of this and he'd stick his neck out.

The Canuck saved him. He got up abruptly and started away; but before he went, he had another word to say.

"I'm pretty hard on a guy don't get working when I say 'work.'" He came back to say it. "I like also to see him eat when I say 'eat.' Otherwise, he usually don't. Now you know that, remember it."

He meant every word of it too, and a couple of days later Barney was given an illustration of how it worked.

One of the Micmacs was late getting in to supper, coming in to start when the rest were nearly through. He'd barely got his plate on the table and the first two mouthfuls into him before he was as alone as Barney had been that first night.

When Adelbert—that was the boss's name, Adelbert Therriault, and when you spoke to him, you used all of it. Not the Therriault, he wasn't that formal; but you didn't shorten the Adelbert—got up to go out, he reached across the table and put the tip end of one big forefinger under the edge of the tin plate full of food.

Barney stood wondering what the hell he was going to do; but the Indian knew. His hand moved like a snake striking. He grabbed the big slab of beefsteak and hauled his head back just in time. Adelbert crooked his finger and the plate shot up past where the Indian's face had been a minute before, clanged against the low roof with a sound that said it was really traveling, and lit back on the table again, upside down.

The Micmac sat stolidly in the shower of gravy and vegetables. Then he got up and brushed boiled potato out of his black hair with his free hand, the other one still clutching the steak.

Nobody seemed surprised, least of all the Indian. He glanced at Adelbert with a flicker of light that might have been amusement in his sloe eyes; but the expression on his face didn't change by so much as that flicker.

"Someday, Joseph," Adelbert smiled sweetly at him. "By christ, someday I'll get to you before you get to the steak."

Barney could see clearly why it paid to eat when Adelbert said "eat."

If, for five minutes, Barney had thought he would feel on many mornings the way he felt when he woke up in that stinking bunkhouse on the first one, he would have crawled out of the bunk then and there, gone down to the lake, and waded out until his hair floated.

Outside it was barely beginning to make daylight. The west-facing window behind the stove was still black; but the blackness had a mitigating look reflected from the graying east.

Either his nose was numb from a night of breathing in that drab fog of sweat and tobacco, or he didn't care. He had an upper bunk, and down below in the gloom it sounded as if a herd of baby elephants had started to come to for the day.

He lay and listened and felt as if his insides had drained out in the night. He wasn't still hung over or anything. That was it, really. He wasn't anything. He had never before looked down the long way of six months and felt as if it was longer than a lifetime. That morning, he did: Thought about the six months; thought about those two kids and their "new uncle"; thought about Sabra.

It wasn't even real thinking, only a parade through his head, one thing after another and none of them good. And he knew as well as he knew his own name, if he didn't turn it off exactly the way you'd turn off a faucet and do it fast, he'd be crazier than a loon by the time the first one of the six months had passed.

So he did. Work! What he'd been doing all summer was so much square dancing alongside what he did all winter. He wanted to be too tired to have anything above his eyebrows but a vacuum.

When there wasn't anything else to do, he walked. That was a thing he'd never done much simply for the sake of walking. He'd always figured legs were given you to use when there wasn't any other way to get around and he'd spent a good part of his life seeing to it he had some other way.

He covered that northern country for miles around, plowing through blowdowns and pulp clearings and sphagnum swamps and everything else there was going and the more the merrier. Half the time he didn't know where he was or where he was going and he didn't give a good god damn.

It was a clean country, once you got away from the stink of that god-awful clearing. And so big it could have held a million men without getting that handled-over feeling there was along the coast where you don't stand a chance of setting foot on a piece of ground somebody else hasn't stepped on about five minutes before you. Down there it was old. The people started there and some were still there. The ones who couldn't stand it kept on going. But up here in the woods, they'd done their mangling and handling over so long ago it was hard to find signs of their ever having been here.

You could if you looked hard enough and knew what to look for. There was one day, it must have been Sunday because it was early afternoon, and he wasn't either wrestling with a power saw or a load of freight. He'd gone way up along the eastern shore of the lake almost to its head, making good time through what looked like a stand of spruce that had been there since time began. Suddenly he noticed that all around through this clean woods there were spotted big green moss-covered humps, some of them as large as the top of one of those round dining-room tables.

When he gathered enough active curiosity to go over to the next one and give it a kick to see what it actually was, a piece of thin moss maybe two feet square peeled back just like hide and under it had been wood once; but now it was so close to being loam again that it was a new substance altogether, halfway between one thing and the other.

So he saw that this spruce woods he thought had never been touched was nothing but second-growth stuff. Once this whole eastern shore must have been covered with trees bigger than he'd ever live to see. They could only have been white pines, and the stump he had kicked must have been at least six feet through at the butt to leave so much of itself after all this time.

A stand of pines like that would be a fine thing to see—and hear. Big trees, a lot of them standing together, sing. Big pines have got a song all to themselves. Barney had heard it at night under smaller ones than these had been. Going along through the woods thinking about your business and wondering where the hell the warden was and all of a sudden hearing this sound and knowing you've come out from under spruces into a stand of pines.

These big old devils must have sung bass. Not singing, really—more like a kind of music that might come from a string instrument men hadn't thought to invent yet.

Well, it had been a long time ago for the mess the loggers had left behind to be so cleaned up and rotted away and the stumps of the trees got past to the place where you couldn't even be sure what they were and these new trees to grow up until you could mistake them for the original ones.

Adelbert was going to have fun in these spruces. He'd see to it that somebody else, coming up along the lake shore in a hundred years—or however long it took—through a stand of fine hardwood growth, would come on the moss-covered and rotting stumps of long-gone spruces.

Evenings Barney used to lie in his bunk listening to the crew that was going to do Adelbert's erasing for him. They were a funny bunch, but no funnier, he supposed, than any other crew of men hauled together off every skid road north of Bangor to do a job like this, pretty evenly divided, French-Canadian and Indian. Most of the Indians would sit around and listen all night long; but they never had much to say.

There was Alec with his one yarn about the cup of tea and after he'd told that he'd done his bit. They never lacked for talk though, because the Canucks never stopped. If there was nobody to listen to one of them, he'd talk to himself.

It was the line of least resistance to listen and they were the damndest bunch for funerals and sudden death and all kinds of horrible destruction. Barney had never known a crowd of fairly young men get together like that before and not talk about women. Of course, they did. But sooner or later they'd be back to the other end of the line. He used to think, listening: Brother, the Army was never like this! But it made things considerably easier that they didn't chew over Marie and Elaine and Emilie and their comparative abilities any more than they did.

There was one particular funeral that made a big hit with them all—it was just about the funniest thing they'd ever heard tell of.

The fellow who told about it was a young guy who'd been cutting wood one winter on an island up somewhere near Grand Anse north of Cape Canso when he went to it.

Years ago some people—not French or he wouldn't have made such a good story of it—had settled in on this island and set up a kind of kingdom. But, the way it usually goes with a setup like that, the old folks have all the guts and enterprise and for some reason, in three or four generations, it's all petered out to a kind of half-foolishness or ignorance—anyway, small potatoes and damned few to a hill.

The old man of the family up and died one day. And the pulp crew, for want of any other excitement within reach, decided to go en masse to the funeral. About the usual time they appeared at the house, and when they came around the corner there was the coffin, brand-new shiny pine box, lying beside the front porch. The kid telling about it said he didn't dare look to see if it was empty or not. Three or four half-grown young ones were jumping up and down on the lid yelling: "See the pretty box our gramp's going to be put in the ground in."

Pretty soon a couple of bigger kids came out of the house and shooed off the chorus and took the coffin inside. When they came out again there were four of them carrying it, so it was heavier. They didn't have any kind of a hearse, just a farm dump cart backed up to the porch and only an ox to haul it. They loaded the coffin aboard and went down to the church with it.

The young Canuck made that church sound like a packing box set on end. From his description, Barney knew it was a good deal like any one of the little meetinghouses you find in most small towns; but to the Frenchman it wasn't much of a church because it wasn't one of those big stone piles that tower over every French village in Canada.

They carried the coffin inside and opened it up and of course everyone had to go and admire what was in it. The old man and his wife hadn't lived together for years—she'd gone out and moved into a shed and fixed it up and they hadn't even spoken to each other since. But there she was, right up in the forefront, to pay her respects. One of the girls—she must have been nearly forty but she was still a girl because she hadn't ever married—was dripping tears all over the place when the old lady came up to look.

"Oh," she says. "Ma, don't you wish you had him back?"

Ma took a cautious look at the old devil who, judging from the description, looked just as ornery dead as he ever had alive.

"Well," she says thoughtfully. "I dunno as I do."

They all settled down to a fine howling match. The church was some kind of a Protestant one, of course, and years back, when the island had amounted to something and there were enough souls worth saving, there'd been a preacher lived right there and had services regularly. But now it appeared as if the church fathers figured that what was left wouldn't have been worth the trouble. Nobody else would want to be in the same heaven with that bunch if they *had* been saved. So one of the men said whatever there was to say and it didn't matter anyhow, because the howling and yelling that went on drowned him out.

The whole thing, the enjoyable part, lasted for as much as an hour before everyone was satisfied. One after the other would get up and testify to the fine qualities of the deceased at the top of his lungs, and lungs were one thing that hadn't run out.

They finally got it settled to their satisfaction that the old man had been one of the finest citizens the Dominion ever had the misfortune to lose, and when that was established they all filed up and stood around the coffin for as much as five minutes and they were worked up to a fine pitch and the tears nearly filled the thing before they got the lid closed.

While four of the big boys were loading the coffin back into the dump cart for the trip to the graveyard, the oldest son went shooting out of the church and when the funeral procession formed to follow on foot behind the cart, he was standing there with a big paper bag under his arm. As each one of the mourners passed him, he'd stick his hand into the bag and come out with an apple and hand it over.

"Thought you might be hungry," he said. "After all that hard work."

They got the old man appled down to the graveyard and the cart up to the grave end to, so they could stand alongside on each side and slide the coffin off and it would be all ready to lower away. There were a few more words to be said and a little more yelling to be done. When that was finished, the same four boys stepped up to the cart and got ready to do the heavy lifting.

One of the kids who'd been dancing on the pine box when the pulp crew arrived had been watching this performance kind of scornfully. When he saw there was going to be some unnecessary work done, he couldn't stand it.

"Hey, wait a minute," he yelled and ran around the front end of the cart and tripped the dump mechanism. The cart went up, the coffin shot off it and hit the far lip of the grave, did a ricochet, end to end, and settled into the hole with a crash, just exactly where they'd wanted it.

The kid stood watching, his hands on his hips and this smug smile on his face.

"There!" he said, real satisfied and pleased with the trouble he'd saved them. "Ain't that some old slick?"

They all thought that was a pretty funny story, the Canucks. They laughed and hooted over it and, come to think of it, Barney thought it was funny too. That was the first laugh he'd had since he'd hit the job and it felt good. It reminded him of the story Sam told about old Arthur Shook who'd insisted on having his coffin made long before he needed it to be sure he got what he wanted. He had himself a cedar box and a hemlock lid, so he could go through hell a'snapping.

The job itself didn't take much brainwork. All he had to do was what Adelbert told him to and he did it. If being a good boy was going to mean he'd get out of this in six months, he was going to be good. He could see Adelbert trying to find something wrong. Sam had apparently primed him for trouble and he was doing his damndest to get it without starting it.

Once a week a truck loaded with supplies came up from Greenville, and Alec and Barney would get the old hooker started and go across the lake to get them. The truck was always driven by the same half-witted kid who would stand on the opposite shore yelling his head off to get them started, and once they got started, yelling it off to keep them coming. He was invariably in a tearing hurry to get away from this outpost of less than nothing.

That far north it got cold early—close enough to Canada to get the overflow of that cold Canadian air that doesn't hit the coast because the salt water's warm enough to push it back. By the second week in November they were having to break away the ice along the shore to get the old boat out of her little slough.

The Greenville Cannonball used to bring the mail too, and for a while the grimy canvas sack looked bigger to Barney than anything else in the whole load.

He had written to Sabra twice in the beginning. It took him some time to get up his courage. At first he didn't dare for fear the letter would come back to him, or worse, because of what she'd say when she answered. He didn't like to write to her from that bunkhouse either. But finally he had to. He lay in his bunk with all that hoo-raw going on down below, not even hearing it, and wrote all the things he'd been wanting to say to her, and when he got through, the first two words were all that mattered: Dear Sabra. And maybe his name at the end. Nothing in between had to be there.

There hadn't been time for an answer to come to the first one before he wrote the second. Then he waited. And nothing. No answer. Every other week or so he got a letter from Jude; but there was never anything in it that he wanted to know. He got emptier and emptier. He wished he'd never set pencil to paper because he was finding out, being shown, what it all amounted to for Sabra— and for him it hadn't even started.

There was never much in the sack but papers and Tru-Stories and the rest of it would be ads for patent medicines and trusses and stuff like that. Occasionally a Sears Roebuck package for Michel's wife. And Barney would go through the heap like a vacuum cleaner, so stupid with misery he didn't even see the light when Adelbert said, one day:

"What's the matter, kid? You ain't expecting a letter, are you?"

The second trip they made to Bristol, Sam didn't know it, but he gave Barney back something he'd thought was gone for good. They were nearly there when Sam reached into his pocket and hauled out the two letters and handed them over, held them out between his fingers as if they might burn him—and there was her name staring up from the dingy white envelopes and the stamps hadn't even been canceled.

"Here," he said. "Tear them up, Barney, or do whatever you want to with them—except mail them."

Barney took them and turned them over to see if Sam had read them, too.

"They haven't been opened," Sam said shortly and there was a quick flush of red along his cheekbones.

"Thank you for that," Barney said.

He sat there tearing the cheap paper into pieces the size of a fingernail and snowing them out through the window all over the countryside. And something inside him was ringing like a bell.

Even inside the courthouse it was hard to get out of Sam's sight. He watched, though it was like watching something already caught in the trap. But there was one thing Sam couldn't do for him. After they'd seen the probation officer and come out again, Barney stopped beside the door to the men's room.

"Go on along, Sam," he said. "I'll only be a minute."

Sam hesitated even then and it was lucky there were a couple of other guys going down the hall with them. If it hadn't been for that, Barney had more than an idea that Sam would have come right in with him, or waited outside the door. As it was, when he went on down the long hall, his feet coming down hard on that nice smooth marble floor, the back of his head had a tight look that meant he was having all he could do to keep from looking back over his shoulder.

After the three went out through the big front door, Barney shot back up the corridor to the public telephone so fast he skidded past the folding door and had to come back to it. His hands and feet were cold and when he got the operator his tongue felt dry and so big he could hardly get the number out around it. But he did finally and then waited—and waited.

He heard the Port Kezar operator say at last:

"DA, Operator."

DA, he thought blankly, what the hell's *that* mean?

The Bristol operator translated it.

"That number does not answer. Shall I ring you ba—"

Just then, it answered. The old, unoiled-hinge voice Barney heard in his dreams said: "Hello?"

Barney thought: I love you, you old bastard!

"Let me speak to Sabra," he said aloud, as if it were the easiest thing in the world to say.

"She ain't here," Arthur said. "She's out somewheres. I don't know where. Who's this?"

Barney hung up. He wasn't disappointed. He thought he even felt better than he would have if he'd managed to talk to her. He'd found out what he wanted to: that she was still there and he didn't have to think of the Port without her. He didn't need the sound of her voice over a wire, or a picture, or anything like that. He had all that and more. He simply needed to know that she hadn't lit out and gone.

On the way back upcountry Sam kept looking at him as if he was trying to figure out where Barney had got the liquor and why he couldn't smell it. Barney felt drunk, that pleasant drunk when you've had just enough to make you sit on top of the fluffy white cloud and everything you see looks so damned funny to you you can't keep from laughing.

The only drink he got a chance at all winter, though, was a cupful of something the cook had brewed up one day. Barney was feeling grouchy anyhow, because he'd waked early to hear a flock of geese going south. That country was full of wings. Ducks, crows, those damned thieving whisky jacks, and the Canada geese, flying high, but not so high you couldn't hear that constant gabbling they kept up amongst themselves. And he had waked to hear them going south and maybe it was because he hadn't had time to start getting tired for the day, but part of him felt as if it hauled right out and went with them.

When the cook beckoned him into the shack, with the unmistakable look of a man who's got a drink to offer, he would have settled for even some of that New England rum that tastes like turpentine and feels like sandpaper.

The cook had brewed up this mess and Barney could never find out what he'd put into it, but it was potent. The minute Barney went into the shack, he could see clearly the cook would have been swinging by his tail from the collar beams, if he'd only had a tail. The shack was full of the damndest animals, right out of the middle of a d.t. nightmare. While he was pouring something the color of coffee out of the coffeepot, the cook kept looking over his shoulder at the black leopard with the bright blue eyes that happened to be lying on the nearest table, lashing its tail and watching every move he made.

"*See* that damn thing, will you?" he said, so matter-of-factly that Barney nearly did. "Him and me's got to know each other pretty well. His name's Peter."

Barney took a step toward the table, more to reassure himself than anything else. The cook screeched like a banshee, grabbed him and whirled him away.

"Jesus Christ, you crazy?" he yelled. "That cat would tear your heart out as soon as look at you! I'm the only one can get anywheres near him!" He led Barney back in a wide careful detour to the stove, pointing to the floor as they went. "Besides, you stepped on George's tail and he ain't used to that kind of treatment."

"George?" Barney said. "Tail?"

The cook's eyes narrowed suspiciously.

"You're just like all the rest of the god-damn jokers," he said. "Jealous as all hell because I've got all these friends. George is my pylon. He lives under the stove. He likes it warm. But I got it good and hot for him this morning, so he come out. You know how them big snakes is. He gets sluggish when it ain't hot. He's a foot longer than when I last see him."

"Good for George," Barney said.

The cook handed over the cup he'd poured the coffee into and Barney took a good swig. It wasn't coffee. It probably wasn't battery acid either, and he had never tasted battery acid; but for a minute he felt as if he had. He saw stars. He saw Peter and George, too.

"Christ almighty!" he said. "What's that?"

"Oh, you mean that *good* flavor?" The cook grinned. "I dress it up a little. Jamaica ginger, boy, that's the answer."

It was lucky for the rest of them there was a hundred-pound sack of dried beans in the storeroom. For a week Alec had to do the cooking and the only thing he could cook was baked beans so they had them three times a day. Barney used to vary it a little. For a treat he'd have ketchup with them for breakfast; maybe plain for dinner; then at supper time he'd dig out a raw onion and slice that over the top. Beans are filling—but a week of them gets a little monotonous.

It took Adelbert that long to find and smash the bottles and jars the cook had filled and hidden all over the cookhouse and even out around the clearing. The last one Adelbert found was lashed in the crotch of a big alder down near the lake and the cook was in tears when Adelbert broke that, so they were pretty sure it was the last one. It was another week, though, before the animals went back into their cages for good; but the cook didn't seem so fond of them without his Kickapoo Joy-Juice.

Barney began to feel sorry for poor old George. The cook would stand above the stove shaking like a popple in a breeze, his face shining with sweat and just the color and texture of an old lemon, not even smoking he felt that bad, and every time George poked his head out from under, if the cook could manage to get one foot off the floor without falling down, he'd let him have it dead center.

"You get back in there, you son of a bitch, and stay there!"

Two of the Micmac boys got the idea there really *was* something under that stove and during the week the cook spent kicking George back into his den, they made a wide detour around it. Barney even caught one of them squatting down to look, from a safe distance, just in case.

"What you found?"

"Nothing." The Indian looked disgusted, but still not too sure. "That feller, that damn cook, crazy as a bedbug. Nothing under the stove!"

"I'm not so sure," Barney said, dead serious. "You keep an eye
open. Someday you may find it."

"What looking *for*?" the Micmac asked. "Who the hell's George,
anyhow?"

"Big snake." Barney couldn't show him the length of a python,
real or imaginary, but he made a circle with both hands. "This big
around."

The Indian nearly turned a somersault trying to get away from
the stove and he kept on making the detour. He also started looking
at Barney the way he had been at the cook. He was right. Barney
wasn't seeing snakes; but in his own quiet way, he was crazy too.

Time is a thing that goes by you, even if you don't happen to be
living in it at the moment. It wasn't all bad. Things happened that
he remembered, and they were usually worth looking at.

There were winter nights, still, and with the stars as big as his fist
and low enough to touch. No wind to make a sound in the trees
so he could hear the sound of the cold. It has a lot of sounds—cold.
On a still night—cold enough so that when you breathe in, the
little hairs on the inside of your nostrils freeze together—you can
hear other things freezing.

The trees kept up a constant snapping and cracking. Underfoot
the snow gave out a dry whining squeak. On a really cold night the
lake would lie there and boom. The sound ricocheted along under
the ice until it faded into the little chuckling noise you'd get if you
threw a rock out across the surface of the ice and listened until it
died away.

It was before the lake froze that something happened Barney
might have enjoyed once. Maybe not quite enjoyed, but joined in
on and felt proud of himself about.

With Alec, he was starting across the lake for a load of freight,
and the half-witted kid was dancing up and down on the opposite
shore hallooing them on. That kid's mouth was almost as big as
Alec's, and Barney wished a good many times he had a sofa pillow
handy and was standing right beside him when he opened it, a sofa
pillow and a cram stick.

He looked away from the kid so he could keep his temper when they landed and had to talk to him, looked down toward the far end of the lake, and saw what he thought was a big old tree, floating mostly under water with only a few roots sticking up. Then he saw the roots were leaving a lot more wake than a floating tree would have.

Before he thought, he nudged Alec and pointed it out. Alec took one look and Barney was watching his face instead of the swimming buck and saw something he'd heard about happening but didn't really think ever happened that way. Sweat popped out on Alec's upper lip—one minute it wasn't there, the next minute it was.

Alec put the old boat over so hard he nearly broke her back. The clangs began to come faster and closer together and Barney found out that when Alec was in a hurry the make-and-break could work up quite a burst of speed. He'd never been in a hurry to haul freight. Back on the shore the kid howled like a wolf when he saw the boat heading away from him. Barney turned and thumbed his nose happily.

Alec was chattering like a chipmunk—no words, just that funny sharp chirring back in his throat. Suddenly he did say something understandable.

"Holy christ," he said without a trace of accent. "All my life I been waiting to catch one of those buggers like that."

With some guys there's a real kick in killing things. That's the way it was with Alec. There was the deer, big old buck, helpless in the water, and he was going to kill it if he had to do it with his bare hands.

The buck wasn't sure at first they were after him. He kept turning his big head to watch the boat, keeping a weather eye on it all the while they were coming up. When they got closer Barney could see that eye itself, big and shining and beginning to be a kind of liquid black with fright, because the deer knew he was helpless, poor old devil. When he was sure the boat was after him, the smooth dog paddle that might have got him somewhere stopped, and he began to try to run in the water. He simply forgot there was anything as betraying as water under his feet. His big shoulders would come clear of the surface and muscles writhed under the tawny hide of his neck and that tremendous head with its beautiful crotched stand of antlers was really swiveling now.

Barney took another look at Alec to see if he might not have changed his mind, knowing he wouldn't have, and looked away fast. Alec's face was shining all over and there was a little trickle of spit coming out one corner of his open mouth.

"Hammer," he said. "Right in that toolbox. Hammer! Quick!"

What he was going to do wasn't any worse, nor so bad, as what had happened right behind Barney that night in Joe Samuels' old car on the Parry Hill Crossroad. That night it had been a big deal, though—funny as all hell.

To get it over with as soon as possible, Barney grabbed the hammer out of the box. He hefted it and was relieved that it was a good stout one, anyway. There was a length of rope in a mess of dunnage under the hood. When Barney reached for it, it got tangled in half a million other things and he had a hell of a time getting it free to make a running noose in one end.

All the while he was fooling around, Alec had the boat going circles around the buck, trying to turn him and keep him off shore long enough for them to dot him one.

"Hurry! Hurry!" he kept yelling, and he was beginning to shake now for fear they'd lose the deer.

"Aw, shut up!" Barney shouted. "You clear up some of this mess, I wouldn't have got tangled up in it in the first place."

Alec didn't even hear him. He hauled up alongside the buck and Barney managed to get the noose over the big stand of horns. The minute he felt the touch of the rope on him, Barney thought the buck's heart would burst. He went crazy in the water.

"Alec," Barney yelled. "For god sake!"

Alec let go the wheel and leaned overside, the hammer in his hand, trying to get a swing. Barney took up on the slack as much as he could; but the boat was still going and Alec hadn't even slowed her down. As she passed the deer and the rope tautened, it was all Barney could do to hang onto it. He thought for a minute it was going to cut his wrist off where he'd taken a couple of turns with it. Just before he had to take the full weight, he snubbed the rope around the stanchion that supported the sprayhood and that began to bend.

"Haul him in here!" Alec was yelling. "Let me get a swing at him."

"Alec, slow down, you damn fool," Barney said. "I can't move him with us going like this."

Alec didn't, though. He leaned as far out over the cheeserind as he could stretch and took a swipe at the buck with the hammer. Missed him by a scant inch. Barney let out another protesting shout and Alec hauled back, aimed, and let go the hammer. It took the buck between the eyes and knocked him cold. Barney felt the surge through the rope and his arm right down to his heels.

There was the stanchion bending like cooked macaroni, the rope stiff as a bar of iron, and the old buck a dead weight now. Something had to give and the rope did. It broke about two feet from the slip knot and the boat, freed from her unwilling sea anchor, came as close to running away as she could.

By the time Alec could swallow his excitement and get to the wheel to turn her, they were nearly ashore. They made a sweep back over the place where they'd lost the deer. Alec hadn't seen him go down but Barney had been watching. The last thing under was that big spray of horn and it sank quietly with no fuss, so there was hardly a circle in the water to mark the spot. By the time they got back to it, even that was gone.

Alec leaned on the side of the boat and stared thoughtfully down through the quiet cold black water where the wild secret had vanished and was free now.

"Son of a bitch," he said softly. "And I lost my hammer, too."

All that afternoon he couldn't think of anything else. He couldn't even tell about it when they got back to camp and the boys were all standing around waiting for the mail. All he could do was shake his round silly head and say: "Lost my hammer, too."

After the real freeze-up, they had to haul back and forth with the old truck Sam brought in. She wasn't much—a big International with a stake body that rattled enough to make you think the devil was riding your tail. She had a pretty good motor but there was nothing faintly resembling a brake lining left in her and the clutch sounded like something chewing at her with steel teeth. Barney couldn't get her into high; but where he was going in her, second was fast enough.

Actually she wasn't much of an improvement over the boat; but easier to load, and he could yarn her right up over the bank and deliver at the storeroom door, so that took care of an extra packing job.

He was hauling over the ice in her one night when he nearly got scared to death. This once the kid had arrived a day ahead of schedule. It wouldn't have killed him to haul the stuff across the lake himself; but he'd been hired to deliver it at the far side and if there'd been a six-lane freeway over the ice, he wouldn't have come another inch.

When Barney came in to supper that night there was a mountain staring across at him. It was impossible to believe, without seeing it, the food that came into that place to keep thirty men and two horses going. It didn't seem possible so much bulk could go down so few gullets; but by the end of the week the cook was scraping the bottom of the barrel.

"Ain't it some old lucky there's a full moon," Adelbert said with a big happy grin. "Looks like you got a chance for a little overtime, Barney. Too bad we ain't got a union shop."

"You don't mind if I have my supper first, do you?"

Adelbert thought he'd care if he spent the whole night getting the damned grub back to camp and Barney thought he might as well let him if it did him any good.

"I advise you to," Adelbert said. "It would break my heart to think of you going hungry."

There was no point in taking that any farther. Adelbert wasn't anyone who mattered. There was only one person in the world right then who did. It was like driving down a long straight road at night with nothing to see but one car in front of you. You get watching the taillight of the other car until you're fascinated and there isn't anything else in the whole damned world but you and that little moving light ahead.

Barney was seeing only the moving light and it made it easy to take whatever was dished out to him. Things he would have tried to push Adelbert's face in for six months ago went so high over his head now he didn't even feel the wind of them.

He ate supper to keep Adelbert from a broken heart and as soon as he got it down, went out and started the truck. That was an adventure involving a double-throw switch and a couple of bare-ended wires and sparks flying; but after you got the combination, she was a hard old bird to stop.

When he got across the lake to the place where the road ended and the pile of freight waited, it didn't look as if a man had had anything to do with putting it there—not a thinking man. If the kid had had a dump truck, he couldn't have left it in more of a mess. It took almost as long to feel around the clearing after whatever had rolled as it did to load the truck. Barney got it loaded finally and started grinding down across the crusted snow and out onto the lake again. There wasn't a cloud in the sky and the old truck lumbered out into the moonlight with Barney feeling as if he were driving into water.

That was a beautiful night, January, and there hadn't been any kind of thaw yet. Old man winter had both his bony old hands tight around the breathing throat of the country.

The full moon looked bigger than the world and silver so you could see the queer dark spots on it. The lake, under moonlight, was striped like a zebra, with the black ice and the waving lines of white where the snow had blown and drifted and frozen.

The moon, frozen too into the winter sky, so bright you didn't see the stars at all, turning everything he'd been looking at since October (everything that was so familiar now that when he closed his eyes he could find it burned out against the underside of the lids like a negative) into a landscape out of another country and one he had never seen before.

The outlines were there where the moonlight lay, the contours of the familiar lake—and beyond that, nothing. It was hard to figure out, until he saw that the light, bright as it was, couldn't penetrate the way sunlight did. It simply bounced back off the hard shapes of trees and ledges.

There he was, out in the middle of that lake in a hard-to-believe kind of never-never light, and all around where the big trees came down to the edge, it felt like something was waiting to pounce on him, something that couldn't bother to come and get him because it was absolutely sure he would come to it.

He was jogging along in second, hanging his weight on the wheel the way you do when you're going slow and there aren't any turns. All at once and just over him and the truck—nowhere else—the moonlight went black out. He could look out of blackness and see it shining away as bright as ever all over the lake. But not here in the middle of whatever had happened to him.

He felt as if the blood inside him had all drained out of its usual channels and made a puddle in the bottom of his stomach and frozen over. He felt as if the old he-angel of death was sitting right on top of him and he was heavy. He thought: God, God, that's the last thing I want!

He wanted a lot of things and wanted them bad; but for about two seconds, the only thing in the world he wanted that night was a good deep breath and he was afraid if he didn't get it pretty soon there wouldn't ever be another one.

After the light flooded back, he found he'd stalled the truck and was sitting frozen to the wheel and shaking so he could hear his own teeth clicking. And he could lean forward and look out and up through the windshield to see the plane pulling up and away with her engine going now.

That country is big and the wardens do most of their traveling from one lake to another in little two-seater planes. This boy was a great joker. He'd spotted the truck crawling across the ice, had shut off his motor and come coasting down over it. When Barney looked out to see him pulling up, his skis weren't more than ten feet above the cab.

If Sam had ever paid Barney for the years he lost off his life in that two seconds, he wouldn't have been able to meet his payroll for the next ten years.

When Barney got back to camp and unloaded, he felt as if his knees would have bent backward as easily as they did the right way. He crawled into his bunk and went out as if somebody had fed him a mickey. The next morning he woke wishing it could be arranged more often. That was the first night he'd spent all winter without moving, the first night he didn't wake up in the middle with Arthur's voice in his ears saying: This is your new uncle.

But, of course, the minute he *did* wake, he realized he hadn't and so, right away, could hear Arthur saying it. Hell, he thought, climb up one step and slide back two!

Sam and Barney went again to Bristol in January, and February; but Barney didn't try to call Sabra again. He knew better now than to try and write.

Then it came around time for his March trip. Sam had always arrived early enough on the first day of the month to get him down to Bristol, back again, and get himself home to Port Kezar by bedtime. The first of March, it was on a Tuesday, Barney was ready and waiting by nine o'clock in the morning. And no Sam.

Barney sat around the cook shack, drinking coffee and reading a couple of the comic books the cook always carried in his hip pocket. The Greenville Wonder had orders to bring in a dozen or so every week and they went the rounds. By the time they'd been through the bunkhouses and got back again they were pretty dog-eared; but it was a kind of literature you could follow along from the pictures, if the words happened to be gone.

Noontime, when the crew came in for dinner, Barney was still there, sitting doing nothing, and that sparked Adelbert up.

"Thought you was halfway to Bristol by now," he said, coming over to see what the magazine was.

"Well, I'm not."

"So I see. Would I be out of line if I asked what the screaming hell you plan to do this afternoon? You gonna sit here and wait all day? If he ain't come yet, he ain't coming, is he?"

"I don't know." Barney shrugged and stood up. It was bad enough facing Adelbert from that level, sitting down, it nearly broke your neck.

By this time they were closed in with the sound of eating. You get thirty hungry men in a room like that, being fed, and you've got a symphony. Barney had got used to that; but today it sounded like twice as many and he wasn't used to sixty.

"You better get busy and eat your dinner," Adelbert told him. "You ain't going to do any more sitting today."

He had a point there. Barney went over and grabbed a tin plate and was standing beside the stove waiting for the shovelful to descend, when the door opened and Sam walked in.

He nodded at Adelbert and glanced around at the crew with that abstracted look that meant he owned them, too; but he was so sure of it he didn't even see them as men. He looked at Barney levelly, straight and thoughtful, and he *was* seeing then. Watching him, not speaking, Barney thought:

Now what's he cooking up? *Now* what? Why's *this* time different?

He had no more idea of what was going on behind that look of Sam's than he was laboring under the impression he could fly if he flapped his arms.

"Well, Barney," Sam said.

"Well, Sammy." Barney grinned, but it was a stiff grin. He was wondering if Sam had a pulp operation going in upper Canada. Or maybe Siam. Or Timbuctoo.

"Well, Barney." He said it again and it was clear he was nervous and wondering about something.

"You said that before."

"Come outside, will you? I can't talk to you with these damn yahoos watching."

They were watching, too. Every bright black eye in the joint and Adelbert's baby blue ones for good measure were glued to them. Barney went out the door and started down the path to the spring as fast as if he really had to get there.

"Where the hell're you going?" Sam said.

Barney swung around to face him.

"I give up," he said. "Where *am* I going? You're the boss."

"God almighty!" Sam said. He was only three feet away and he had that familiar stifled look on his face that meant he was trying to say something and didn't have Jude there to say it for him. "You don't make it any easier for me, do you?"

"Well, Sam, I don't know what I've got to make easier for you. I don't know what we're talking about."

"Look, kid, I'd kind of like to forget about this winter, if you can."

If Barney had had anything handy to kill him with and it had been six months earlier, he would have dropped Sam in his tracks. Forget this winter! He would like to forget this winter, if Barney could! And if Barney ever wanted out, he couldn't say: Sam, I will hate your guts for the rest of my life for this winter. He was going to have to say what Sam wanted him to and make his voice sound easy and not like a wire stretched across that endless ravine of time wasted and time lost forever that this winter had been for him.

"I can try, Sam," he said and now he was going to have to smile.

He did it well enough so he could see relief come up behind the eyes watching him, and Sam held out his hand. They stood there in the path, closed in with alders and nothing to see them but whatever it is that starts you up the steps, and shook hands solemnly with each other.

"It's not very easy—" Sam began to say. He was looking right at Barney when he started; but his eyes moved enough to settle on something behind Barney's left shoulder. "Well, hell, Barney, what I'm trying to say is: I guess I've been treating you like a kid and I've got to learn to stop. Makes it hard because I'm so much older than you. You see? I forget sometimes you're my brother and a grownup yourself."

He still had that I-want-to-say-something-more look; but he turned abruptly and started back toward the clearing without saying it. Barney stood looking after him, knowing from that, it hadn't been Sam talking. It had been Jude. Sam didn't believe it for a minute. Barney wasn't grown up and as far as Sam was concerned, he never would be; and Sam couldn't look him in the eye while he was saying the things Jude had told him he had to say if they were ever going to get on together again.

That made it just that much easier for Barney. At least Sam hadn't asked him for any promises or reassurances, much as he'd wanted to. That was what he'd left unsaid. He *had* wanted to. Maybe he didn't dare for fear of the answers, or maybe Jude had told him that wasn't what to do either.

They came bursting out the path into the clearing and by that time Sam was going so fast and so was Barney, trying to keep up with him, they must have looked as if they were running a race. But they always had been and Sam was slowing down, he wasn't half so far ahead as he'd been once. Barney was catching up with him, and suddenly he discovered he didn't want to. He didn't want anything Sam had or anything he did—nothing of his. And why the hell had he been racing with him all this time when it wasn't worth the trouble?

Sam stopped beside the bunkhouse door and his face wasn't smoothed out yet the way it should have been if he'd really believed all those things he'd been saying. He looked as if he'd found out about the race too.

"All right, Barney," he said. "Get your duffle."

"What?" Barney sounded stupid to himself.

"Well, how about it?" Sam said impatiently. "You ready to come out of the woods?"

Barney shoved both hands hard into his pockets, turned, went a couple of steps back down the path they'd just come out of. He didn't dare let Sam see his face yet.

He was looking at the same things he'd been seeing all winter: the frozen lake with the ice treacherous and spongy now; the tarpaper shacks; smelling the smoke from the cookhouse; hearing the horses; standing where he had stood once before and thought he was dying. Now there was nothing. A curtain had come down somewhere inside him and there was absolutely nothing.

When you want something so much that every waking thought and every minute of time has all been concentrated to one single end and then, all of a sudden, all you have to do is reach out and there it is, sometimes you're scared to reach. He could have reached and he wasn't even scared because there wasn't anything to pick up.

He tried. He took the letters and set the word up behind his eyes and looked at it. SABRA. Nothing else. No future. No past. Only a word he hadn't thought of for nearly a month and couldn't find a meaning to now he *had* thought of it.

For christ sake! he thought. It was for that—all the misery and thinking I might die and wishing to god I would, and all the "where is she?" and "what's she doing?" and "who's she with?" all gone, and no reason for it.

He commenced to laugh. He felt fine. He turned around and took a swing at Sam just for the hell of it and because Sam was closest. He'd have swung at anyone, not to hurt, just to let off a little steam. Sam's face, worried until Barney turned, relaxed.

"Hell, Sam," Barney said. "Why not? But I'm out of the woods right now!"

"Barney, I think you are. Come on. Get your junk and let's go. Jude's getting a real fancy supper for you. She said if I didn't bring you home with me, she'd come and get you herself."

For the last time they drove down through that deserted wilderness of back country—not really deserted because there were still people living there, going through the motions of living; but slower than the motions used to be and not so important, so their being there made the place all that more deserted.

When they finally hit the coast and there was the ocean, just where he'd left it, it was low tide and Barney could smell the iodine smell of rockweed and flats mud and realized he'd been homesick for it. It nearly made him dizzy and he sat sniffing like a hound dog trying to decide which way the rabbit went.

Port Kezar looked the same. It hadn't moved two feet out into the Sound while his back had been turned. Only another winter had gone over it and there had been a good many of them and the changes they made were so slow you didn't really notice them until there'd been a lot. The town had that dingy, end-of-winter, spring-coming-and-hurry-up-about-it look, and with night coming down over the side of the Mountain and nobody around in the streets and the lights coming up in the houses, it looked cold and lonesome; but Barney couldn't remember when it had ever looked so good to him.

He felt quiet inside. He wasn't even looking around to see what he could see. It didn't make him turn a hair to know Sam was watching cornerwise to see if he *might* be looking. Sam couldn't know that all that churning around and wanting and to hell with everything else was gone as if it had never been there. Barney wondered himself if it ever had been as bad as he'd thought it was. The quiet was new and good and he sat there and let it slosh around inside him.

They stopped by the house, alongside Cliff's old Ford, and Jude must have been watching because she came out the door before the engine died. Her face looked tight too, under the smile; but she took one look at Barney and the tightness went away and left the smile.

"Barney, you look like a million dollars!"

Barney knew he felt better. He'd put on weight this winter and had a lot more sleep than he was used to. There was such a change in him that Jude didn't even bother to give Sam that questioning, is-everything-all-right look. All she had to do to know it was look at Barney's face.

He'd only been a hundred and fifty miles away, but he felt as if he'd come back from the moon. He'd never been so far away before —in miles farther, in time farther—but never half so far.

He put his arm around Jude's shoulders and pulled her against him hard and they walked into the kitchen that way, both of them laughing at nothing.

"All right," Sam said, once they were inside the old low room. "Let go of her now, kid. She's *my* wife."

"You've seen her every day." Barney went along with Sam's joke; but he let Jude go then and stood staring around that room, checking to see if everything was the way he'd left it. This place, their place, was the only home he could remember and coming back to it now and to them was the best thing that had ever happened to him.

Either they hadn't let him see before, or he hadn't bothered to look, but they were honestly glad to have him back. All of a sudden, he could let them know he was glad to be back too.

He could see what a hell of a lot of time he'd wasted, horsing around, not being willing to admit he was grown up. Hell, he'd wasted nearly twenty-three years being a smart bastard, letting himself think he was the only thing going and nobody else was worth taking the trouble with!

What it came down to was, he was home, and he was so full of good intentions he almost caught himself reaching up to see if his halo was on straight.

That evening was one of the nicest ones Barney ever had. Jude had evidently tried to remember everything he'd mentioned he liked to eat and most of it was there. He ate until he thought to god he'd bust a gusset. Sitting opposite him, Cliff watched the process, that big punkin-devil grin of his getting bigger. But he managed to keep up pretty well and he wasn't even breathing hard when he shoved back from the table. Sam held his end up too; but Jude didn't eat much. She sat and watched the three of them and when anyone's tide went down enough so she could see the flowers on the plate, she'd fill it up again.

Funny! People. When anything happens or there's a big holiday or something, the first thing they do is sit down and see how much they can eat. It's almost as if it was a safety valve—eat to keep from doing something else.

And afterward, they talked, in a new way, too. Plans! If they had really been doing half the things they talked about that night, they'd have been busy for the next two geological eras.

They were going to start on a big new broiler house first. Sam had it all planned out. He'd made a deal with a broiler company down in Belfast—one of those we-bring-them, you-raise-them, we-take-them deals—and it sounded good to him. So the first thing Barney had to do next morning was head for Bristol to see Ansel Jarvis, the big secondhand lumber dealer up there, where Sam always got his rough lumber.

Once Jude put out her hand across the table to Barney and, against his will, he remembered the last night they'd sat here, last October, when she had done the same thing and he'd refused her. But he remembered it as if it had happened in another life to somebody else. Her hand in his now felt the way her eyes looked, sure and steady. He had never stopped long enough before to think about anyone: That's good, or That's bad. But she was good and he thought it, looking at her. She trusted you and believed in telling you so.

"We've missed you, Barney. It didn't seem possible you were coming home."

"Well, you know now I have, don't you?" he said, hearing, with surprise, words coming out of him that he couldn't even have thought, much less said, six months ago. And neither of them was talking about the physical fact that he was back in this house. The home they both meant was one that had never seen him before and it wasn't four walls and a roof of wood.

"I think I do."

"Hang onto it, then."

"Oh, my god!" Sam got up and yawned. "Hearts and flowers yet." He stretched and to Barney, sitting down, he looked almost bigger than Adelbert. And he looked happy and sleepy and relaxed.

"I'm going to bed," Sam said. "The rest of you better too. School tomorrow, Cliff. And look, bud," to Barney, "if you don't stop holding hands with my wife, there'll be works."

"*You*'ve got a lot to be jealous of," Jude said, and all she did was look at him; but she didn't need any more words for that either.

Barney got up and headed for the stairs. Suddenly he was sleepy himself and thinking how good it would be to go to bed in a clean decent bed and sleep. He could hardly wait for it to be morning.

When it came and he opened his eyes and looked at it—the sharp early spring sunlight coming in through the familiar window, falling on the known furniture, lighting the walls of the room where he had not wakened for months, he felt as if he'd never been away.

Or it was more as if he'd been asleep or dead or just suspended between then and now, and had finally come to, and the sleep or the death or whatever it had been had wiped out the part of him that used to wake up in the morning feeling if he couldn't get up and go his head would blow off his neck like the stopper out of a bottle of soda when it's warm and you shake it.

"Then" was gone. It was behind the sleep or the death. And "now" was going to be forever.

He got up and went over to the window and morning wasn't really any prettier than any other March morning. But it looked brighter and bluer. He stood looking down on his kingdom, the one they had opened the gate to and let him into last night, the one he had never seen before as part his. He could see the roofs—even the roof of the big broiler house they had talked into being, though it wasn't there yet and there were scrub spruce growing where it was going to be.

He heard Jude getting breakfast, so he dressed fast. When he went to Bristol he could get his registration too. The sight of his Chevrolet sitting out there in the yard made him anxious to get her rolling. He'd done enough walking to last a long time.

"Hi, Judith," he said to her back. "Where's your young brother?"

"I've been trying to get him out of the hay now for half an hour. Here's your coffee, Barney."

Cliff came in then, still half asleep.

"Cliff," Barney said.

"Unh."

"Can you hear me?"

"Yeah. Just."

"I want to use your car this morning, if it's all right with you."

Cliff didn't answer right away and Barney looked up to find him exchanging a questioning look with Jude. Even the kid, he thought, and Jude wasn't sure, or maybe a night had given her time to start wondering again.

"It's all right," Barney told her. "I want to go to Bristol to see about that lumber."

"Sure," Cliff said. "Only watch out for the right front tire. It's kind of spongy."

Barney lit out right after breakfast, went to Bristol and got his business done. It was early in the afternoon when he drove back into the yard. Jude was coming around the corner of the house from the barn and when she saw him she looked like a kid on Christmas morning.

He sat in the old Ford and his hands got cold on the wheel and he thought: Barney Cousins, what a son of a bitch you can be! And where did it come from?

He nearly got out and went over to her and said all the things he was thinking; but, because it would have scared her to death, he didn't do it. Poor Jude, just seeing him back there was enough for her.

He spent the rest of the afternoon trying to kick a little life into his own car. By five o'clock, when he went in to wash up for supper, he had her purring to him. That was a sweet engine. The body didn't look like much; but the engine was the kind they didn't make any more.

He was washing his hands at the sink and the kitchen smelled like heaven; but he didn't feel hungry. There was a funny sensation in his stomach like sometimes when you wake up in the morning hung over and you want a drink and you don't want it at the same time. He was standing there, his hands covered with sand soap, trying to figure it out, listening to something he hadn't realized was there to hear until he stopped moving.

He was so busy listening to himself he didn't know there was anyone else within forty rows of apple trees until Jude spoke right behind him.

"Barney," she said, and he nearly jumped out of his skin.

"What's the matter?" Jude sounded as startled as he felt.

When he turned to face her, though, he was all right again. The funny feeling was gone and he was starving and ready to eat.

"Nothing," he said and was relieved to hear his own voice. It was the right one and came easily and there wasn't anything wrong after all. "Just didn't hear you coming."

"Well, I think you scared me more than I did you." She went to stir something that was making a bubbling noise in a kettle on the stove. "I forgot the milkman doesn't come tomorrow and we're all out. Would you go uptown before supper and get a couple of quarts?"

"Sure thing. If I can wait. I'm starved. You need anything else?"

"No. I did the shopping this morning. Guess that's all I managed to forget."

Cliff was upstairs. He could have gone. Jude could have gone herself.

"Homogenized," Jude yelled after Barney shut the kitchen door but was still in the shed.

He went out, climbed into the Chevvie, and went uptown through the cold blue March evening. There was still light tenting up overhead; but the sun was well down. The street in front of the A. & P. was deserted, nobody walking, no cars. He made it in the nick of time. The boys were up back in the store putting on their coats and as Barney opened the door the lights went out.

"Hey," he yelled. "Wait half a minute, will you? I only want some milk."

He got it from the cooler and came back to the check stand where the kid was waiting, overcoat on, hat pulled down across his eyes. He took the money but didn't put it in the register, left it lying on the marbled edge.

"Checked out my cash for today," he said. "Damned if I'll do it again for fifty-two cents."

"Don't blame you," Barney said. "Thanks."

He took the milk, one carton in each hand, and they went out together. As he went through the door the kid snapped off the last dim light and the long aisles died into darkness behind them.

Barney wasn't thinking anything, just had it in mind to get home with the milk. He still wasn't thinking anything when he looked at her standing there and said:

"You going home?"

"I was."

Inside him he felt it start up again, the feeling that was almost like a sound, whatever it was he'd been listening to when Jude had come into the kitchen and startled him. The rest of him felt like a blackboard after somebody hauls the eraser across it.

"Get in the car," he said. "I'll take you down."

Sabra hesitated a minute, then walked over and got in. Barney went around to the driver's side and got in too.

When he was behind the wheel, no more able to reach out and turn the ignition key than he was to pick up the car and carry it home, Barney was thinking about a forest fire he'd helped fight years ago when he'd been a kid in high school.

It was a heart breaker. It ran wild for days, back and forth in the pulp clearings, getting, the second or third time across the land, whatever green and living it missed the first time.

All through the screaming hot dry September days with the west wind howling across the countryside like a bulldozer, it was like living and trying to work in hell. There was nothing that resembled life during the days. But the wind would go down with the sun and the fire would quieten and when they should have been digging it out, they'd be too damned tired to do anything but pray the wind wouldn't blow again in the morning. But it did. For a whole week it went on like that. On Sunday night the wind died and they got a little spit of rain, not enough to touch the fire, but enough to tell them the weather had changed. For another week they had it quiet—gray peaceful days without enough wind to move a grass blade, and they worked like a crew of devils out of that same flaming hell they'd been living in for seven days. They had it licked. You couldn't find anything but a faint spiral of smoke here and there over the blackened and sodden earth.

That night Barney went home to bed for the first time in fourteen days in an honest-to-god bed and he was so tired it didn't feel any different to him than the back end of the dump truck he'd been snatching cat naps in.

They told him afterward the wind came up again about midnight. It came from the northwest, whistling down over the shoulder of Mount Hagar like a tornado that's been held in check until it got a lot backed up, and then let go all at once.

There were a couple of guys patrolling the edges of the burn and they all should have known how fire could drive into two feet of powdery duff and hang on like a piece of Fourth of July punk. If there had been a hundred of them, they couldn't have done any more than those two, stand there and watch living fire pour up out of what had been safe and quiet ground—right out of the earth they'd been walking on minutes before, just as if somebody had punched a hole down into the middle of the world where there's always fire burning and let out the flames of eternity itself and this was the end.

It crowned before they could get into the car and downtown to blow the fire whistle, and by the time the crew was out of bed and back there, it was like all the spread-out fury of that first week, hauled together and concentrated. The fire wasn't so big but it was hotter, fiercer, more dangerous than it had been before.

And Barney sat there in the front seat of his old Chevrolet in front of the darkened A. & P. with two quarts of homogenized milk, one in each hand, and felt the same thing happen to him. It had been burning underground for a long time and now it was crowning.

He rolled down the window and put the two quarts of milk outside on thin air, the way you'd put them on a shelf. He didn't ever hear them hit the ground or know until later on what he'd done with them.

He turned around then and took hold of Sabra's hands and they were just as cold as his were and closed into tight fists. It was like taking hold of something as dead as driftwood and cold as death.

"Listen," he said and it all started coming out of him, the way he'd felt and how it had been, the words coming out had nothing to do with him voluntarily and he couldn't have stopped them if he'd wanted to. He wanted to reach in and haul his own heart out between his ribs and put it in her hand. He wanted to wrap up whatever it was that had kept him breathing, wrap it up tight in the way things had been with him, and give it to her to do anything she wanted to with.

He wasn't sure what he was saying by the time Sabra got one hand out of his grip and laid it along the side of his face.

"Barney, don't!" she said. "I know all that. For me, too. But I didn't even know where you were."

"All right. That's what I've been wanting to hear you say. Now we've got to do something about it."

She smiled at him, but it was like the smile you'd give to a kid who's just said he can't live if something he wants can't happen and you're a grownup who knows what he wants is impossible—but knows, too, that he will live. One corner of her mouth smiled, the other didn't, and the gesture didn't come anywhere near her eyes that were watching him, quiet and dark and hopeless.

"What do you suggest?" She glanced away, out through the windshield, down the darkening windy street. "You're back and I'm here. And there's just as much as there was before and more with me, Barney. Can't you settle for that?"

"No. I've got to have it all. I want you out of that house, away from that old man. I've got to be the only one."

"It's too late. You must know you couldn't be now."

"What in hell are you talking about?"

Barney put his clenched fist against her jaw and made her turn until she looked directly at him and he had seen the look in her eyes before, once. He couldn't remember when or what they had been talking about to make her look that way. All he knew was it had got to him enough so that he recognized it now for something that was dangerous to him.

"People live along, Barney, and they can't help letting other people get a hold on them."

"Well, my god, he can't have such a hold on you that you can't marry me. Hell, he's only your father!"

"I'm not talking about *him*. There's two others with more of a hold and look at you! You've forgotten all about them. But I can't. As long as I've got them, you can't be 'only,' Barney. You can be first; but not only."

"Oh," Barney said blankly and she was right. He had forgotten all about the two kids. And the half-recognized look Sabra had given him was the same one she had the night he'd asked her what their names were—the night Arthur had spent in the kitchen howling his unholy prayers up through the ceiling at them—the night she'd looked at Barney like that and said: "Those kids are *mine*, Barney."

"Well, look," he said desperately. "I can't stand this! Hell, I don't care. There could be forty kids if there was you too."

"I can see how there could be forty and maybe it wouldn't matter, if they were all—" She couldn't say the word about Chris herself. "If none of them was like Chris."

Barney knew what she meant. Just thinking about Chris he could feel a funny shiver go down his backbone. And she was watching him like a hawk and if he was ever going to have her, he couldn't let her see. It was all he could do to keep his face from showing how he felt, thinking, all of a sudden, that he would have Chris around for the rest of his life, growing up in the same house, getting bigger, getting worse, getting more whatever it was and harder to handle.

"You see?" Living had gone right out of her voice. "That's what

I mean, Barney. You couldn't do it and you'd have to. You'd always be asking me to choose between you and that would be something I couldn't do."

Right then and there, and for the first time, Barney balanced the scales with Sabra and the two kids on one side and what his life would be like without her on the other. Because that was the way it was going to have to be, one or the other, and there wasn't a second's hesitation after he got the scales loaded.

"Come on," he said and got out of the car again.

"What?" she said. "Where?"

"Marriage license," Barney said. "It takes a week. We've got to get started."

She didn't move, didn't say a word, just looked at him.

Finally she said:

"You wouldn't ever ask me to do it, would you, Barney?" And he knew she'd seen what he wanted her to. "You'd know you were first, wouldn't you?"

"As long as I knew that I wouldn't have to ask you, if you mean choose. Hell, why would I?"

"You wouldn't; but I'd want you to be sure right now, so you'd always know."

Barney didn't go back to Sam's for three days. He didn't dare leave Sabra alone with the kids, or either to the old man's tender mercies, before that. As it was, even with Barney right beside her, she changed her mind every time she looked at those kids; and Arthur was willing to do anything he could to help her change it.

He was sitting on the sofa under the kitchen window when they went into the house the first night, and he had one kid on each side of him. Sabra went in ahead. When she saw them all there she stopped as if somebody had put a hand against her chest. She and Arthur exchanged a long steady look. Then his eyes fumbled past her and met Barney's. Red came up behind his skin until even the mean little eyes looked red too.

"There you are," he said. "I was beginning to wonder when you'd be back."

"Now you know."

"Pa," Sabra said and she hadn't even heard him speak to Barney or Barney to him. The queer strained sound of her voice attracted Arthur's attention fast. He knew what she was going to say before she got the words out, or maybe didn't know how far she intended to carry it; but knew that this was the end and that even while he was looking at her she had started to walk away from him. Before she had a chance to tell him, he said:

"No." And if he didn't know surely what he was saying it about, he had a good idea. He used almost the same words she had when he spoke to Barney.

"Can't you be satisfied?" he said. "Isn't it enough for you to have your way with her under my roof? Do you have to take her away, outside, away from her children? I've let it go because I knew there'd be someone, if it wasn't you."

"Oh, Pa, shut up! Let me say what I've got to, won't you?"

"What can you say? What is there?"

"There's this." Barney put in his two cents' worth loudly, before Arthur could tell him anything else he didn't want to hear. "We're going to get married. Does that suit you?"

"Why?" Arthur's mouth opened and shut twice before he could go on. "You don't have to, do you? You've got what you want, haven't you?"

Barney shook his head.

"What about the kids?" Arthur said. "You needn't think you can go off and leave them for me. I'm not going to take care of them."

"Well, I am." Barney looked, in spite of himself, at Chris sitting there propped against his grandfather's shoulder and needing that shoulder to hold him up, his head nodding. Chris had both hands around a sad-looking tortoise shell kitten that was lying still as death against his chest. The old she-cat was pacing the floor, watching the kitten and talking to herself about it.

"You going to take care of him too?" The jerk of Arthur's head echoed the nodding of Chris's. "Sabra," he said. "Take a look at his face! Just look!" And he meant Barney. "See him look at your precious son!"

Maybe Barney *had* looked at Chris the way Arthur was saying he had, maybe it *did* show. But what did that have to do with it? Nobody could have liked it; but if Chris came with her, then Barney had to have him too, and that was all there was to it. By the time Sabra had swung around to face him, Barney had managed to get under wraps whatever it was the old man had seen.

Arthur's little eyes had turned from red to the shiny colorlessness they usually had.

"You going to trust him with that baby?"

Sabra's hand was cold again when she took hold of Barney's; but she was smiling.

"Yes, I am. Yes, I'll trust him."

Arthur didn't. The last night Barney had seen him, he'd told Arthur in so many words he'd probably kill him someday. He hadn't meant it. He'd had too much to drink and he was mad clear through. But now Arthur was telling him the same thing without finding words or liquor necessary. And *he* meant it.

"The sooner I get them all out of this house and away from you," Barney said, "the better off we'll all be."

Arthur didn't answer. He just sat there staring at Barney and all of a sudden Chris let out a yell and began to cry. Ann got up and scrabbled around to the other side of her grandfather and began to pry at his fingers where they had closed on the boy's shoulder.

"Stop, Gramp. Stop! Let go! You're hurting him."

Arthur's bony old fingers had shut to on that kid's arm like a vise and he didn't even know it until Ann yelled at him.

He said "Oh" in a surprised voice and let go; but he was still looking at Barney and he didn't glance down at the screeching child until Sabra went down on her knees in front of them. The kitten, suddenly sensing release, went across the floor and under the stove like a streak of greased lightning.

"It's all right. It's all right, baby," Sabra said.

Barney stood looking at Chris's limp white hand against her warm throat, thinking what it must feel like, being touched by something that couldn't think or know anything or come near being human; and not only that but to have to know, too, that, whatever it was, it belonged to you and you had to do for it whatever it needed as long as it lived. And now he was going to have to do the same thing. But she looked over her shoulder at him and she was his and anything that had to do with her was his and he'd take whatever it was and glad to get it.

"You're right, Barney," she said. "We've waited long enough."

Even after that Barney didn't dare leave her alone with them. For three whole days they carried on a silent argument, Sabra and Barney against Arthur. Her mother just sat around and dripped slow tears all over the place and watched Arthur to see what he was going to do next. Sometimes it was just Barney against the old man, and that was why he hadn't dared leave Sabra alone. Sometimes it was as if she'd gone away from behind her face and there was only that left and, when it happened, Barney would feel as if Arthur were winning.

In any battle, though, there had to be a time when the side that's going to win eventually knows it, and from that point there's no going back. Barney knew which side it was the night Sabra said to him, right in front of Arthur:

"Barney, we're going to have to be thinking about a place to live. Tomorrow we've got to do something about that."

Barney felt the way you do at a carnival when you take a slam with the sledge hammer and the little gadget starts up the pole and way over your head in the dark the gong gives out a loud clear note and the guy hands you the cigar. When Barney turned to look at Arthur, he had the cigar in his hand and Arthur saw it.

For a while and in spite of his attempts to bolster it, Arthur's faith had been shaken. He had been confident that God would never let things go this far, and He had. But, by the time it happened, Arthur began to see that maybe it wasn't God who'd failed him after all, but he who had failed God. He had been intended to do something more than he had. He couldn't see what it was. He was old and Barney was young and he didn't know what he could have done; but now all there was left was to watch, and wait. Old or not old, he could do that.

If he watched and waited patiently enough, his time would come, bound to. All he hoped was, when it did, God would give him the ability to recognize it and know what to do.

He could see now that he had lost his daughter the minute he sent her out of his house, years ago. She had come back; but he had lost her and it wouldn't do any good to brood over that now. So, with a single-mindedness of purpose, he transferred everything in the way of hopes he had ever had to expend on Sabra, to the next logical recipient.

There was still a chance, and perhaps a better one, because Ann had Sabra's brains, unaccompanied by the looks that had given her mother a choice of two roads to go. Maybe that was the solution. Ann wouldn't have the same choice and Arthur had that much to thank Baxter for.

If God was with him, someday he would be able to see what he had to thank Barney for. Right now it was hard for him to feel that such a time might ever come, even knowing as he did that it had to. Right now he hated Barney Cousins and hadn't been given the ability to hide it.

His chance would come, when it did, through those kids and he had to hang onto Ann somehow, anyhow.

"All right," he said. "If you've got to go, then for the love of God, go, and get it over with!"

In a town like Port Kezar you'd think there'd be any number of places you could get to live in for a decent price. But most of the places they looked at were either too big and they couldn't afford them, or too small for four people. It was still winter as far as work went, and all the dough they had was what Barney had saved this winter and what Sam was going to pay him, if Sam was going to pay him anything at all, and he wasn't sure of that now. Sabra wouldn't sign up for her unemployment for a while longer and they had to eat under the roof as well as get it over their heads.

They finally found something, not much, but neither one of them cared. It meant they'd be together and not under somebody else's roof. It was that shack Diddy Wallace put up to sleep his kids when he finally had fifteen and the oldest ones were beginning to poke their feet out through the windows nights because there wasn't room enough inside the house to hold them all. One big room with a bed and a stove in it and a loft overhead where they could rig up a place for the kids to sleep.

Diddy's boys were long gone. The place had been standing empty for years and he was glad for the chance to pick up a few dollars out of it. Barney didn't offer him much and he began to stutter about it.

"That's a god-damn comfortable little house," he said. "Why, any man would be glad to get the use of that for twice as much!"

All the time he was looking at Sabra with his eyes getting brighter by the minute. She wasn't paying him any never mind; but Barney was. For what Diddy was thinking about her, he should have paid them to live in the place.

"Take it or leave it," Barney said. "Besides, it's right under your front windows and we'll have to keep the shades down all the time or you'll be right aboard."

That slowed Diddy down a little.

"It's just standing here empty," Barney pointed out. "And I know damn well you told Jack Bartlett he could have it for hauling it away."

"Oh, all right!" Diddy gave up in disgust. Then he began to hem and haw around and Barney wondered what was coming now. When it came, he had to grin.

"I don't reely believe in it," Diddy said. "You take a man and woman living together like—by rights they ought to be married."

"That so?"

Determined to give him no satisfaction, Barney was waiting to see which was more important to Diddy, seven dollars a month or his suddenly discovered righteousness. A fine one *he* was too, the old s.o.b.! Fifteen kids he owned up to and probably as many more spread around all over town he didn't.

Though what any woman could ever see in him! Barney thought they must have been kind of tired when Diddy got around to them and he didn't give a damn anyway, as long as it was a woman. When Diddy went out the door, Barney had stared him down and Diddy had seven dollars in his hand.

"Why didn't you tell him?" Sabra said. She was looking at Barney with a half-mad, half-amused smile.

"I like to keep them guessing."

She came and put her hands on his shoulders and, looking down at her, Barney knew something he'd been trying to figure out ever since he'd got back. She was different. *How* different, he couldn't see. But something had changed, and it made her more beautiful and he hadn't thought she could be.

"Oh, my god," he said. "Aren't you—" But he couldn't find any word to tell her exactly what she was.

That night Barney figured it was safe to leave her for the first time.

Sam was coming out the back door when Barney pulled into the yard. Sam took one look to see who it was and kept right on going. Barney sat watching him head for the barn without turning his head again. What he should have done, Barney knew, was turn around right then and there and go and never try to come back. Because they weren't going to believe anything he ever said to them again. But there hadn't been a time before, with one exception, when they ever *had* believed him.

He'd picked an hour of the day when they might all be reasonably expected to be busy with something, to make it simpler. He went into the kitchen trying to feel easy and wondering how he'd done the same thing so often before without having that funny quivering deep in his belly. The other times there had been more reason for the quiver and it hadn't been there.

Jude was getting supper and when he stopped to think, every time he'd seen her since he'd come out of the woods, she'd been getting a meal or about to and, my god, didn't women ever do anything else besides feed men? She looked over her shoulder at him and didn't bother to smile before she looked back at what she was doing.

"Hi," he said.

"Hello, Barney. You ready to eat?"

Well, all right, he thought, I guess that's the way it's got to be. It was like going backward in time. They were right back in the middle of last summer and the whole winter had been erased, the winter and the other night when he'd come home, and all the things they'd talked about. Nobody was going to give him a chance to say he wasn't any different than he had been that night. That was the sad part about this mix-up. He was still right there and feeling exactly the way he had when they'd been so glad to see him. And if they had been willing to give him half a chance, tonight he could have said so.

Jude set another place at the table. Barney washed at the sink and sat down beside Cliff in a silence you could have cut with a dull knife. When Sam came back in, he went over and washed too, and came and sat down before he bothered to say anything.

"Where the hell's the milk?" he said.

It was then Barney remembered what he'd done with the two quarts of milk he'd gone uptown to get four nights ago. Damn it anyhow, they should have been able to tell by looking at him that this time was different. He hadn't been on a bat. He hadn't even had one drink!

"Well, Barney." Sam's eyebrows looked heavy and black across his forehead, the way they did when he didn't like something. "Back in the old rut, hanh? How does it feel?"

Barney should have said it then, what he was thinking—how they were all wrong this time. But there was Cliff and Jude and he couldn't. Besides, it seemed to him he'd spent most of his life whistling down a rathole and anyone can get tired of that. He figured he might as well save his breath. Their minds were made up.

So he thought: Well, shut up, Barney, and just hang her tough.

Port Kezar wasn't the only place in the world to live. He liked it and he had to stay for a while, for the rest of the spring and summer anyhow, until they could get a little bit ahead. But then he'd go. He'd take Sabra and the kids and go to Connecticut or somewhere. Half the state of Maine was there now, working in the factories, two more of them wouldn't even show. Maybe down there, too, they could find a doctor who could do something for that kid.

"Fine," Barney said and started eating.

"Can you manage to go to work in the morning?"

"Why, sure, that's what I'm here for."

He gave Sam a wide innocent look as if he was saying: For god sake, why not? Sam didn't care for that either.

"You want to start clearing for the broiler house?" Barney said. "I see the lumber's here."

"No." Sam was chewing steadily and looking right down at his plate. "I've changed my mind. Guess I'll coast along with what I've got now and when I empty the big one, I'll use that instead of building."

No more "we." All "I."

"Okay," Barney shrugged.

It was Sam's kingdom, after all. Barney didn't really have a say in it. He wouldn't have had even if things hadn't happened the way they had. Sam and Jude might have tried to make him think so— maybe ask him what he thought about doing this or that, tried to make him think his opinion mattered. But when it came right down to brass tacks, it was theirs. He should have seen that sooner, and he thought perhaps he had. Around there, his address was tomorrow, never today. His name was wait-and-see, not right-here-and-now.

He looked at Cliff and suddenly he thought: There's the crown prince. Because Cliff would probably stand as good a chance as anyone of having all this someday. Barney wondered if Sam and Jude thought they could leave him to Cliff too, maybe with a clause saying: And care for my brother Barney as long as it shall be necessary. Thinking when they had the lawyer write it down that it would be necessary as long as Barney could draw in a breath!

Yes, it was definitely time for him to stop coming back to them every time he bumped his head. But he had to hang on through this summer coming up and Sam had just said that he expected him to, so that much was settled. Barney could do it because he'd done it before; but this was the first time he'd ever got the one-syllable-word treatment when he felt he didn't deserve it and he found out that justice has nothing to do with justification. It was a lot easier to be lippy when you were getting what was coming to you than when you weren't.

PART THREE

IT FELT to Jude as if they were going backward in time too. But it wasn't so new to her as it was to Barney. It had never happened to him before—for Jude it had happened every time. Each time they had extricated him from some mess or other, she had dared to let herself feel, until the next one started building, that this might be different. Maybe he'd learned his lesson. Maybe now, with the newly surmounted crisis behind him, he would see that his life was lying waste.

There was something different about this return, though. Barney was back, he was sober, there had been no explosion to end with the phone call in the dark house. So what was gnawing at her?

Simply, there was nothing she could find fault with, except that he had gone and she knew where. And now he was back, but not back the way he had been. All the confidence she had felt in him that first night had vanished, leaving the old defensive Barney behind his expressionless intent undemanding façade. But there was more of a difference, there was a finality that bothered her, as if he himself recognized the irrevocable now.

Whatever it was, they all felt it, even Sam—perhaps Sam most of all. He hadn't even been able to talk to her this time and, in his silence, the resemblance between the two, Sam and Barney, had come out even more strongly for Jude.

Last night they'd all gone to bed early because of the constric-

tion that lay over them like a cloud as they sat together in the
kitchen after supper, but a cloud to be ignored and the human
faces and voices to be forced into natural look and sound—and
because of the force achieving nothing but complete lack of ease.

Sam was a restless sleeper and, after the light had been turned
out, Jude knew he was lying there awake simply because he lay so
quietly she could scarcely hear him breathe, and the narrow aisle
between the two beds felt miles across to her. After a while she
knew, too, that he wasn't actively thinking about Barney—he was
lying there hoping she wouldn't speak to him, wouldn't try to talk
about anything at all.

Here we go again, Jude thought helplessly, seeing them all poised
at the top of a roller coaster; but one with no ups, only downs.
We had our "up" a week ago, she thought, already with nostalgia
at how transitory it had been, the relieving and new thing about
Barney that night. He had been so sure of himself. That was what
broke your heart about him—it had all been true for him and he
had been able to convince them because its validity had been so
strong for him.

"Sam," she said, trying to think how to tell him they didn't have
to talk about it.

"Not tonight, Jude."

His voice in the darkness was expressionless and quiet and so
strange to her that she didn't try again. Instead, she lay there in
the stillness hating Barney or anyone else who could make Sam
sound like that, or who could come so strongly between them that
they couldn't even talk together any more.

And when she went down to face Sam in the morning, she
found that what he was feeling had lasted over the night. His
eyes said to her for a desperate second: We can get it back. Help
me! And Jude knew she would have to play along with his hopeless attempt once more, knowing that its hopelessness must be as
clear to him at last as it was to her. But Sam couldn't afford to
admit defeat and for his sake, neither could she.

"You're all dressed up." Sam eyed her unaccustomed blouse
and skirt, eyebrow lifted. "Stepping out today?"

"Town Meeting Day," Jude said. "I told you a week ago I was

going." What she couldn't say was that it would have been impossible for her to stay in this house today and any excuse to get out and away from it would have been welcome.

"Oh, yes." Sam glanced out the window at the feathery fall of snow that had taken all night to cover the ground and was now melting faster than it had come down. "It's the weather for it, all right. Can't remember a Town Meeting Day we didn't have a thaw."

"Come with me," she said on a sudden impulse.

"Me?" He turned an aghast and violated gaze upon her. "Hell, no!"

"Well, it'll be your money in part they're spending," she pointed out patiently, going along with him, fumbling for words to say that would not immediately remind them all of what she was not saying.

"Honey, I've got to stay home and make it. Besides, they'll spend it anyhow. *I* couldn't stop them."

Jude's eyes hesitated for a minute on the narrow back of Barney's head. We're going to have it that way again, are we? she thought. You're going to get away with it again. It never happened. But when she stopped to think, she didn't know what *had* happened. There was nothing. It was like trying to put your finger down on a puddle of quicksilver.

Barney pushed back his chair and stood up, looking down at his brother who should have been his father, should have had the authority as well as nearly the age.

"Better get to work, hadn't we? If we've got to work up all those taxes before the day's over."

And *he's* working at it, too, Jude thought, seeing with pity she told herself was completely impersonal the look of tight strain around his young mouth. Everything's all right. Everything's just fine. Everything's exactly the way it was before. Come to think of it, it was. Just exactly.

"What the hell's the matter with you?" Sam put half a doughnut into his mouth and with the end of the same motion grabbed his cap off the back of a chair. "Never knew *you* to be so anxious to go to work. You afraid she'll try to get you to go with her?"

"She could ask me. She hasn't invited me yet."

Jude couldn't carry it along from there. She was completely incapable of helping them any further and her silence was the answer to the question they'd all been asking. Hastily, to cover the abyss, she started clearing the table, thinking tautly: Go away, both of you. Just get out of here. That was a fine masculine solution to something you couldn't grab with both hands. Run!

It was late when she started uptown and she was in a hurry. The road was still treacherous with melting snow and water and it took all her attention and she was glad of it. But when she passed the factory she saw the Road Runners, largely because she had been expecting to see them and it would have been more remarkable if she hadn't. There they were, the skinny little girl toiling up the hill toward the main road, almost there, pulling the homemade wagon with the little boy's handsome nodding head sticking up above the sideboards.

Jude expected the boy to wave. He waved at every vehicle that passed them, while his sister plodded unnoticingly ahead. But this time, as Jude passed them, something else happened. She was so surprised that she was well beyond them before she realized just what it had been.

At the sound of the approaching truck, the girl had turned, snatched something from the cart, and held it high over her head, calling out in a voice as shrill and piping as a plover's. When Jude glanced back, the child still stood, hands high above her head, with the limp kitten dangling docilely from her tight grasp. What she had screamed in that high thin voice was:

"Kitten for sale."

The kitten looked to be dead; but as Jude drew away from them, the little girl turned, her shoulders sagging, to put it back into the wagon and it gave a slight, not definite enough to be protesting, wiggle.

"That poor little mite," Jude said aloud, meaning both the defeated child and the dismal animal.

On this beautiful March morning, the town, drenched in golden light, with the cream white of the sharp gull wings circling high over the sunny street, made her feel unreasonably that the people who lived here should be a little better than most, a little larger than life. God knows most of them are that, she thought bitterly, larger than life, but in the wrong way. Barney was, because, wherever she turned, his shadow lay before her instead of her own.

She had thought she could leave him behind her today, could forget him for a little while; but the Meeting plodded and dragged, and Barney was with her.

He was with her until the Meeting reached the road articles which contained one everybody seemed to think was a sleeper. It concerned a short piece of town road, perhaps an eighth of a mile long, never needed except by the man who had bought the shore property it led to and who had built a house there and used it as a driveway. The town had done no work on the road in years and had not been asked to. But would they discontinue it or wouldn't they? Back and forth. Over and over.

There was an old graveyard in on that road. Nobody would ever want to be buried there now; but the folks who *had* folks there would want to keep the right to go in to it whenever they felt like it. Nobody knew where the graveyard was, exactly, but it was there and you couldn't be cut off from your dead even if some summer man did want to keep you forever away from the gray slate stones over the once-human dust long ago at peace and not at all worried about the road or whether any foot could ever find the way again.

Pretty soon, if things kept on the way they were headed, They would own all the shore and all the ways down to it and then where would you be, cut off and penned in, and the town would have to appropriate money to build a tower so's people could climb up it to get a look at the salt water.

Every sea lawyer in town had his say on that one—it was what they had all been waiting for—the safety valve they could blow after the slow steady process of draining good money and endless and necessary money down the insatiable holes of Necessary Town Charges, School Buses, Snow Removal, Highways and Bridges, this, that, or the other which, under the law, had to be maintained and, consequently, to be paid for.

Late in the afternoon, with the flare of interest dead, the road still safely in the possession of the town, and Barney back with her as if he had never been away, Jude slipped out the door just before the Meeting adjourned, a day's indoor stickiness and weariness on her like a second skin. The wind, which had been soft and south-westerly that morning, had rounded into the northwest and the March afternoon was cooling rapidly to dark. The snow, turned to water, was already freezing in the puddles and occasionally in a treacherous sheet across the tar.

When she drove past the factory, there were the two forgotten children very nearly in the same place she had seen them this morn-ing. They looked cold and miserable and hunched in on them-selves, as if by making the target area smaller they could shut out some of the searching wind. Once more, hearing the engine, the girl turned to the wagon, but despondently this time, holding the kitten outstretched before her, not over her head, and holding it supplicatingly in silence.

Cursing her own foolishness, Jude slammed on the brake. I can always have Paul put it out of the way, she thought, backing fast. It would be better off.

"What do you want to sell your kitten for?" She rolled down the window and leaned out to look at the children. The boy, at close range, was still beautiful, too beautiful. His beauty cried out for a flaw and it lay in his eyes which were strangely shallow, cold, light blue, as inhuman as a young animal's. They were the only feature he shared with his sister. She had them too, set closely on either side of her sharp little nose. But where the boy's were blank, hers were sentient, completely avaricious, and too intelligent to find in a small girl who was not too long from having been a baby herself.

"For a dollar," she said, making it clear that she understood Jude's question to refer to what was foremost in her own mind. "I been trying all day long. I saw you this morning. I didn't think you'd stop tonight when you didn't then. I've tried all over. Look." She thrust the tiny animal up at Jude. "It's a good kitten."

"No, that's not what I meant," Jude said helplessly. "I meant, isn't it your pet?"

"We got an old cat has kittens every six weeks." The girl gave her a wise thin smile. "We got plenty."

The boy was watching the procedure intently, his mouth slightly open, his head moving. When Jude glanced at him, his eyes slid carefully and slowly away from her direct look. She stretched out her hand and took the kitten gingerly, putting it down on the seat beside her where it stayed without moving.

It was a tiny sick miserable scrap of a calico kitten, obviously unwanted, completely uncared for, and what was worse, uncaring. For anything as vitally alive and flittery as a kitten to behave the way this one did made Jude know that its short harried past had been just as awful as its unbelievable present.

The girl climbed quickly onto the running board and clung, peering in over the window at the cat.

"I thought I'd just get up here," she said. "In case you might try to drive away without paying."

Wordlessly Jude started fumbing for her billfold, thinking sickly: What kind of people raise their kids like this?

She held out the dollar bill and the child's hand closed on it. She had exceptionally long thin fingers, raying out from a comparatively small palm, and Jude felt as if a five-taloned bird claw had taken the bill. Having accomplished what she set out to do, the little girl dropped off the running board, no longer even thinking of Jude, picked up the cart handle and started down the hill. The dollar had vanished, tucked into some secretly safe and invisible pocket in her tattered jacket.

Jude's face felt hot with unreasonable anger as she pulled the truck out around the children and drove on away from the village toward the sea. The kitten lay limply on the seat beside her waiting for whatever might happen to it next. When she glanced at it, she found herself saying aloud and without having consciously thought anything at all:

"Oh, Barney—Barney—"

There is an impatient pushing feel about a house where men are waiting to be fed and Jude could sense it in her own house when she went in with a sack of groceries under one arm and the tiny cat lying in her other hand. They were all in the front room, she could hear desultory voices, and she didn't go in, thinking they would hear her soon enough and come to find out what she intended giving them to eat. Meals, she thought protestingly. And the protest grew more acute when she looked at the kitchen sink, piled with and completely obscured by dishes from which they'd managed to make out a lunch at noon.

She dumped the groceries on the table and set the kitten down gently in the middle of the floor. It gave a tentative flirt of its needle tail and stood looking around dazedly. By this time Sam had heard her come in and was standing in the door watching the performance thoughtfully. To beat him to the gun, Jude said:

"For pity sake, what did you all have for lunch? It looks to me as if you'd managed to use every dish in the house."

"We got hungry." He grinned unrepentantly.

"Well, you left a sweet mess for me, didn't you, you big dope. When the cat's away—"

"Speaking of cats," Sam said thoughtfully, "where'd you get *that* little sad sack? And why?"

"This?" Jude indicated the only possible cat with her toe. "This? Oh, I picked it up in my travels. Looked so damn miserable I thought I'd get Paul to take care of it. Poor little devil would be better off dead."

"Well, Paul will have to. You know *I* won't. And he can't do it till morning, so you better give it some milk." Without waiting for her to do it, Sam went over to the refrigerator, filled a saucer with milk and put it down in front of the miserable scrap of fur. The kitten extended a curious paw, got it wet, and began to lick. It was obviously galvanized by the experience.

"Look, Jude, for chrissake, it didn't know what milk *was!*"

Jude, watching the kitten make its fascinating discovery, hearing it begin greedily to drink and at the same time to make a rusty purr like a buzz in the quiet room, felt as if somebody had struck her sharply over the heart. My god, she thought, I wonder if those kids know either.

"If that isn't just like you, Jude," Sam said, half despairing, half amused. "Hauling home some godforsaken thing like that nobody else would want! If you wanted a cat, why didn't you get something worth looking at?"

"I'm not going to keep it," she said sharply. "I'll tell Paul to put it out of the way in the morning."

"I see you," Sam jeered.

Jude did too. Saw herself nursing the little cat along through whatever might turn out to be its life span. The minute it began to purr, she'd known she was stuck with it. I should never have brought it into the house, she thought, watching it. I should have taken it right out to Paul and let him do it tonight. She stooped and refilled the gleamingly empty saucer.

"It'll puke," Sam warned.

"Let it."

Barney, no longer able to contain his own curiosity, and closely followed by Cliff, had come along the hall too, and was standing looking over Sam's shoulder.

"Money cat, hanh?" he said, wondering where he'd seen a kitten like this one not too long ago. But all kittens looked alike to him and this wasn't a prime example. "Sam, didn't we—"

Sam gave him a puzzled look.

"I shouldn't think you'd remember that far back," he said. "Yes. Pa used to like them. We always had money cats, years ago."

By the simple statement, he made them see the long-dead money cats, their fur brilliant against the shining June grass of springs that had dwindled into autumn in fields long ago lost to pucker brush, alders and young thick spruce.

"Let *me* look," Cliff said protestingly from behind the barrier of the two broad pairs of shoulders that filled his view completely. He pushed past the two older men into the kitchen and stood spraddle-legged, fists loosely on his hips, looking down at the little animal with the air of a connoisseur of cats.

Well, Jude thought in helpless amusement, watching the three of them completely absorbed in the kitten, I couldn't have done anything better than bring it home. Men were children, really, and it took only very simple things to tie them together—it was the complicated and difficult to assimilate that bothered them. They had to have something with a material existence, something they could touch or see. And god knew, if anything as simple as a sick calico kitten could bring back even for a second that feeling of togetherness they gave off now, then she'd nurse the creature until she was blue in the face, and glad to do it.

The shed door opened suddenly and somebody stepped into the entry and no farther. The four people in the kitchen stood looking at each other curiously, waiting the identifying step or voice, which didn't come.

"Must be Paul," Jude said. "But what's he doing?" Raising her voice, she called: "Who is it?"

"That's where you are, is it?"

The voice that preceded the impatient hand on the thumb latch was unfamiliar to all of them, but one. Jude happened to be looking at Barney and saw him, in turn, look with sudden horrified recognition at the kitten. So she knew whose hand was on the latch, whose voice it was.

Oh, my god, she thought, now what?

She stood waiting, unable to move, watching color drain out from behind the stillness of Barney's brown face. His hand was on the frame of the door where he leaned behind Sam, and it didn't move; but the fingernails were suddenly colorless too.

When the door opened, Jude was hardly able to take her fascinated eyes from Barney's face, thinking: Is it really like that with you? Before she turned, she saw Cliff's jaw drop with recognizing astonishment; saw Sam beginning to get his what-the-hell-do-you-want expression. Then she turned herself, to face the girl who stood in the doorway.

Perfect physical beauty is impossible to define; but it has to be admitted in its rare actuality and Jude knew she would be the last to deny its existence, after having seen this girl closely for the first time. Youth lay on her like an incandescence. She was shaking slightly with some emotion Jude didn't recognize at first and she had her arms folded tightly across her chest, as if physical restraint could hold back the explosion.

She ignored the three men, and her eyes met Jude's squarely and Jude, recognizing now the unknown emotion for the fury it was, wondered suddenly: My god, can she see me? It was a moment before the eyes seemed to focus and when they did, Jude knew she had seen two other pairs of eyes just like them today—not physically like, because these were dark, not blue. Like only in knowing, in defense against humanity; but these eyes knew why and the children's had not.

"You people sit around in your big houses and think you're God," Sabra said evenly to Jude, still ignoring the men. "You think you can have anything you can pay for, don't you. Well, *my* kids don't need your charity!"

It was then she threw the thing she'd been holding in one clenched fist onto the table, as if she were pushing something away from her. Jude's eyes, following fascinated the arc of flight, saw that it was a dollar bill that had been crumpled into a tight little ball.

"I want that kitten."

"What's she talking about—"

"What is it—"

Cliff and Sam spoke simultaneously, cutting off whatever Jude might have said before she could even think it.

"If that's her kitten, Jude," Sam said harshly, "for chrissake, give it to her and get her out of here. What a hell of a—"

"Nerve, were you going to say?" For a minute there was an expression that went through the motions of a smile—if a smile could be activated by anger—across the lovely dark flower of a face. "I wonder sometimes who has the nerve and who doesn't. That kitten is my kids' pet and I want it."

"Well *take* the god-damn thing." Sam was furious too, and had every intention of showing it.

"A dollar doesn't mean much to you, does it?" Sabra looked directly at him for the first time.

Jude bent stiffly, wordlessly, feeling Sabra behind her, feeling as if there were a wild animal loose in the narrow door, wanting to look over her shoulder to see at least the beginning of the spring; but too mad to give her the satisfaction of that glance. The kitten had left the saucer, empty for the second time, and lay under the skirt of the stove, curled up nose to tail in the warmth. Reluctantly, as if she were betraying something that couldn't help itself, Jude picked it up gently and gave it into the ungentle waiting hands.

"When me or mine need anything from people like *you*," the tight voice said, "we'll let you know. Till then, keep your hands off!"

Guiltily, for some reason, Jude didn't want to meet those eyes again; but Sabra stood there as if she waited for something to loose her and let her go. Jude was compelled to look, to see if that beauty really was as she had seen it in her first quick glance. And it was—unflawed, complete—an absolute and undiluted perfection.

For a second they were in league against the surrounding masculine enemy, and alone, simply two women looking at each other in a hushed room, one apparently from a peak of happiness and security as great as any one person could ever achieve in uncertainty, the other from an unimaginable and opposed depth. But the second vanished unacknowledged.

"I know you. I know you. You have to do us *good*." Sabra made of the last word something it had never been intended to mean.

She was gone so quickly that, if the kitten hadn't been gone too, Jude might have doubted she'd ever been there. But when she turned reluctantly to meet Sam's affronted eyes, the doubt would have vanished. Weakly she sat down in the nearest chair and, because it would have been silly to cry, she began to laugh.

"Well, for god sake," Sam said heatedly, his anger, unexpended, shunted from one female to another, inexplicable and forever beyond his understanding. "I'm damn glad you can see the funny side of things, Jude! Who *was* that crazy woman?" But he knew.

Barney made the first decisive motion he'd made since the back door opened. He passed in silence, but not unnoticed, across the kitchen and out through the door. No sound attended his going at all but there was a frightening singularity of intent about it, particularly to Jude who had seen his face.

Ought I to stop him? she thought. I shouldn't let him go after her when he's that mad. But she knew it would have been like trying to take the northeast wind in your hand and say to it: Stop blowing.

After he had gone, the others accorded his going a moment's silent consideration. Sam's eyes, coming back from the door through which his younger brother's broad shoulders had just vanished, met Jude's—shadowed with worry. He shrugged helplessly.

"Her name's Sabra Baxter," Cliff said nervously into the adult silence. "She lives in that old white house down by the factory. With her father and mother. They all work there. Been living there for a couple of years. She—Barney—they—" He petered out, not knowing how to say it.

Sam had stood with his head bent, listening, but not hearing the quick boy's voice telling him what he had known and really hadn't had to ask.

"God almighty, Jude," he said, as soon as Cliff's voice stopped and as if the boy had never spoken, "you sure have got a genius for trouble. How in hell *do* you get mixed up with these people? What did you do? Steal that god-awful kitten from her damn kids?"

"I gave them a dollar for it." Jude was still laughing helplessly; but behind the hysteria she too was beginning to lose her temper. Sam's purely masculine attitude toward what he chose to treat as a women's spat infuriated her. There were times, and thank god they were in the majority, when Sam filled every blank she presented to him. There were others, and it seemed to her important ones, when she could have screamed and thrown whatever was to hand at his uncomprehending head.

"My god, I think she's right," she said hotly. "Here we are talking about 'these people' and their 'damn kids.' They aren't anything but human beings and, god knows, you aren't either."

"She behaved like anything but," Sam said in his most irritatingly pontifical tone.

Jude turned and left the kitchen quickly.

"Hey," Sam called after her, jolted out of his anger by her departure at this crucial moment. "How about some supper?"

"You're both big and ugly enough to get your own." Jude didn't hesitate on her way up the stairs. "You managed to get lunch all right."

She went into the bedroom and lay there on the bed in the dark, feeling as if, once she had passed out of the company of other people, she had entered a state of suspension and her mind, without somebody else to give it focus, had gone out of her down the dark road to the village after Barney, after Sabra who had told her that hell was paved with good intentions.

She could not imagine, remembering those two faces, what was happening out there on the road. Perhaps nothing. Perhaps it had already happened as she waited, and was over, whatever she lay dreading. She knew herself that violence and anger, pushed to a point, could go out like a blown match—so that nothing at all might have happened.

Downstairs Sam and Cliff were getting their supper, she could smell the frying steak, and she shut her teeth against nausea. Then Cliff went out and she heard his car start; but Sam stayed in the kitchen and there was a loud clatter of china and she knew that he was, half angrily, trying to atone for having injured her, angry because he didn't know what he'd done, atoning because he didn't like to do it.

After Sabra was three minutes gone, Barney could still see her standing in the doorway, and nothing else. He felt as if he'd been alone there in the kitchen and there still was nobody else there when he went out.

He didn't catch up with her right away. When he did, she was walking fast and he could tell, looking at her from behind, from the way she held herself, that she was carrying something and it had to be the kitten. He drew up alongside and rolled down the window. Sabra didn't stop, didn't even hesitate. So he put the car in low and jogged along with her, watching her out the window. Her face was pale and it looked thin.

"Sabra," he said finally. "Get in the car."

She didn't answer him.

"Get in the car," he repeated and his voice was expressionless.

"I won't," she said, but she hadn't looked at him yet.

Barney let her get a little ahead and then he hauled in until the right wheels were on the gravel and drove slowly along behind her wondering what the hell he was going to do now. It was going to be something, because he could feel it building.

He reached down and grabbed the emergency without even bothering to put his foot on the clutch, and the car bucked and stalled. He opened the right-hand door and left it swinging. Then he climbed out his own side and started after Sabra.

She must have heard that, his feet coming after her. She didn't hesitate long enough to look over her shoulder, but she began to run and so did Barney. Just before he caught her, he remembered the deer he and Alec had found swimming in the lake.

The minute she felt his hand on her arm she stopped dead, stood there as if the touch had turned her to stone and maybe it had for a minute. When he picked her up, she felt cold and as if it weren't flesh and blood he was carrying.

He went back to the car with her, went around and half threw her in through the door. She stayed right where she landed, too. When Barney got in under the wheel she hadn't moved, was just sitting there staring at him with eyes that looked as big as his fist. The kitten was staring too, with its mouth open. Barney had never known that a cat could breathe through its mouth before, like a dog panting.

When he slammed his door, of course the light went out, and he couldn't see either one of them and he had to see them, so he reached out to the door post and snapped on the overhead light and turned halfway around in the seat to look at her and she was laughing—or going through the motions.

Laughing!

Barney had forgotten that night something he had discovered about her. She laughed when any other woman would cry, and he forgot it.

Because he had forgotten, he did something he'd sworn to himself he would never do to her again. He hit her hard with the back of his hand and then, while he sat watching her, Sabra put up her own hand flat and covered the place where he'd struck her.

He wasn't hitting her. She had just been standing too close to the dynamite. It was Jude and that damned smug brother of his and Arthur and all of them he couldn't hit. But Sabra was within reach and they weren't.

At that moment, another car came up with them and passed and Barney sat stupidly watching the taillights pull away and all he could think of to do was start up and go too.

By the time Sam was ready to go to bed Jude had come back downstairs and was sitting in the front room with a magazine propped uncompromisingly in front of her. Sam stopped in the doorway on his way up to look at her, and her attitude was so remote that for a minute he contemplated letting it go, saying nothing. She wasn't reading the magazine, he could tell that, her eyes weren't moving at all. But she looked enclosed and beleaguered.

"Jude," he said softly.

No answer.

"Jude, come on to bed. He won't—"

"He won't what?" Jude said, not looking up. "Who won't?"

"Barney. He won't be back tonight. What makes you bother to wait?"

"I don't care whether Barney ever comes back," she said levelly. "But Cliff will, and I want to see him into the house. I want to be sure whatever's wrong with Barney isn't contagious."

She flipped a couple of pages and held the magazine up stiffly so there would be no possibility of their eyes meeting if she should, by mistake, look up at him. Sam shrugged and turned away—cursing mentally all the people you let matter enough to you so they could drive a wedge between you and the people that mattered most. That was where you made your big mistake, letting somebody with no responsibility matter to you. If you could only take them or leave them alone—pick up where you left off with them—instead of going right on from one time to the next, getting increasingly involved and wound up until there was no way to let it drop until the end, wherever and whatever that was. And in the process somebody got slighted. Well, he thought wearily, I'm only one man and there's only so much of me, and I'm damn tired tonight and I can't go in and talk to Jude because it would just end in another hassle and "what-are-we-going-to-do?" and "Cliff—Cliff—Cliff."

He couldn't see where Cliff was giving her anything to worry about, he was a good sensible kid, as steady as any of them were at his age, and Sam couldn't see a trace of anything wild in him to worry about. He thought sometimes Jude simply used Cliff for a club to hold over his head about Barney—but he couldn't see what she wanted him to *do*. Apparently she didn't want him to tell Barney he couldn't come back to the place again, because she'd been the one who'd forced him to go up and haul Barney out of the pulp camp. And if it wasn't that, then what the hell was it?

Women were damned irrational! That was all there was to it, he thought angrily. And if she wanted to sit there half the night waiting for those two to come back, he wouldn't stop her. There was no point in trying, because if she'd made up her mind Sam knew he couldn't change it, just by trying.

He was nearly asleep at ten-thirty when the car drove into the yard; but not too close to sleep to know it was Cliff's car.

Well, thank god, he thought, not knowing why he should ever have felt that Cliff wouldn't be back either, unless Jude's foolishness and worry over the kid was as contagious as whatever she was worrying about. He turned over comfortably, forgetting Barney, putting him completely out of his mind, and was instantly asleep.

Jude caught her young brother halfway up the stairs—she had waited to see if he'd come into the living room and when he didn't, she was sure that he hadn't come intentionally and that there was some reason for his wanting to avoid her.

She spoke to him from the living-room door and Cliff turned to look down at her, one hand on the banister, and it seemed to her that his eyes looked big and alarmed; but the light was dim and she would be looking for things that weren't there anyhow.

"Been to the movies?" she said quietly.

Cliff nodded.

"Good show?"

"So-so," Cliff said. "The usual blah."

"Waste of time, hm?"

"Better than nothing," Cliff said. And then: "Did you want something, Jude? I got to get up early tomorrow."

Then she was positive there was some reason for his wanting to avoid her, because Cliff never voluntarily went to bed until the last gun fired. So she had to ask him the question she'd been trying to think how to ask, bluntly, before he got away from her.

"Did—did you see Barney anywhere uptown?"

"Why, yes." He drew in his breath as if he'd intended to say more and stopped with the unsaid words so close to the surface that

Jude could almost hear them. Then, that *is* it, she thought. That's what's bothering him. Something certainly was.

"Was he—"

"Was he what?" Cliff's voice was getting tighter. "What d'you want me to tell you?"

She couldn't say to him: How do I know what you've got to tell and how much of it I really want to hear?

"All right?" she said quickly. "Was he all right?"

"As far as I could see, he was."

By some unexpected and not truly voluntary exercise of control —because she wanted to ask and be answered, but not by the boy— Jude didn't say: Was he alone? What was he doing?

And Cliff didn't go on to tell her what he had seen and what he could still see now in his mind: the car parked with the inside light on so that the man and the woman sitting in the front seat could see each other's faces. Didn't tell her how, in the second when he drew abreast and glanced over at them, something about their absolute stillness had burned on his memory those two, half turned to face each other in a globe of deadly stillness and light, saying nothing, just looking. To Cliff they had appeared armed, and not with weapons you could see, nothing as easily discharged as a gun nor wounding as easily as the slick thrust of the sharp blade; but weapons invisible and more dangerous, entirely beyond his experience and recognition.

As he passed them he had seen Barney lift his arm and strike her hard across the face with the back of his hand. Before Cliff had been able to move his shocked and fascinated gaze, he had seen her smile and cover the place where the blow must still echo through the firm young flesh.

That was what was in his mind and on his tongue; but he had no words to tell about it and he couldn't see why Sabra had smiled. That had been the most shocking thing about it to him, and he didn't want to tell Jude now, so he said:

"As far as I could see, he was all right."

There was an embryonic idea of privacy in his mind and, such as it was, it had been deeply offended by what he'd seen and if he repeated it to Jude now, the offense would go deeper.

"Well," she said indecisively, and to Cliff's immense relief, "go to bed then, Cliff."

She watched his speedy retreat thoughtfully. For a second she had been sure there was some other thing he was holding back from her consciously; but, after all, there had been nothing else. And if whatever she had been waiting for hadn't happened by then, the chances were it wouldn't happen at all.

You could be surprised without being, Jude found the next morning. She was standing with Paul outside the big broiler house. The northwest wind, still blowing, funneled down between the buildings, roistering and ungentle, finding the chinks in her jacket as she stood talking to him but with her eyes going past his intent listening face to the unbelievable clouds, to the savage-colored water.

Sam was still eying her warily this morning, but he had calmed down a lot and Jude was beginning to feel sheepish herself at the way she'd behaved. Sam had been right, though, and Barney hadn't come home last night, wasn't home yet; but she would forget that— would forget all about Barney and his actions. It had nothing to do with her, really, any longer.

There was too much to do. The new chicks would come tomorrow, five thousand of them, and although Paul knew they were due, he hadn't known just when, and the brooders would have to be started tonight.

"Let 'em come." He grinned at her, his freckled face wrinkling under the crew-cut red hair. "We got here first. I'm all ready for them anyway. All's I've got to do is light up."

"I don't know what we'd do without you, Paul." Jude put her hand on his denim-covered arm for a second. "There's so cussed much to do around this place."

"Probably just what you've done with me," he said. "Anyone can nurse a batch of hens."

"That's all right," Jude said. "You know what I mean, you joker."

That was the trouble, right there. They all knew, but nobody would say, as if they were preserving a secret from each other, all the while aware that it was common knowledge, that Paul was doing his own work and Barney's too, while Barney was—well, wherever he was this morning, when he should have been right here.

Turning away, Jude nearly fell over the two children. It was then that she felt the queer unsurprised surprise and knew she had been half expecting to see them somewhere this morning.

"Oh," Paul said. "I meant to tell you. I've run them off once this morning already."

"What?" Jude said, startled.

The little girl said something in a quick excited gabble, something that didn't even sound like English.

"I can't—what did you say?"

"My gramp says we need the dollar more. Here's the cat."

The boy was holding the kitten squashed tightly against his chest and the little animal was once more reduced to taut trembling misery.

"I can't take it," Jude said firmly. "Your mother wants you to have it."

"Fifty cents."

"It's not the money—but if I pay you for it, she'll come and get it again, the way she did last night."

"She won't now, because Gramp says not." The girl gave her a wise level look. "He says the kitten will die and if you're foolish enough to pay a dollar for it, we might's well have it. This is the hard time of year. Mama ain't signed up yet."

"Oh." Helplessly Jude glanced over her shoulder at Paul, who was watching with what looked like fascinated horror. "Oh, well."

She pulled her billfold out of her hip pocket and took a dollar from it. It might have been the same one that had passed between them the day before and been thrown back at her last night. Doing it, she was aware of an actual pressure, as if the child were trying to hypnotize her into action and had succeeded.

Once more she watched the conjuring act with the bill, seeing it stowed quickly away and not seeing where, before the little girl turned to take the kitten from her brother. She had to use force to get it this time, because he didn't want to let go. In the middle of the tug of war, the kitten opened its mouth wide, but made no sound.

Once more Jude took it, feeling the little thing settle into the comfortable cup of her large hands and burrow like something trying to dig itself deeper into a cave of safety.

"All right," she said, more roughly than she had intended. "But now that's enough. I don't want to hear any more about this kitten from anyone! Nobody is to come and get it and if they do, I will say I haven't got it. Do you understand?"

She found herself speaking with a clear careful enunciation, as if by clarity of sound alone she could pierce the wall of protective callousness the child had found it necessary to build around herself. Then, meeting the old-young eyes, Jude was silenced, seeing understanding there, but understanding more complete than she had asked for.

"That's good. That would be the thing to do, all right. I'd do it myself."

At that point, Jude began to wonder which of them was the older.

The baby in the wagon burst suddenly into a bereaved roar. As if she had been as anxious for the diversion and as relieved by it as Jude was, the girl spun and slapped him soundly. This produced indescribable volumes of sound, sound so great it was hard to see how his small lungs could encompass air enough to produce them. She rounded on him again, her hand raised threateningly.

"You shut up, you little bastard, or I'll really let you have it!"

The boy closed his mouth on the next roar, letting out nothing but a slight hiccup of sound. As composed as if she hadn't just been screaming like a little fishwife, the girl said to Jude:

"He can't believe there'll always be another batch of kittens. He yells like that when we drown them too."

Jude's ears were still vibrating to the sound and then the cessation of sound, still echoing to the unbelievable words that had poured out of that contained small face. The girl, who had been pretending during the entire exchange that Paul didn't exist, looked at him now and was re-established as a child. She ran her tongue out at him, making the sound that went with the action.

"She *did* want it, didn't she?" she said triumphantly. "*You* didn't know so god damn much, did you, you old fool?"

Paul lifted his hand and covered his mouth carefully, without being aware that he had done it. He met Jude's despairing glance and his eyes were expressionless and still.

"You don't have to worry, honest," Ann said firmly. "She won't come for it again. Besides, she don't know we're here. She had to go to court this morning, to her hearing."

"Hearing?" Jude's attention was pulled to a point, out of the despair. "What—"

The girl shrugged.

"Oh, her and Uncle Barney had another fight last night and he beat her up again. So Gramp went and got the man who comes to get him when he does that and they signed the paper and took him up to jail. But Mama had to go up this morning to swear to it."

Jude set the heel of one hand firmly against her forehead, feeling as if it might burst outward if she didn't hold it back.

"They made an awful racket," the child said. "It woke us up. And Mama's face was all black this morning. Worse than before."

Jude took a deep breath and said, between clenched teeth: "Go home! Just go home!"

"I don't know, Jude," Sam said and he looked thoroughly miserable. "I honest to god don't know what's the best thing to do."

"But *something*," she insisted fiercely, trying to force him to meet her eyes by the steadiness of her own gaze. "Sam, you can't leave him alone in a mess like this."

"I think I can."

"Well, *I* can't."

"Look, Jude. Just last night you were telling me I'd taken care of him too long. Now you're telling me I've got to take care of him longer. He makes his own messes. I think he'd better get out of one by himself."

"Not this. That old man is crazy, Sam. There's no telling what he'll say, swear to. And the judge will have it in for Barney, too, after last fall."

"In the first place, all you've got to go on is the say-so of a seven-year-old kid. There may be nothing in it at all. She might just have made it up."

"Why on earth would she do that?" Jude recalled the child's eyes. "Oh, no, she didn't make it up."

"Well, hell, I suppose I'd better go up and see what's going on. If I don't, you will. I can see that. And if it's anything like the hassle we went through last time, I don't want you mixed up in it."

"This time I'm coming with you."

"I'd rather you didn't."

"Sam, I don't want to butt into your business. I don't want to argue. I just want to be with you."

They had kept their voices low, standing there in the kitchen looking at each other with determination. Jude had forgotten that she still held the kitten, had forgotten it while she was still out beside the chicken house looking at Paul with what wanted to be disbelief, but couldn't because there was no room for it. Now in the kitchen, telling Sam, she tried to keep her voice down; but her hands closed convulsively on the little cat, squashing a faint mew out of it.

Jude grinned ruefully, thankful for something else to think about for a second, tending carefully to the kitten as if it were the only thing that mattered any longer, saying to Sam's stare of outrage:

"This cat's caused more trouble now than its hide is worth. I intend to see it's damn well cared for."

"That crazy woman won't be back for it, will she?"

"No," Jude said shortly. "She won't. And don't keep saying 'that crazy woman,' will you?"

"Well, for god sake, she *was!*"

Oh, no, Jude thought. No, I cannot face it again. I know who *will* be crazy, if this goes on much longer.

"Sam," she said pleadingly, "it's not important. What matters is what we're going to do about Barney."

"Wait till I get my checkbook," he said heavily. "I might just need it."

In the small room across the hall from the living room, Sam leaned over the slanting top of the big yellow oak desk, pawing hastily through the welter of bills and loose papers that snowed it under. The house was shutting to on him and he scrabbled impatiently, not thinking, only feeling the constriction of four walls

around him, in a hurry to find the checkbook and go and get the
business over with.

Once outside in the brilliant sunlight and under the high sky
where he could breathe again in comfort, he crossed the drive at a
stride and stood looking in at Jude who was sitting in the truck
waiting for him.

"Jude, for the last time, please!"

"Sometime—one of these rigs—you're going to need me," she
said implacably. "When you do, I want to be sure I'm there."

Sam shrugged, one corner of his wide mouth quirking up in a wry
gesture toward a smile.

"What do you think you can do?" he said soberly. But they had
twenty miles to go and he had no time to stop and argue with her
now. Remembering the last time he had gone on this errand, he
would have given anything he had to leave her behind him. She
was down enough on Barney now so she didn't need anything more
to put against him in the ledger, and if she came with him today
she was bound to get something more.

Sam drove fast and well—not finding it necessary to think when
he could give his total attention to something he could do with his
hands—and inside half an hour they were topping the last high hill
from which they could look down across the flat to the soft shouldering low hills of the river valley where the county seat lay, apparently
at peace, under its anonymous canopy of elms. Out of the welter of
gray that would be green soon, under the brilliant light, the starkly
clean spire of the Congregational Church—sitting whitely on the
rise behind the courthouse—stabbed blue sky as sharply as the
sword of the very God of Wrath who set it there.

Jude thought blankly: How could there be anything soft or
peaceful about a religion that needed a symbol like that one to
mark its place of worship? God of Retribution, God of Vengeance,
God of anything but Peace and Quiet! In this case, a God set to
watch over the complicated workings of the law, the tortuous answer the law held for its questioners, the long slow process of ac-
cusation, argument, rebuttal, judgment.

And to watch over the thousands who came for justice, the hun-
dreds who daily went in and out of the great ant hill of a court-

house, up and down the long flight of tamed and polished granite steps—tamed and polished and artificially roughened again for safety, but whose safety, since most of the feet that trod them were in jeopardy and walked with fear, who had no need of steps at all. Granite carved out of the wild old foundation of the state itself, hauled in from an offshore island, holding inside itself (quiet and waiting for the day to come) the knowledge that the un-man-touched heart of stone would be there when the men were gone. Hauled in to make a long approach to the asking and to the answer, and when the asking and answering were nothing but wind blowing through ruined windows and all the written judgments dust on that wind, would still be there, making a long approach to nothing.

Jude sat in the truck with the steeple before her, sharp against the sky, watching Sam walk up the long flight of granite steps to the shining brass-bound glass doors. He looked bigger than the other men—there were two or three others, two coming down, one going up—neat in their quiet tweeds, controlled and stiff in their way of walking. Sam shouldn't have been there at all. He still wore the black-and-red checkered shirt he'd put on this morning to go down to the shore, tucked inside his heavy trousers, its bulk contained by bright red suspenders, the legs of his pants stuffed down inside the unlaced tops of his larrigans. He went up the steps with a loose ease, taking two at a time every third or fourth step, like a man walking the ties of a railroad and cursing the just-not-long-enough distance between them. His big hands swung tense and ready as if he expected to be able to do with them what he hadn't been able to accomplish with twenty years and all the words in the language.

Once at the top, he put out one hand to the door. Before he had touched it, it swung open and a woman stepped through it to stand confronting him. Sam stopped as if he had run into a barrier of something as impenetrable as it was invisible. Then he took a step away and aside and Jude saw what had stopped him. If she hadn't been so sure herself who that woman was, she would never have known from her face. Where there had been perfection the night before, there was now only a battered ruin, a swollen caricature of beauty.

Apparently the only thing that passed between the two people at the head of the stairs was a look, no words. Sabra came down the steps, one hand on the middle rail, moving with a slow care that told Jude more clearly than if she had seen them, that there were other and invisible bruises. It was hard to say whether Sabra glanced at the truck and saw Jude or whether she didn't, her eyes were so sunk and slitted into the abused yellow-brown flesh. In any case, it made no difference; she made no sign, went quietly and slowly— as if every trace of her lithe youthfulness had been pounded out of her—along to the old Chevrolet parked two spaces down the hill, and crawled painfully in to sit there, waiting.

Two little boys who had been hauling an express wagon back and forth along the cold-pack driveway that led in to the jail, spotted her just as she got into Barney's car. With one accord they left the wagon for the greater attraction and came over to stand on the sidewalk staring in through the windshield, their soft unformed still-baby faces blank with wonder. Sabra either didn't see them or didn't care. She just sat there in the front seat as inanimate as a sack of meal.

"Is she an Indian?" the younger boy said curiously.

"Maybe."

"She might scalp us."

"Run, if you're scared." His older brother looked at him scornfully. "I'm going to stay here and look at her. She didn't have nothing to scalp *with*."

Jude looked back at Sam and found he hadn't moved, had stood there watching Sabra go down the steps. And while he stood, Arthur Kenney had come out and past him and was going down too. He moved unsteadily, with an uncompromising impatient swing of his left foot, coming down one step at a time; but even at that, faster than his daughter had.

Sam's attention transferred itself from the girl to the old man without a jerk; but a little late for him to see what Jude had seen— the quick sideways glance Arthur had given him when he found Sam there, the furious recognition, the half-made motion with one hand, as if he thought of striking out at Sam, who represented Barney but who was too far away to hit; the quick acceptance of futility, knowing that if he had hit Sam it would have had as little effect as a flea bite.

Jude wasn't expecting the door to open a third time; but Sam had been watching it and knew before she did who would come out. She saw Barney hesitate, watching Sam, seeing that Sam had waited there at the head of the steps. Barney stopped halfway through, until the door swung back with heavy slow force and staggered him. Then he pushed it again and came out to stand himself, silent, watchful, his face wiped as clean of expression as if it had just that moment been created and there had been no time for whatever he was thinking to show.

To Jude it seemed as if they stood unmoving and in utter encased silence for a full minute. Maybe it wasn't. The two dark profiles against lighter stone and brick lost for her their look of humanity. They were more like two big animals, completely aware of each other and absolutely forgetful of anything else.

There was, in her chest behind her breastbone, a place as big as a clenched fist from which all warmth had been sucked out with her breath and replaced with ice. She didn't recall getting out of the truck—neither Sam nor Barney had moved or apparently spoken— but she was out and across the sidewalk and standing at the foot of the steps looking up at them and by that time they had begun to talk. She could see the impatient slight motion of Sam's head that meant anger, could see Barney's defensive face break up suddenly into expression.

She must have been there for five minutes, still with that ball of ice that scarcely let breath down past it. At the foot of the hill, the clock on the bank at the corner began to strike and, carefully, she counted eleven booming flat notes.

As the last one faded, Sam made an impatient movement with his wide shoulders, flung one hand out sideways in an unaccustomed sweeping gesture of helplessness, leaned slightly forward and said:

"Barney, what in hell has she got? What is it? If you could tell me that much, maybe— What is it?"

"I don't know." Barney's lips felt stiff and it was hard to form the words, the way it is when you've been working outdoors on a cold day and your face gets so cold you can hardly move it. "All I know is, whatever it is, it's what I want and I'll have it, one way or another."

He was seeing and feeling in slow motion. He saw Sam's shoulders move impatiently; his body stayed where it was, but his face seemed to get closer, or bigger.

"Look," he said. "You god-damned young fool, *anyone* could have it who asked her. Can't you see that? *You've* had it! And a lot who don't bother to ask, but just take it."

Barney felt as if somebody had picked up a handful of dust and thrown it into his eyes. He shook his head hard, trying to clear it away, and couldn't. There was no idea of violence in his mind. He wanted only to get Sam out of his way so he could go on down the stairs to where Sabra was waiting for him. He put out his hand the same way he had to open the heavy door and when he felt it meet resistance against Sam's chest, he pushed. To get him out of the way.

Sam grabbed desperately for the only thing that might have saved him—the betraying hand—missed it, and was not a lithe and able animal any longer; but a man off balance and in a dangerous spot. He flung his arms up wildly, clutching at empty air, staggered, almost regained his balance; but one foot went off over the first step and he fell helplessly, backward, still moving with the momentum of that push and his own futile attempt at recovery.

Before she started up the steps, incapable of anything but motion, Jude thought she heard the sound he made when he hit the first step. Afterward she wasn't sure. But she certainly heard the noise tearing raggedly out of his lungs because he was still making it when he struck the landing and lay there, his eyes open but unseeing, his mouth open, and that sound like rough cloth tearing coming out of him on each hard breath.

She knelt beside him and put both hands flat against his chest to keep him from moving, unaware of what she was doing, hardly conscious herself, until she looked up to meet eyes so much like his own and almost as unseeing, across his big helpless body, and heard Barney say:

"Oh, jesus, Jude, I didn't mean to do it!"

For the space of a second, before people began to shout and they had to do something, she knew how easy it would be to murder and was afraid of herself as well as for Barney.

PART FOUR

―――――――――――――――――――――

BARNEY never really believed there was ever any such thing as an innocent bystander and now he knew it for sure. If there was anyone thought he might be, then he ought to get wise to himself. You can't stand back and let things happen to other people and just watch them happen and think: Well, I'll keep out of it. I'll stand here and watch and feel damn superior because it can't happen to me as long as I mind my own business.

You've got to mix in. And you might as well get into it, whatever it is, neck over crop. If you do, of course, you'll get clobbered. You won't be able to help yourself. The sad thing is, if you don't—if you stand back and be the innocent bystander—you'll get clobbered too.

He'd a hell of a lot rather earn his clobbering than not deserve it. That was the one way he and Sam were alike. Sam never was one to sit on his hands, and he sure wasn't doing it the day he got his.

It took Barney quite a while to decide Sam had had it coming. In the next few days he thought about it a lot and got it figured out that it really hadn't been his fault, or Sam's either. It was something bigger than he was and outside of him that handed retribution out to Sam, and whatever it was it was so much bigger, it could decide just how bad Sam ought to get it. Barney knew himself for the means, and was going to have to take the blame; but he could see now, even if nobody else would be able to, why and how it happened the way it did and as bad as it did.

It was bad. They'd taken Sam to the hospital and if he was still

190

there after four days, then it had to be bad. Barney really did some sweating at first—when he still thought it was all his fault—until he got thinking straight about it and could see it was like anything else that ever happens. It begins so far back you can't ever stop it and whatever's going to happen, will. Sam had had just as much to do with the beginning as he had.

When he got that far, Barney began to feel better.

It was about nine o'clock in the morning and he was lying on the big bed with his hands behind his head, thinking. It seemed to him he hadn't really heard anything else going on in the room around him; but when he sat up, he realized he must have been hearing on a kind of second layer of attention.

Ann wasn't there and he knew she'd gone off to school nearly an hour ago, so he must have heard her go. He expected Sabra to be doing the breakfast dishes after she'd fed the kids, so he must have heard her start. And he wasn't surprised to find Chris hauling wood out of the wood box behind the stove and piling it right where anyone would be sure to fall over it, if he wasn't looking for it to be there.

Well, Barney, he thought, there won't be anything to wash off those dishes pretty soon if you don't get up and get started. He knew, too, what he was going to have to do—again. He'd done it so many times he could have gone through the motions with his eyes shut. But this time he couldn't afford to keep them shut. Every sense he owned was going to have to work overtime, because nobody out at the house was even going to be relieved to see him. That was going to be the difference.

Maybe they hadn't been glad other times; maybe they hadn't rolled out the red carpet—but somebody, Jude or Sam, had always been relieved when he finally turned up. Sam wasn't there now. There'd only be Jude and Paul and Cliff and none of them would know what Barney could see so clearly, that he'd just got caught between whatever was pushing him and whatever had pushed Sam.

He honestly hated the idea of going out there and having to say to her what amounted to: Jude, you're the only one I can turn to.

He looked at Chris, fiddling around with the wood down there beside the stove, and thought: He's one reason. If it hadn't been for Chris, he could have lit out right then and there. Gone. Put the whole business behind him where it ought to be, and gone so far he wouldn't ever have wanted to come back. But there was Chris, solid flesh and bone if nothing else, and he had to eat.

Barney had enjoyed his life, as far as it had gone, and seen to it it was worth enjoying. But he supposed he could have arranged it a little better if he'd stopped sometimes to think how things were going to bounce back and hit him later on, if he'd taken a little trouble, instead of bulling ahead and to hell with it. He'd probably have got as much of a kick out of whatever it was as he did anyhow, and maybe there wouldn't have been so much recoil.

Hard to say, though.

He sat and watched Chris and thought of the guys he knew here in the Port—how many of them there were in the same spot he was, getting along from one job to another, not trained to do anything. Most of them married now too, and with families, because they'd got around to it younger than he had. He couldn't see where they had any more on the ball. But any one of them, if he got fired or laid off, could go out and pick up another job without trying too hard.

And here *he* was. There was only one place in the whole christless town he could go with any hopes of going to work and getting paid for it, and the hopes were pretty thin right now.

What'd I ever do that was so bad? he thought. Any one of the other guys he had in mind—Packy Hill or Bill Sutherland or Harris Baker—there wasn't a one of them hadn't got into the same scrapes Barney used to, and sometimes right along with him. Then why didn't it work the same way for them? Why was *he* always the one who either got caught or took the blame if nobody got caught? Well, hell, he shrugged—there has to be one and Barney was it.

Sitting around thinking like that wasn't getting him anywhere, so he got up and took his cap off the hook by the door and put his jacket on. He glanced over his shoulder and Sabra was watching him, so he dredged up a confident grin for her.

"This isn't getting the baby a new pair of shoes," he said. "Guess I better go see if I can mend a few bridges."

Her face said so clearly that she'd been thinking the same thing,

Barney went out the door in a tearing hurry before he said something he didn't mean to.

Didn't mean to! Didn't mean to! He'd been saying that to himself for a long long time. For nearly twenty-three years. As far as he
could remember, he'd started saying it early—to himself. The first
time he'd ever got the words out to anyone else was when he had
said them to Jude the other morning on the courthouse steps. He
was counting on her remembering that much anyhow. He knew
pretty well, when she saw him coming, she was going to have trouble
remembering anything good about him—if that was good.

Spring was a stingy and teasing kind of season down along the
coast. It was almost as if it was trying to get back at them for winter,
because winter was never as hard there as it was inland, away from
the water. One day spring was on the land, soft and sweet-smelling,
and there never was any such thing as winter. The next day there
could be a howling blizzard and that would be the way spring was
too.

This was one of the soft days—sky not really blue, too hidden
behind a kind of mist that said: Spring on the way, to have any
color but a pale sky color—and the sunlight sifting down through
the mist so it seemed to be coming from all over the sky and not just
the one spot in it where the sun happened to be.

When Barney drove into the yard, the house looked closed and
deserted and as if nobody had gone in or out the back door for days,
but there was a wisp of smoke from the chimney.

The only other visible sign of life was the little money cat sitting
on the back doorstep in the warmth of sun washing its face with its
paw, as calm and contented as if it had always sat there and always
would. It was probably right on that one. If Barney knew Jude, it
would.

He stood and stared at the little cat and suddenly he thought: By
god, maybe *you're* it. Maybe you're the reason Sam's where he is and
I'm here. That's something, isn't it? Because some ranting tom ran
across the old she-cat one night two or three months ago, here we all
are and we're people and you're nothing but an animal and a damn
small one at that. And it's almost enough to make you think maybe

people aren't all that important. Maybe they don't matter half as much as they think they do. Not if a silly calico kitten is enough to splatter their good solid lives all over a ten-acre lot.

He stooped and picked it up and it sat in his hands as contented as it had on the doorstep. It made just a good handful, comfortable, with plenty of room, and when he looked at it Barney felt sick to his stomach to see how small the match that lights the fuse can be. And still it doesn't make the explosion any smaller, it doesn't take any of the kick out of the dynamite. But, of course, the match is only incidental and the fuse was there and waiting and one match is as good as another.

He hadn't heard Jude come to the door and he was still eying the kitten and it looking back at him, as if they both might find an answer if they looked hard.

"Put that cat down, Barney," Jude said. The only reason he knew it was Jude without looking was because it was a woman's voice and there wasn't any other woman in that house. He had never in his life heard that voice from her before. After he *did* hear it, he couldn't have looked if he'd been paid for it, because if her eyes backed up the voice, for a minute he didn't want to see.

He leaned down again and set the kitten back on the exact spot he'd taken it from in the first place and it began licking its forepaw and swiping around its ear, the way they do, as calm as if it hadn't been interrupted. Barney still couldn't look at Jude, so he stared at the kitten until the regular, circular motions of its paw nearly hypnotized him. He stared, wondering if Jude was thinking the same thing: How small a thing disaster needs to set it off.

She had to speak again. He couldn't. If they had stood there all morning, she would still have had to be the one to speak, or either turn around and go back into the house and shut the door so he would know for good and all that he was through. If she spoke, he told himself, he still had a chance. He kept repeating that, like those charms you make up when you're a kid: If I can get to the next telephone pole before two cars pass me, then I'll get a bicycle for Christmas.

She said: "What do you want now?"

Barney tried to answer her, but if he let the words out he was afraid he'd vomit, too. That was how her voice made him feel, as if his windpipe was closing to on being sick.

"What are you doing here, Barney?"

"I just wanted to ask you how he was." He got that much out on an emergency supply of air, and felt a little bit better. He hadn't managed to look at her yet and if he didn't, in a minute he himself would have to turn and go and god knew he couldn't afford to do that.

"It's very nice of you to come and ask," she said evenly. "And since you've taken the trouble, I will tell you that he has a broken back. I doubt if you know what a thoracic vertebra is, Barney, but they're important and one of Sam's is fractured. It was fractured three days ago. I'm surprised you didn't hear it around town and that would have saved you the trouble of coming to ask me."

He didn't say he hadn't been around town to hear anything.

"Jude, I can't tell you—" he began and looked up at her and stopped there.

"No, you can't," she said. "So don't try, will you."

Her face was the color almost of white-lead putty and she looked as if somebody had got both thumbs covered with soot and used them to push her eyes a quarter inch farther back into her head than they usually were.

"I've *got* to do that," Barney said and the minute he said it, it was the god's own truth.

"Why? So you'll feel better? To ease your conscience? My god, Barney, how can you sleep nights? How can you come here and ask me how he is?"

He didn't tell her he hadn't been doing too much sleeping. He didn't say he couldn't do anything but lie there and think. She wouldn't care whether *he* could sleep or not.

"Jude, I—" he began and then thought that the words he needed would have to be words that could make what was done, undone; or make what couldn't possibly be better, better. "What can I say?"

"Not one damn thing!"

"Well—can I—is there anything I can do?"

"Do!" She repeated it as if it were a dirty word. "Haven't you done enough? You broke his back."

Barney closed his eyes for a second. He'd known this was going to be bad—hell, he'd known it would be stinking—but it was so much worse than he'd ever dreamed it could be! And Jude was making it just as hard for him as she possibly could and all ready to make it harder. He nearly said: I didn't do it, Jude. It wasn't me. But he didn't dare try to make her see what he meant.

"Will you ever believe that I didn't mean to push him?" he said desperately.

"Of course I believe it. But what earthly difference does it make whether you meant to or not? You did."

"Jude!" This time he really wasn't thinking—the words came out before he could stop them. "For god sake, give me a chance. Let me help. Can't you see I've *got* to."

"It's a fine thing to see your conscience bothering you for a change, Barney. I've often wondered what it would take. Now I've found out, it's expensive knowledge."

"I *swear* to you," he said. "Bring me a Bible. I will swear."

"If I could make things any easier for you by turning my hand over, Barney, I wouldn't do it."

He saw then that she was standing there hating every move he made simply because he could make it. She was hating the way he could stand up, could walk, could bend his back to pick up the little cat. Before he could stop himself, he blurted out the stunning knowledge:

"You really hate me, don't you."

"Hate?" Jude turned the word over curiously and looked at it. "More than that. I never before in my life knew what it was like to want to kill somebody with my own hands. It's not a civilized feeling. I don't like it. But if I could strike you dead, I think I would."

Oh my god, Barney thought, listening to her, how can I do anything with that? What can I say to that? She wasn't anyone he knew. A week ago she couldn't even have thought words like that, much less said them—and she thought he was the reason she could do it now.

She not only hated and wanted to say so, she wanted to hurt, too. She was standing there having all she could do to keep from striking out at him. She really wanted to do him physical harm as bad as she thought he'd done to Sam.

Realization horrified him and however he looked, it was enough to set her off and she came at him off that step like a wild woman. Jude!

She nearly scared the living tar out of him. She was almost as tall as he was, and when she hit him the force of it all mixed up with astonishment and a kind of croaking horror drove him staggering backward. He saw out of the corner of his eye, the little cat arch its back and spit—he couldn't hear it—and vanish around the house like a flame moving. You noticed the damndest things when something happens—like a kind of protection to keep you from thinking of the thing that's going on and is so awful you can't believe it.

He thought first: Well, let her! Get it out of her system! It'll make her feel better. But the way she came at him, he began to be afraid if he did let her, she *would* do damage. She was strong. And big. And he didn't dare let her go. So he did the only thing he could do, he put his arms around her at her elbows and hauled her hard against him.

He had her all right and she couldn't move. But she was fighting harder against that than she had fought to harm him. She didn't like touching him the way she was having to do it. You could tell things like that with a woman and Jude was all woman.

Trying to soothe her, quiet her down a little, Barney found himself saying:

"Jude. Jude, stop. Jude, for the love of god, listen to me."

He was so scared that all he could say after that was just her name: "Jude. Jude." Over and over.

He might have been calling to somebody miles away and making as much impression. He was frightened—who wouldn't have been? But it was more being frightened by what was happening to her now than it was of what she might do to him if he let her go. She had always been so calm and easy to talk to and knowing what she wanted. And here she was going to pieces in his hands like sand running out through a hole in a sock.

Suddenly either she heard him or she realized she wasn't going to be able to do anything to him that way, and she stopped. When she did all the stiffening seemed to go out of her, too, and Barney knew if he hadn't been there holding her up, she would have gone flat on her face. She didn't seem to have any bones left.

When he felt her begin to quieten, he stopped talking and just held her and she put her forehead down against his shoulder as if she couldn't manage to hold her head up another minute. He had to think of the right thing to say to her now. If he could it would be all right—or not all right—but they could begin again. He'd won.

He said as quietly as he could:

"Let me come back, Jude. Let me tend to things for you, anyway. You can't do it all."

"How could I ever trust you to do anything again?" She didn't lift her head and Barney could feel her lips move with the words against his shoulder. "I trusted you too long. How could I ever again?"

"Forget all that."

"*Forget!*" At that she did manage to lift her head. At close range her eyes were all pupil and black.

"No," he said, trying hard for the right thing. "I mean, forget about the trust, Jude. You can't trust people anyway. Forget about we ever had anything, the three of us." Thinking back, it seemed to him there wasn't much to forget, because what had they had, really? Damn little! "You might as well," he said. "I can see we'd never get it back. Let it just be a job for me to do—until he gets home."

"Oh, Barney, why?"

"Look," he said. "Let me tell you how it was." He had to tell her what he'd felt when he stood watching Sam sprawl down over those steps. "When it happened, I felt like I'd pushed God Himself, Jude. But it was what he said!" When he thought of what Sam *had* said, Barney could feel himself begin to get hot all over again, and he knew if it happened again and Sam said it to him, he would do the same thing; but he couldn't let Jude see that part of it.

"What he said to me. If anyone had said it, I'd have done the same thing. I wasn't even thinking about it being Sam."

"What on earth did he say?"

"About *her*." Barney's lips stiffened against the words. "He said something about her I don't want to say to you. But I didn't even see his face when I did it. It wasn't Sam. It was just everyone."

"Barney," Jude said. "Stay away from her. Promise me only that much and we'll try to get it back. I'll try. Only—my god, *look* what she's doing to you! You won't even have a decent life left to live. She's ruining you. Promise me."

She put her hands flat against his chest and pushed herself away. Barney didn't have the strength left in his arms to hold onto her. Because he was going to have to tell her something else now and she wasn't going to like it. She was watching his face and she must have known there couldn't be any promises and she should never have asked for them, never gone that far, because it was too late now for anything: too late to take back the words and pretend they hadn't been said; too late for him to promise. If they could have been unsaid somehow, he thought she might have tried it. Or if she could have kept him from saying what he would to answer her, she would have done that too. But neither one of them could do a damn thing about it now and he said it.

"I can't very well do that, Jude. We were married last night in Bristol."

Barney got a stunning welcome from Paul when he finally found him that morning. Paul was grading eggs in the little room off the grain shed. Barney heard the grader going a mile a minute in there and he stuck his head in through the door and said: "Hey, Paul."

He was going to try and be casual, as if he'd left just as usual the night before and was now back in the morning. Paul looked up at the sound of the voice and Barney thought he had seldom seen such a succession of expressions go over anyone's face. First, the astonishment—that I'd-just-as-soon-expect-to-see-Joe-McCarthy look. From there it went down through a subsiding series that ended up with: What-the-hell-do-you-want? And Paul hadn't had to open his mouth.

"Where d'you want me to start?" Barney asked when he saw Paul wasn't going to speak, or couldn't. With Paul he was never sure which it was, because he had one of those red-headed tempers and sometimes it got him to the place where he couldn't talk. Other times, it sulled him into not wanting to.

"Where's Jude?" Paul said.

"I left her up at the house. Why?"

"Does she know you're down here?"

"Well, for god sake," Barney said. "I wouldn't be here if she didn't."

Paul got up without turning off the grader and went out as if there had been nobody standing in the doorway. Barney looked to see where he was going and, sure enough, he was legging it for the house as fast as he could make his feet work. He watched Paul out of sight and then went in and sat down in front of the grader and started in where Paul had left off. If he hadn't, there would have been the makings for one of the finest omelets you ever saw spread around over that floor.

It was about ten minutes before Paul came back, a lot slower than he'd gone. Barney looked up to find him standing in the door.

"Satisfied?"

"By god," Paul said. "I wish you'd tell me how you do it."

"Do what?" Barney was the picture of injured innocence.

"Get away with it."

It wasn't any of his business; but he was making it his.

"You're the only guy I ever saw," Paul said in a puzzled slow voice, "who could kick somebody's teeth out and then have them thank you for it and say they were going to have them out anyhow and now you'd saved them the trouble."

It just showed Barney how right he had been. He hadn't expected one of them to see his side of it, and what Paul had said would be what everyone else would say. Not that Barney gave a good god damn what anyone said about him, or thought—never had and never would. Everyone had the right to live his own life the way he wanted to and if anybody else got hurt when he mixed into it, then he shouldn't have been in the wrong place at the wrong time.

"All right, son," he said. "You keep your nose out of what doesn't concern you and we'll get along all right."

"I'll agree to that," Paul said. "The less I have to do with you, the better I'll like it. Oh, I'll get along with you if I have to. Because of Jude."

"That's big of you!"

"But—" Paul leaned forward a little and gave his head a nod about the way Sam had once. "Let's have this right out clear, Barney, and if you want to make something out of it, now's your chance. For my money, you're the lowest son of a bitch in sixteen counties."

"That's pretty low, isn't it?" Barney said. "And from you, I like it. Okay?" He was thinking: Funny. He can't make me mad any longer.

He'd found it paid to know exactly where you stood, then nobody could sneak up on you when you weren't looking. Knowing the direction from which they would come, you knew where to watch. For a second he felt lonesome; but he always *had* been alone and known it. The only difference was, now they'd stopped pretending he wasn't and were all telling him right out what he'd known himself from the beginning. What the hell, he thought. Let 'em come! I got here first.

It was all right. Now he knew where he stood and there was no room in the same place for doubt, and that's the safest spot to be in.

"Go ahead and finish up here," Paul said, as if he'd been talking to a total stranger. "The automatic waterer in the big house is on the blink and when you get through, you can fix that."

"Okay, boss," Barney said.

Paul spun on his heel and Barney sat there grading eggs like crazy and wondering what it would feel like to be right. It might be kind of nice. Everybody else seemed to enjoy it. God's good man, who'd just gone out the door, was getting one hell of a kick out of it, whether he knew it or not, and Barney couldn't help but wonder what Jude had said to him.

Probably she hadn't said much more than what she had already said to Barney after he told her he was married. She'd stood for a minute staring as if she could see right through him to something on the other side that scared her. She had a funny look on her face and it wasn't surprise. More as if she had known all along what she

was talking against. Then she'd said, as if none of the rest of it had
happened—as if he hadn't been standing there holding onto her
for grim death to keep her from beating his brains out—as if it was
any ordinary morning:

"Paul's grading eggs, Barney. Go ask him what ought to be done
first. There must be plenty."

So he had, and here he was.

That night when he got ready to go home—it seemed queer to
think of going home and not have it be going into that house—
Barney thought he might as well stop by and pick up his things.

Some people, even in only twenty-two years of living along in the
world, manage to collect enough junk of one kind or another to
keep them in the same spot for the rest of their lives. Because things
you own do that. You don't really own them after a while. It's more
the other way and they own you and tie you down and anchor you
to the place you've put them in, just like a stout kedge sunk in a
mud flat.

He never wanted anything like that. He'd spent all his life trying
to keep from owning anything he couldn't put in his pocket and
walk away with. He'd always wanted to be able to get up and go
whenever he felt like it. Now there was only one thing he wanted
out of that house besides his clothes and that one thing was port-
able.

It was the only thing he'd ever had that belonged to his father.
The old man had been a great one for hunting. All his life, from the
time he was big enough to smash the windows out of the school-
house with an air gun, he'd had guns around, so maybe the way he'd
died had been right for him. By the time he died, he'd collected a
regular armory. Rifles—everything from an old single-shot .22 up to
a Mauser that would have torn the head off a bull elephant if he'd
ever got a shot at one.

Before Barney got old enough to use any more than a slingshot,
Sam had had a chance to take his pick of those guns, and his pick
was all of them. They were up on racks on the wall in his office,
neat and shining and oiled, and he dusted them once a week and
wouldn't let anyone else lay a finger on them.

Amongst the lot there were three shotguns. One was a big Parker 10-gauge. Pa had never used it much and Sam didn't, except to take it out and let it off now and then the way you'd exercise a dog. It was a beautiful gun but a little too heavy. The one they both liked best was a Smith .12. That was really an expensive gun. It had a lot of fancy work and fancy gadgets on it. It had a raised matted rib and a beaver-tail fore end and a cheek piece and a soft recoil pad. It had everything that had ever been invented to attach to a shotgun and the old man had had it made to order. God knew what it cost him. That one was Sam's pet, too. It amused Barney because Sam wasn't much of a guy for frills and it didn't look like his kind of a gun. It was more something one of the sports who'd never so much as set eyes on a partridge would buy at Abercrombie & Fitch to go out and shoot pheasants at one of those places in Connecticut where you pay your subscription and the gamekeeper goes about a hundred yards in front of you and lets two birds out of a cage and you have to stamp your foot to drive them into the air before you can knock them down, because of course it wouldn't be sporting to shoot them on the ground.

When Barney turned fifteen, Sam gave him the third shotgun, and that was what he wanted now. It was a beautiful little gun— an Ithaca 20-gauge—just what a gun should be, no more, no less. One barrel was modified, one full choke. It was balanced like a feather and nearly as light. It only weighed five and a half pounds and Barney thought that was probably one reason why he ever got it. It seemed more like a toy than a real gun to Sam.

It had had good care. Though, as far as he knew, Sam had only shot it a couple of times and then he claimed it nearly tore the shoulder off him. But for Barney, there wasn't a thing a rifle would do at fairly close range that little 20-gauge wouldn't. He'd met more deer in old orchards on dark nights that didn't walk away from that gun than you could shake a stick at.

There he was. He packed his whole life in one suitcase and had room left over. The gun, a few clothes, and the old Chevvie and he was ready to roll. His discharge papers were in the bureau drawer and he took them for sure, because if he ever wanted to make a claim for veteran's benefits, he'd need them. When he got all through you wouldn't ever have known he'd been inside the room at all, much less lived there for fifteen years, when he'd lived anywhere.

That was the way to be, all right.

When he came downstairs, Barney had to go through the kitchen to get out the back door. He saw Jude eying the gun and the suitcase; but she didn't make any talk about it.

"Where are you going to live, Barney?" she asked. "Not—you don't plan to—"

"No. No, we've moved into that little place of Diddy Wallace's, for the summer anyhow."

"It'll be better to get away from—" She still couldn't say it.

"That's what we figured."

He answered what she'd been trying to say, thinking it might help her out a little. If she could once get Sabra's name off her tongue, he thought it might make things a little easier.

Jude thought so too, because she was still trying and this time she made it.

"Tell—Sabra that I will be up to see her as soon as I get a minute."

"I'll do that," Barney said.

But he was thinking that Jude already had as many minutes as anyone else. She'd simply said one of the things people say and she had no more intention of doing any such thing than the man in the moon. He wouldn't tell Sabra anything and Jude knew he wouldn't. But she had made the gesture and she turned away with relief and Barney went out the door, suitcase in one hand, shotgun in the other.

He went out the door that had been the entrance to everything solid and comfortable, and a place to come back to all his life, and knew he wouldn't ever come through it again to find what had always been waiting for him. But it wasn't happening right now. All the solid and the comfort and whatever it is you find behind familiar doors had gone, little by little, down a lot of holes. And the last of it, whatever might have been left, had gone down the granite courthouse steps a few days ago and broken its back.

Well, hell, who wants it? Especially when it's second hand and never really yours and just what somebody else has so much of there was enough left over to make you think maybe it really *was* yours until something happened and then you knew it wasn't and never had been.

That afternoon he felt as if he had a cork leg. He couldn't remember having a thirst like that since he'd tried the cook's hell broth in the middle of the winter and the first taste knocked every idea of thirst right out of his head. He stopped in to Aunt Bessie's on his way home and got a pint. He set out to make it a fifth; but he wouldn't get paid for nearly a week and there might come a time between now and then when he'd need the extra two dollars. It seemed queer to be thinking like that when he never had, but in a way he liked it. So he got a pint instead.

Aunt Bessie wasn't in one of her talky moods, but she wasn't taciturn either and she gave him a going over while he was digging down for the cash.

"Hear you got married, Barney."

"Word gets around, doesn't it?"

"Didn't think you'd ever be damn fool enough to get stuck," she said. "I always figured you were as smart as I was."

Barney laughed.

"Well, you must have been wrong," he told her.

"Yup." She cut her black eyes at him and grinned. "You know something? If I'd been forty years younger, she never would have got you."

"That's my girl," Barney said and they had to have a short one on the strength of it before he headed for home.

It *was* home, too. When he saw the light in the window and knew Sabra would be there waiting for him and all his, he knew it was home.

Before he pulled up over the sidewalk into the yard where he parked the car, he passed somebody walking in the dusk. At first he didn't think anything of it; but after he got out of the car, he looked casually down the street and then not casually. Because it was Arthur. He hadn't turned his head and he was still walking away

with that twisting swing of his shoulders that was unmistakable
and that counteracted the drag of his limp. Arthur apparently
hadn't even seen his son-in-law.

So Barney went shooting in through the door wondering what
the old devil had been up to.

"Arthur been in here?" he asked Sabra.

When he'd come bursting into the room he'd scared Chris, and
before Sabra could answer she had to go quiet him down. He raised
a howl that stood Barney's hair on end.

Chris had all different kinds of howls to mean different things.
He might want something and it would start with a funny whimper
in his throat. If Sabra didn't pay attention to that, and Chris didn't
get whatever he was starting to want, the whimper would grow to
an awful animal yell and he didn't seem to have to stop for breath.
When he yelled like that there wasn't a thing—not a sound you
could make—that would get through the wall of sound he was
making himself. So it seldom did any good to threaten him. Once in
a while Ann could frighten him into silence; but Sabra could never
be that firm about it. It was like a big noisy transparent bubble of
wanting and he could see you through it and you could see him;
but there simply wasn't any way for Sabra to reach him except the
way Barney had seen her use, take Chris's hand and put it against
her throat and let him feel instead of hear. Everything in him that
came near human was concentrated on wanting.

He had other noises to mean other things. There was fright and
frustration and anger and they were all clear and different. Barney
had to feel sorry for the poor little bugger when he made some of
them. They were like tongueless cries for help, and when Chris
made them he needed something badly.

The wanting was different, though, and it made Barney so mad
he wouldn't be able to watch Sabra still Chris down. That was the
biggest noise of all and there was only one sure and permanent solution and that was give him whatever he wanted.

Tonight Barney had been so interested in finding out what Arthur
had been up to, he'd forgotten about scaring Chris. When Chris
let out that unbelievable screech of terror, he scared Barney almost
as much.

Barney leaned the gun against the door frame, put the suitcase on the floor, and covered his ears.

"For god sake, Sabra," he said, knowing she couldn't hear him. "Shut him up."

She was trying to and Barney was just as glad she hadn't heard him. Finally she got Chris down to a mutter.

"You've got to remember how easy it is to scare him," she said reproachfully. "You came in like a hurricane. You scared me. It'd be bound to scare him."

Ann was sitting in a chair beside the stove with her nose in a book and she was so deep in it she hadn't even looked up to see what was going on. She was used to the noises though, and Barney wasn't yet.

"Was Arthur in here?" he said again as soon as he could make his voice heard. "What'd he want?"

"He wasn't in." Over Chris's head, Sabra looked at him and her eyes were puzzled. "You know what he did? He was waiting for Ann when she got out of school and he took her down to the house and gave her supper and then brought her home. He didn't come in. He just brought her to the door and didn't even wait to speak to me."

Ann still wasn't hearing a thing that went on, so Barney said:

"What in hell you suppose *that's* all about?"

Sabra shrugged.

"Funny he didn't come in, though."

"Not really," she said.

"I suppose not," Barney said doubtfully, but it still seemed funny to him. Arthur liked those two kids, in his way—Chris, too. And he must have known Barney wasn't there when the car was gone. Barney would have been a lot easier in his mind about it if Arthur had been inside. It gave him a queer feeling to think of the old man coming as far as the door with Ann and then not even stopping to speak to his own daughter.

"I'll tell you who *has* been in, though," Sabra said quickly. "And I'd just as lief he hadn't."

"Who's that?"

"Diddy."

"Oh, the neighbors been calling, hah?" Barney grinned. "Well, I can't really blame him. If you lived next door to me, I'd come calling. Often, too."

"I'd be glad to see *you*." Her eyes were bright when she looked at him and all of a sudden they were thinking about the same thing and it didn't have anything to do with Diddy Wallace. But there wasn't much point in even thinking with the kids around and supper to get, so she went back to him.

"Filthy old thing!" she said explosively. "Know what he did? He was chewing tobacco and he kept spitting in the stove."

"Knowing Diddy, you were lucky it wasn't on the floor."

Barney was thinking about Diddy—he was thinking he wouldn't want the pint tonight, so he went over and stood it in the cupboard against the time when he would want it. When he moved, Sabra looked past him and caught sight of what was leaning against the casing of the door where Barney had put it when he came in. Her face got that frozen look most women's do at the sight of a gun.

"What's that?"

He picked it up and stood turning it over in his hands.

"Put it down," Sabra said. "I don't like it."

"It's just a shotgun."

"Is it—is it loaded?"

"Of course not."

She got up from the bed where Chris was lying quietly now and came over to look at it, her face all wrinkled up as if she was looking at a snake.

"How does it work?"

Barney showed her. Got a shell out of his suitcase and showed her how to break the gun and load it and unload it again. He showed her the safety and she even held the gun up to her shoulder and pulled the triggers. She had her eyes closed when the hammers clicked, as if she expected an explosion out of thin air. She handed it back to him with a shiver of distaste.

"No," she said firmly. "I don't like it. Put it somewhere where I can't see it and the kids can't get hold of it."

"It can't do you any harm when it's not loaded."

"Well, you might forget sometime."

"That's the kind of forgetting I don't intend to do," Barney said. "They'll never put 'I didn't know the gun was loaded' on *my* tombstone!"

She didn't say anything more, just went over to the sink and started getting things ready to eat. Barney put the gun in the corner behind the bed for now. Then he went and stood behind her while she pretended she didn't know he was there. Finally he said:

"Hi."

He could see her cheek round out and knew she was smiling.

"What do *you* want?"

"You," he said.

"About time!" She still wouldn't look around at him. "Here we've been married twenty-four hours. About time!"

"Poor kid." Barney put his arms around her and pulled her back against him for a second. "It was a hell of a wedding day, wasn't it!" He kissed the nape of her neck where the hair starts to grow and then worked around until he could say low in her ear: "Get the kids fed and off to bed early. Yesterday wasn't it. Today is."

"If you don't stop, Barney, right now is it—kids or no kids. Now stop."

Barney let her go and went over and sat down beside Chris. They had managed to attract Ann's attention this time. This performance must have been something new for her. She was so used to Chris's yelling she didn't hear that; but she was watching Barney now and her eyes were big around as silver dollars. He grinned at her, wanting to say something to her and not knowing what.

Kids were funny in what they noticed and what they didn't. Already he could see he had a job on his hands with Ann. Chris was a total loss and he wasn't going to bother—let Sabra tend to him. But he wanted to get to know Ann and it wasn't going to be the easiest thing in the world to do. If she'd been his own, they would have been familiar with each other now, instead of strangers forced together by circumstances. Already he knew her well enough to know there was a real brain sharp enough to scare you behind the ugly little face, and Ann didn't miss a thing she didn't want to miss.

Trouble was, she'd been knocked around so much, too, that she was just like him, didn't trust anyone. It wouldn't hurt her a bit to see that grownups could like each other a lot. So he smiled at her, trying to begin to show her that things were going to be different. Ann gave him a steady thoughtful look and went back to her book. Barney felt rebuffed until he caught her stealing another look at him when she felt it would be safe and he wouldn't see her do it. He didn't let her know he'd caught her; but that was a beginning.

It *had* been one sweet wedding day, come to think of it! He could still see the front room in old Benny Clark's house in Bristol. Benny was Justice of the Peace and he'd been doddering along for the last twenty years, hanging on by the skin of his teeth to a job he'd had so long it had grown to him like a shell. He was so old you couldn't help wondering if what he did was still legal.

And that front room! When they went in, there was an old lady running around pulling sheets off the furniture and the last thing she pulled a sheet off turned out to be an old piano and it was hard to see why the sheet was necessary. The varnish was so sun cracked it looked like a turtle shell and every third white key had the ivory broken off right where it narrowed to take the black one. The ones that were left had turned light yellow.

There was a bay window on the side toward the road and in it one of the damndest plants Barney had ever seen. He thought at first it couldn't be real, had to be some kind of a thing somebody had made out of green wax. It was as tall as he was and had great thick leaves, shiny green. It gave him the feeling it might reach out and take a nip at him when he stopped in front of it and felt a leaf to make sure it was real.

Benny stood beside the piano, behind a little table where he had his book laid open. The old lady, who turned out to be his sister, stood right beside him beaming at them and her teeth looked exactly like the piano keys. She asked Sabra if she'd like some music and Sabra looked at Barney and shook her head.

The car was parked outside where Sabra could see it through the bay window and the kids were sitting in the back seat waiting.

That's where they were married, with Benny chewing over the words so you could hardly understand what he was saying and the old lady looking as if somebody had given her the best kind of a Christmas present. They didn't get too many weddings now, Benny said afterwards—most people either got married at home or in a church.

Neither Barney nor Sabra had a word to say on the way back to Port Kezar and the kids were quiet too. They knew something was going on, but they weren't quite sure what. Ann, anyhow. Barney was never sure what Chris knew and what he didn't.

The trouble was, Barney couldn't think of anything *to* say. He sure to god didn't feel the way the bridegroom's supposed to. He couldn't think of anything but what might be going to happen and how he'd messed everything up and now he was hauling Sabra and those two kids into it too; had already hauled them in. That was before he got it straight in his mind that he hadn't really done anything at all.

So it turned out to be a sad kind of wedding night.

It must have been all of two hours later that she asked him how things had gone today. She'd been lying there breathing steadily for an hour or so and Barney thought she had been asleep for a long time. He didn't know why he couldn't sleep. He felt good, relaxed, sleepy—but he just couldn't sleep. He wasn't thinking about anything, dozing, when Sabra turned her head suddenly and spoke to him:

"Did anything happen this morning, Barney?"

The minute she asked, he knew what was keeping him awake and why he didn't want to think about it and that he'd been trying hard to keep it out of his mind. Now Sabra had brought it back and he was remembering the way Jude had come at him as clearly as if it were happening all over again. Then he could hear Paul Hanna's voice say: Lowest son of a bitch in sixteen counties.

"Nothing much," he said as quietly as he could. Because how could he tell her what had?

"I was afraid you wouldn't—"

"Wouldn't what?"

"Well, after what happened the other day, about your brother, I was afraid she wouldn't let you keep that job."

"There are others," Barney said.

Sabra was saying what he'd been thinking—that there weren't

any others in this town for him—but it touched him up a little that she should see it as clearly as he did.

"Yes, of course," she said and didn't mean it. "It's only that this is a bad time of year."

"Well, you can calm down," he told her. "I've still got that one. Hell, I can talk my way around Jude any day in the week."

He hadn't meant to say that but it came out and once he heard it himself, he thought: I guess it's true. It didn't sound very pretty, saying it that way; but truth doesn't sometimes. It made him sound as if he thought he was irresistible—it even made the way he and Jude were together sound like something it wasn't and never had been. It wasn't exactly what he meant, but it was out and a lot simpler to let it stand than try to explain it.

"Did you tell her about us?" Sabra asked, after a silence so long Barney thought she wasn't going to speak again. That put them back on safer ground.

"Yes, I told her." He was going to let it lie at that, but that seemed kind of short. If he knew anything about women, or maybe just people, Sabra was lying there having all she could do to keep from asking what Jude had said when he'd told her. For fear she would and he'd blurt out the whole thing, Barney added: "She's coming to see you as soon as she gets time, she says. She's pretty busy. She goes to the hospital every day."

And there it was right beside him again. Jude went to the hospital every day, to see Sam. Because Barney had ruined him.

"I don't think she really will," Sabra said in a low quiet voice. "Do you, Barney?"

Barney stared breathing steady and slow to show he was asleep and couldn't answer her. Because she *wanted* Jude to come and he couldn't figure that one out. He didn't want to answer her with the truth. He knew Jude wasn't coming. Sabra knew it too; but so long as Barney didn't come right out and say he thought she wouldn't, Sabra could go on thinking that Jude might.

Jude fooled him, though. She came.

Barney thought he would never understand until the day he died how a woman could say one thing and make you think she meant another—and then go on to show you what she meant was exactly what she'd said in the first place.

It was about three weeks after they moved into Diddy's shack. Barney had worked out a routine. When he came home at night, he'd have a drink first. Then he'd lie down on the bed—if the bed didn't happen to be occupied and that was one thing that bothered him because it often was—and let the drink circulate and take hold and smooth him out. Then he'd have another short one before supper.

In three weeks he knew what he was coming home to, and it wasn't quite the way he'd thought it would be. Not Sabra. He always came home to her with the same feeling if he'd seen her only five minutes ago. He had everything there was in the world to have for her and more now, it seemed, than before.

But coming home to that kid, to Chris, was more than he'd bargained for. He never knew when he left the car and came across the yard what he'd find. He got so he'd stop to listen outside the door to find out if Chris was quiet or yelling.

It was hard enough, living four people in one room the way they had to, without having one of the people like Chris.

Barney would get out of the car feeling as if he had a strip of rawhide wound around his head and getting tighter. He'd go over to the door with it tightening all the way. By the time he got the door open and got inside the room, it was about as tight as he could stand and he needed that first drink as much as a man ever needed one.

Then he found out Chris could tell. He knew when Barney was feeling good and when he wasn't. If he wasn't and Chris happened to be lying on the bed when Barney got there, he'd shut his eyes and pretend to be asleep; but he'd be as still as a poker and Barney would know he wasn't sleeping because his eyelids would quiver.

This night, when Barney came in, Sabra wasn't there. No Ann either, just her eternal book, face down on the table, open to the right place so she could pick it up when she came in and not have to hunt. He'd seen her do it so often now, he didn't see her any more: pick up the book and before she even got settled in her chair, her eyes would be devouring the print greedily, the way a thirsty man drinks water.

There was a good fire going in the stove, so Sabra hadn't been gone long. Barney went over to look and right on top was a piece of birch hardly beginning to burn yet. He took the bottle out of the cupboard and poured a drink into the water glass before he turned around. He *was* feeling ugly, not knowing where she was or why. She never went out and left Chris alone. But he was alone now, lying on the bed under the thin top quilt.

Barney leaned against the counter sipping his drink and watching Chris, not realizing there was any particular expression on his face. Maybe there wasn't, not one to scare anyone; but there must have been something. Chris knew what Barney was thinking before he knew it himself and it was from Chris and his actions Barney got it, knew that he was standing there wishing Chris gone—he didn't care how or where—he just wanted Chris somewhere else.

Chris opened his eyes and the pupils were big. Barney didn't move a muscle, stood watching to see what he was going to do because there began to be an odd look of purpose about him. Usually he closed his eyes again and lay waiting for Barney to stop looking; but tonight they were alone together.

Chris crawled out from under the quilt and eased himself down off the bed. He couldn't do it the way any other kid would have. He had to hang on all the way, and his hands clutching at the bed clothes nearly pulled them off after him. By the time he managed to get to where the floor felt solid and safe enough for him to let go, he had them all scrabbled up into a heap on the edge of the bed. Once down he turned over slowly onto his hands and knees and started across the room. Barney didn't know what Chris thought he was going to do or where he thought he was going at first. There was seldom anything that looked like purpose in the way he behaved; but purpose was there now. Chris's eyes were big and scared and staring right at what he wanted and he wasn't making noise about wanting it.

All this time Barney hadn't made a move toward him, hadn't said a word. Maybe Chris had some kind of a sense of protection like an animal, because most animals that live around with people know when their people are mad or out of sorts and they know there's a clear danger for them in the way the people feel. They get out of the way. That was what Chris was doing.

Behind the stove, between it and the woodbox against the wall, there was barely space enough for him to crawl into and turn around and be surrounded with something solid and inanimate.

That was where he went as fast as he could haul himself, and without a sound out of him but the little scraping noise his hands and feet made. He went into that hole as far as he could go, so far and so fast Barney heard his head hit the wall. He turned around and shoved his stern back into the corner and stayed there on his hands and knees looking out. He must have known it wasn't the time to yell—that there was nobody there to comfort him. He didn't let out so much as a whimper. And he didn't look any the less like an animal.

Barney couldn't see anything but his face with those two big eyes glaring out. He had to close his own eyes for a minute. While he had them closed, he heard steps coming up the path from the sidewalk and knew they were Sabra's and that she was hurrying. He took another look at Chris and they'd changed places. Chris had heard her too, and now *his* eyes were closed and Barney felt better, not having that to look at.

She came in through the door in a tearing hurry.

"Hi, Barney. I thought I'd get home before you."

Instead of looking at him, she was looking at the empty rumpled bed.

"Where's Chris?"

"He's around," Barney said. "Where've you been?"

The most important thing was for him to know where she'd been and what she'd been doing. The most important thing for her was that Chris wasn't where she'd left him.

"Just to the store."

"How come you didn't take him with you?"

"Well, I was only planning to be gone a second. Where is he?"

"What else did you do besides go to the store? Where he'd be in the way?"

Barney thought she must have been telling him the truth—her quick glance was uncomprehending and only a glance. Her eyes were still doing that hunting around the room and finally she found what she'd been hunting for.

"What?" she said startled, seeing where Chris was.

She put the paper bag she was carrying on the table and went over to kneel down in front of Chris's cave. Her face was puzzled, but nothing more than that yet.

"What's he doing in there, Barney?"

Barney shrugged.

"How should I know what he thinks he's doing? I sure didn't put him there."

"But—" She looked at Chris again and he opened his eyes and stared back at her. "How did he get off the bed? Did you lift him down?"

"Look," Barney said. He finished his drink and set the glass down in the sink. "I haven't laid a finger on him. He just got off the bed and crawled in there. That's all. I don't know why. I doubt if he does."

"He got off the bed by him*self?*" She had to ask, as if she couldn't believe her ears. "I didn't know he could."

"Well, apparently he can. He did."

Chris began to whimper. Sabra was watching Barney over her shoulder; but at the first sound from Chris she forgot Barney was standing there. She started to croon and held out her arms to the little boy.

"Come on, honey," she said. "Come on out. Mama's here. Come on back to bed."

It took her a few minutes, with him whimpering like a whipped puppy all the time. He didn't start to scream, so he could still hear her, and finally she coaxed him out of his corner and took him back to bed. She smoothed out the covers and got him settled against the pillow and tucked in. When she was apparently satisfied that he was all right, Barney said:

"How about some supper, Sabra? I'm starved."

"Did you say or do anything to scare him?" She was still puzzling over how and why Chris had got off that damned bed.

"I just came in," Barney said wearily. "I just came in through the

door and you weren't here so I had a drink while I was waiting for
you to get back from wherever it was that was so damned important
you had to go without him. See? While I was having the drink, he
got down off the bed and crawled in behind the stove. That's all.
I didn't say or do anything to him!"

The last words were no louder; but he spaced them out and gave
each one the same solid emphasis.

Sabra could see he was tired of it and she came over and started
setting the table; but she couldn't seem to leave it alone. The baffled
wrinkle between her brows didn't go away. Finally she said:

"Well, *he* knows why ne did it. Something scared him. *He* had a
reason for it."

"I don't see how you know."

"I wish he could talk," she said in a low voice.

"Yeah," Barney said. "It's too bad he can't."

She got his supper ready and put it on the table in silence, still
thinking. They sat down across from each other and started to eat.
Every time he looked up from his plate, either she would be watching him, or if he looked past her, Chris would be watching him. He
was never going to get away from the eyes watching for the rest
of his life. Even now, everywhere he could look, there were the eyes,
still watching.

That was the moment Jude had to pick to come calling.

Ann came in the door and Sabra looked up and asked, "Have you
had your supper?" before she saw that Ann wasn't alone and was
nearly speechless with trying to say who was with her. Sabra made
a queer little noise in her throat that caught Barney's attention and
he looked at Ann, and right across the top of her head he met Jude's
eyes.

Come to think of it, it wasn't such a bad time for her to pick. She
could be almost sure they'd be eating, and if things turned out too
uncomfortable she could always use that for an excuse not to stay
long.

"I was just on my way home from the hospital," she said quickly
to Sabra. "I thought I'd stop in and say hello to you." And wish
you joy of your bargain, she added mentally, both of you, you poor
young idiots.

She'd brought reinforcements, too. Cliff sidled in the door after her and stood leaning against the wall grinning at Barney, who gaped back at him, amazed that Jude would bring him with her. "Oh, I'm so glad you did. Please sit down. No, don't think anything of it—we were nearly through supper anyhow. Weren't we, Barney?"

"Oh, yes, indeed," Barney said and Jude glanced at him thoughtfully, and then back to Sabra again.

They started talking as if they'd known each other to gossip with for years. Women! He'd never figure them out. Looking at these two, knowing what had been happening around them in the last few weeks, remembering the way they had stood in the kitchen looking at each other across the little cat the first and last time they'd met, he couldn't believe his ears.

All the while they were chattering at each other like two members of the same sewing circle, Jude's eyes were going around that room. Not obtrusively and almost as if she didn't want to look but couldn't help herself. Barney had never thought much about it before. He'd never looked at it as anything but a stopgap. They wouldn't be there long, only until summer was past and done and they could get out. But Jude didn't know that and the look on her face made him see the place the way she did. Sabra had done her best. There were curtains up to the windows and new paint on the sideboard and stuff like that. But curtains and paint couldn't make more than one room out of it, and one room with four people living in it.

He got up and went over to the cupboard and came back with the bottle which he set in the middle of the table.

"Can I offer you a drink?" he said.

Jude smiled and shook her head. Sabra was watching him, Cliff was watching him—what time he wasn't watching Sabra and he seemed to be fascinated with her. Barney poured himself a drink and sat down again and got his own smile ready. Then, when he was all set, Jude got up.

"Well," she said. "I can't really tarry tonight. Thought I'd drop in for a minute. I've got to get home and get supper for this young one."

"I'll just bet," Barney said. "I'm sorry you have to hurry."

"I am, too," Sabra said and *she* meant it.

Barney wanted to say to Jude: This isn't what *you'd* call living, is it? But, hell, what was the use? He sat and finished his drink while Sabra went to the door with them. Cliff was still looking over his shoulder when he went out. Jude wasn't.

She hadn't missed a clip. Not one thing in that room got by her —Chris least of all. She'd looked at him once, lying there on the bed watching with his empty bright-blue eyes, and after that her glance had done a kind of hop every time she came back to him.

Sabra closed the door behind them and came back to where he was sitting and said:

"Barney Cousins!"

"What's the matter?" But he knew because everything that was bothering her was wrapped up in his name when she said it.

"I don't know what gets into you sometimes."

"I'm just sitting here," he said. "Just sitting here thinking how nice it was of her highness to come and call. Too bad we weren't serving tea. God damn big of her, wasn't it!"

"Barney, listen. We can't live our lives all alone. We need other people like everyone else does. She was only being decent and it must have been hard for her. So I was, too."

"Decent, hell!" His face started to feel hot. He was all crossed up with being mad at Jude and sorry for Sabra until he wasn't sure which way it went and maybe he was sorry for Jude and mad at Sabra, for not being able to see what the two of them, between them, could do to a man in his own home. "Did you see the look on her face? Did you see her look at this room? You blind? All she came for was to nose in, to see if it was as bad as she thought it would be."

"It's not all that bad." Sabra's eyes got bright and in a minute, if he didn't stop, she was going to cry—or laugh. "It's clean."

"Yeah," he said. "It sure as hell is clean."

He reached for the bottle and she turned her back on him. Barney sat there all the while she fed Chris.

"Isn't Ann going to have any supper?" he asked once. Sabra still wasn't ready to speak to him but Ann glanced up at the sound of her own name, looking at Sabra, waiting a minute to see if her mother would answer him. When Sabra didn't, Ann said quickly:

"Gramp gave me my supper tonight."

"Oh, yes, I forgot," Barney said. "You're eating out. Was it good?"

"Yes," Ann said doubtfully, sensing the sarcasm but not knowing what to do about it.

Barney opened his mouth, intercepted a glance from Sabra, and shut it again, ashamed himself for taking out what he was feeling on a kid.

When Sabra finished with Chris, she stirred Ann out of her book and hustled them both off up the ladder to bed. Chris seemed weaker than usual tonight and between the two of them, Sabra and Ann, they could just manage to get him up the ladder to the loft. Once up there he could fend for himself. Barney heard him scraping across the loose boards to his bed and then silence.

"Will he ever learn to walk?" he said evenly to Sabra.

She said: "I don't know."

And that was the last time she spoke that night. She cleaned off the table, washed the dishes, turned out the lights, and got into bed, leaving Barney sitting there in the dark with his own thoughts for company. It was lonesome.

Jude didn't come again; but Cliff did.

The first time Sabra mentioned it to Barney. When he came in, she said:

"Cliff was here looking for you a few minutes ago."

"Oh, was he?"

"He was on his way home from school and he thought you might be here."

"Did he say what he wanted?"

There ought to be a good reason because Cliff had a pretty definite idea where Barney would be at any minute of the day if he really wanted to see him.

"No, he didn't say. He only stopped a second. Then he said he could probably catch you out at the house."

"He must have just missed me both places," Barney said. He didn't give it another thought then. He wouldn't have the next time either, if it hadn't been for Sabra not telling him. But the second time he had something else beginning to bother him too, and it made everything seem worse than it was.

Sabra wasn't much of a cook. At least, it seemed to Barney, after the meals Jude used to serve up, that she wasn't. It was always a struggle for her to get a meal on time. She made a lot more work of it than necessary, and then when he got whatever it was she'd been wrestling with it was hard to say sometimes what she had intended it to be. After a month and a half of it, he'd begun to see why the kids looked peaked. They had plenty to eat—there was enough of it; but Sabra didn't have any more idea how to make it look or taste like food than he did.

The kids were both picky eaters. Sabra used to sit in front of Chris by the hour with a full plate coaxing him to open his mouth and finally he'd take a swing at the plate like a one-year-old and splatter everything on it all over her. The first time Barney ever saw him do it, he wanted to pound Chris properly; but he couldn't with Sabra watching to see how he was going to react to that. After a spell of coping with her cooking himself, he came to see how Chris felt; because he wanted to do the same thing himself.

Ann made out pretty well because of Arthur. He saw to it that she got one decent meal a day all the while she was still going to school. When school let out for the summer, Arthur used to come and get her whenever he could and take her home with him. When he wasn't working. Barney was surprised that Sabra would let him do it, and if Arthur had ever come when he was home, he would have put his foot down. But Arthur took care to see to it that Barney was well out of the way before he showed up.

Sabra would tell at first how Arthur would never come in, but stand outside the door and call. He never called Sabra. Barney could picture the way Arthur looked standing there.

He would call: "Annie. Annie. Annie." Over and over in a steady monotonous creak until Ann could get ready and go out to him. Sabra would stand in the door watching them walk away together and never once would Arthur speak to her. Just to the little girl.

"He makes me feel exactly like a piece of window glass," Sabra said and Barney knew what she meant. Arthur had looked at him—or not looked—often enough. It made you want to grab at your arms and legs to be sure they were solid flesh, and it was a relief to find them still there, still attached to you.

Arthur took pains to see to it he and Barney never met each other when he came for Ann; but it seemed to Barney he was meeting Arthur on the street a hell of a lot more often. Either that or he hadn't noticed before how often they met.

That was what was beginning to bother him. Everywhere he turned that summer, there was Arthur with his tight shiny little face and his bright shiny hating eyes and when he looked at Barney now, he saw him and made it clear he did. After a little, Barney got to placing bets with himself: When I go to work this morning, I'll bet ten dollars I meet him before I get to Fairlee's Diner. Or: I'll bet ten dollars he'll be somewhere near that big oak at the top of the factory hill.

It got to the point where he could have set his watch by Arthur's coming and going. If Barney was a little late getting started, Arthur would be a little farther uptown, that was all. He wasn't a fast walker.

At first it was funny—that Arthur should be so upset about the way things were to carry it that far. Because he had to be doing it on purpose. There wouldn't be any other reason for his coming uptown every morning that early unless it was to let Barney know he was still around and still watching.

The morning Barney first began to be bothered by it, he'd had one too many the night before and his stomach had that uneasy jiggling to it when he got into the car. Nothing definite wrong— only hate everyone in the world and wish there were a few more people in the world so you could hate them too.

That morning Arthur had just come up the factory hill, and when Barney drew abreast the road Arthur was standing there waiting for the car to go by so he could cross. Barney saw him and before he knew it, he was thinking: By the lord harry, old man, I'd like to catch you out in the middle just once. I'd give you a close shave you'd remember!

He would have, too. Not to hit him, of course. But Arthur would have felt the wind of it, if Barney could have caught him in the right spot.

It was that night or the next—along in there somewhere—Barney had the dream, dreamed he was going down this long corridor and it had a stone floor. He didn't know where the corridor led or where it came from; but there was light way up ahead and light behind, although he walked in darkness. His feet didn't make any noise in the dream and he couldn't feel the stone floor under them; and behind him, between him and the distant light, he could hear Arthur's steps—the dot and carry one—coming as slow and steady as a heart beating or water dripping. He didn't know what Arthur was going to do when he caught up, and he did know Arthur was old and little and nothing to him; but the way he came along that stone-floored corridor gave Barney the willies and he had to start running.

He still didn't make a noise and he could still hear Arthur coming, and not coming any faster, either; but Barney wouldn't be getting away from him. It was as if the floor underfoot ran backwards like the treadmill in a squirrel cage where the damn squirrel spends all his time getting nowhere.

Then, slow or no slow, Arthur began to catch up—to get closer. The faster Barney ran the closer Arthur got, until the pounding of Barney's heart drowned out the sound of the following footsteps and he woke up gasping for breath.

He couldn't have been asleep very long because there was still enough fire in the stove to make those bright glancing lights across the ceiling. He was lying there watching them dance and sweating and all of a sudden he knew it wasn't all a dream. He could still hear Arthur's feet, thud and drag, on the sidewalk past the house. For a minute he thought he was still in the middle of sleep, but then it came to him: Barney, you're awake and you can still hear him!

He was out of bed like a shot and across the room to the window staring out into the warm summer night. There was a street light across the road and it threw the big shadows of leaves all over the place so he couldn't be sure what he was looking at or seeing. It made everything look uncertain and moving and it would have been easy to imagine anything.

He didn't see Arthur and he wasn't sure any longer that he had heard him. It had actually been more like a sound inside his own head. He snatched the door open and stood listening. Nothing.

If Arthur was anywhere out there in the shifting night, he had either gone out of hearing or stopped moving altogether. That was the trouble; Barney couldn't be really sure he'd heard him. If he had been sure, he would have shouted at him, yelled:

"Arthur, come back! I know you're out there! Arthur!"

But the dream was still so real, he didn't know.

Behind him he heard Sabra moving around and that was real enough.

"Barney," she said. "What're you doing?"

Barney looked down at his hands, realizing for the first time he was holding something, and he felt damned foolish when he saw what it was. He'd grabbed the shotgun when he crossed the room and he was standing there with it now like Davy Crockett looking for the Indians. Lucky Arthur hadn't been there. Half asleep like that, Barney knew he could have been just far enough away from sense to load the thing.

"What *is* it?" Sabra said.

"Nothing. I thought I heard somebody outside the door, but there's nobody there."

He stayed where he was by the door, hoping she'd settle down again so he could get the gun back where it belonged without her seeing it. But he could hear her sitting up and knew she was trying to see him, so he stepped in out of the open doorway and stood the gun against the casing silently and went back to bed. He'd have to think of something in the morning when she noticed, the way she was sure to, and asked him what it was doing out there. By morning he'd be able to have a good reason for her.

When he lay down beside her, Sabra settled back and took hold of his hand and hers was warm.

"What is it, Barney?" she said. "What's the matter?"

"Oh, hell, nothing's the matter! What d'you mean, what's the matter? If I hear something, I can look out to see, can't I?"

"Yes." She sounded hesitating and doubtful. "But I heard you get up. You got out of bed like a wild man. What—who did you think—"

"Nobody." He couldn't tell her he'd been dreaming about her father, that they'd been meeting every morning, that Barney was beginning to be afraid. He could see now that was exactly what it amounted to. The old son of a bitch had him scared. He couldn't see quite what Arthur could do to him, and not knowing what he *could* made what he *might* something to be scared of.

"There wouldn't be anyone prowling around *this* place," she said. "Anyone with any sense would know we didn't have anything worth taking."

"I didn't know but what it might be Diddy," Barney said. "Come to see if I happened to be away from home."

After a minute Sabra decided to think that was funny and he was joking and she laughed.

"If that ever happened," she said, "I think I *would* use your shotgun."

She fell asleep soon after that with her head against his shoulder. And the gun was the first thing she set eyes on in the morning. He watched her eying it all the time she was getting breakfast. Finally she couldn't hang off any longer.

"What's *that* doing there?" She wouldn't even put a name to it, she didn't like it that much.

"I set it there last night to remind me," Barney said. "There's been some hawks around the chicken runs and I'm going to take it with me this morning to see if I can't get rid of a few of them."

He hadn't planned what to tell her; but it came easily enough since he'd waited for the right minute. She thought that was all right. Only he forgot the gun, after all, and when he got home that night it was back in the corner behind the bed, where it usually was. He set out to ask Sabra if she'd picked it up with a pair of tongs; but then he saw the ashtray and it drove the thoughts of the gun right out of his mind.

It wasn't anything but an ordinary white saucer that sat on the table. Ordinarily when Barney got home it was cleaned out and empty because Sabra didn't smoke. Tonight there were four cigarette butts and a lot of ashes in it—butts with no lipstick on them. He thought maybe they were his and Sabra had forgotten to throw them away and he went over to look and he didn't smoke Chesterfields.

He turned one over with his finger to be sure there wasn't any mistake. Sabra caught him doing it and he was looking right at her and he didn't move his hand. So she glanced down to see what he was doing and it seemed to him she turned a little pink. Maybe it was the heat from the stove, though—it was a warm day.

"What's the matter?" She looked up at him again.

"Not my brand."

"No. They're Cliff's. He was in this afternoon for a few minutes."

"Chain smoker, is he?" Barney went over to the bed which, for a wonder, was unoccupied. Ann must have Chris out in his wagon, neither one of them was anywhere in sight.

When Barney lay down, he was thinking: So that's what took him so long! Jude had called Cliff along in the middle of the afternoon to go uptown and do an errand for her. Barney hadn't seen him around the place again for nearly an hour and it sure as hell didn't take an hour to get from the house uptown and back again.

Sabra didn't answer. She was standing looking at the ashtray with the beginning of a scowl between her eyebrows.

"Were you going to tell me he'd been here?" Barney asked.

"When I got a chance," she said quietly. "You've just come in, Barney. I haven't had a chance to tell you anything yet."

"How often does he stop in to see you?"

All the while he was trying to build this up into something, there was a loud voice inside his head saying: You damn fool! You damn fool! But it was as if the words were in a foreign language. He didn't feel like himself. He had to start something. It was too quiet.

"Barney Cousins!" Sabra came over to the bed but she didn't sit down beside him as she might have ordinarily. She stood looking at him as if she didn't recognize what she was seeing. "What are you trying to say?"

"Don't you care for it?"

"No!" She all but stamped her foot. "I do not!"

"Then you know what I'm saying," Barney said and found he could look her in the eye. The voice inside him wasn't saying anything now.

She was beautiful. She was always prettier when she was mad. It was easy to see how anyone would think she was worth looking at twice, maybe think it was worth his while to come and see her when Barney wasn't there and he knew damned well she'd be alone.

"Yes, Barney, I know what you're saying and I wish to god I didn't."

"Well, then," Barney said, "you probably know I don't think too much of having people come to see you while I'm out working."

"Not people," she said. "Barney, it was only Cliff. *Cliff!*"

"How do *I* know who else?" He went back to his other question. "How often does he come? How many times that I don't find out?"

He knew what he was doing and saying and he couldn't any more stop than he could fly. He remembered how it was when he hadn't had her and he couldn't figure out why he had to do things like this now when he did have her and knew it.

He knew this stuff he was dishing out to her about Cliff was so much bull. Oh, maybe Cliff liked her looks the way a kid does sometimes; but it would never amount to anything, either with him or with her. Still Barney had to try and make something out of it that wasn't there. It wasn't Sabra he was trying to hurt. He felt as if he'd stretched himself out on the floor like a rug and was jumping up and down on his belly.

It was all a part of that business about the old man, too. He knew that Arthur, every morning of his life, came up to the drugstore to get his paper. Out of that Barney had built up a fine frenzy. He'd made himself think Arthur did it on purpose to meet him on his way to work. He'd arranged everything in his mind to be something it wasn't.

He knew as well as he knew his name was Barney Cousins he

hadn't heard Arthur or anyone else outside the door the night he'd found himself staring up and down the street with the shotgun in his hand, all ready to roll. Hell, if Arthur looked at him, why shouldn't he? It wasn't any different than it had ever been. And whatever he thought was going through Arthur's mind, it was what he himself had put there. Arthur sure as hell hadn't said much.

He stared blankly at Sabra, wondering what was the matter, why he had to behave like this with neither need nor excuse. It was just as if, when things got too quiet, he had to stick a charge of blasting powder underneath them and light the fuse.

"Barney," Sabra said. "Listen to me. He's only sixteen. Sixteen years old. He's only a baby."

It was on the tip of Barney's tongue to say: That's plenty old enough. But he thought of the blasting powder and didn't say it. Instead he reached out and took her wrist and pulled her down to him, or tried. She didn't come.

"Oh, hell, I know it," he said. "Skip it. I'm talking through my hat."

"Yes," she said. "You certainly are."

She didn't lie down with him; but she got down on her knees and her face was close to his, still puzzled, still with that scowl between her brows.

"Barney, what's the matter? If you could tell me, maybe talk about it. What's happening to you?"

"I don't know what you mean," he said; but he couldn't face her because he *did* know what she meant, even though he didn't have an answer for her. He didn't have any answer for himself, and until he had that how could he tell her? It seemed as if the bottom was gone out of things—out of him, maybe, and how can you tell anyone else that and have it mean anything to them?

Things were different for her, too. If they hadn't been, by this time, they would have been having it round and round; but she didn't come at him any longer when she got mad. He must have enjoyed that, whether he knew it or not, because he missed it now.

"Barney, I think sometimes you must be crazy," she said, not really meaning it.

Barney realized suddenly that she had come so close, even exaggerating, to what he was thinking himself, that he wasn't easy with it.

After that things seemed to quiet down for a little. Coming that close to the edge—the edge of what, Barney didn't know and that was what scared him—was enough. He didn't want to jump over. The weather helped him. They jogged along through the hot part of the summer and it was really hot. All through the high golden days the heat quakers chirred in the edge of the woods until it sounded like one continuous note and the quiet dazed world was full of the pungent smell of pitch, trying out of the spruces.

Barney hated hot weather, but luckily it made him feel like a dishcloth after it's been used, wrung out and hung on the edge of the sink. It was so hot that nobody even wanted to say: Hot enough for you? any longer.

Along about the last of August, Sam came home from the hospital. He'd had to spend all that time lashed into a wooden frame, not even moving. Barney wondered Sam wasn't crazy with that, knowing he himself would have been raving at the end of the first week.

Sam wasn't crazy; but he wasn't Sam, either.

The day Jude was going to bring him home, Cliff and Paul were waiting out by the door to welcome him: King Sam, coming back. Barney didn't know whether to join in or go on about his business. Sam must know he was still around—Jude wouldn't have let him come back without telling Sam about it. Barney spent the morning trying to decide whether or not he'd want to see himself first thing, if he were in Sam's place.

Finally he made up his mind it'd look worse, more as if he felt guilty or bothered—he did, but not in the way they all thought he should—if he stayed away. So, a few minutes before Jude could reasonably be expected to drive in, he went over to the house and he was standing there a little behind the other two, but not trying in any way to make himself look as if he weren't there, when the truck arrived.

Paul and Cliff had been talking, slow and without saying anything, the way you do in hot weather. As if the effort to shape
the words and make them come out forestalled the necessity of
seeing that they made sense too. They were taking care to keep
well inside the shade of the big horse chestnut. Neither one of
them spoke to Barney, and only Cliff acknowledged his presence
by a quick glance of greeting.

Jude drove into the driveway without the usual scattering of
gravel, and eased the truck to a stop as if she had the back end
loaded with eggs. Sam opened the door on his side and it took him
a good minute to get out. He didn't move as if it hurt him, but
as if he was afraid it might. He was wearing a heavy brace around
his middle that showed clearly through his thin white shirt.

Barney hadn't laid eyes on him since the morning it happened,
and was surprised now to see how Sam had changed. He was
thinner and his face looked frozen into a different older heavier
expression, thinner and heavier at the same time.

Jude's face, though, was going to tell Barney whether or not
he'd made a mistake in being there, and the minute he looked
at her he knew he had. She gave her head a slight shake, only
enough for Barney to see, so he dropped back a little and, not
knowing what else to do, stood there while Sam held his ceremony
with Paul and Cliff. When that was all over and he either had
to get to Barney or not, their eyes met for the bare instant it
took Sam's glance to get to him and past him and that was it.
They'd had it.

Barney turned around and started back across lots toward the
chicken houses and the sun was hot on the back of his head. Not
a word! Not one god-damn word! The sky was bright blue. The
water was smoky blue. There was a west wind like the breath out
of a furnace blowing and when he stepped into the shade of the
houses, the shade was hot too. Hardly any different than being
out in the sun, except the light was easier on his eyes.

He'd noticed when people don't think much of you, they try
to look through you as if you weren't there or they could see
right through what of you there was. But there's an effort involved.

With Sam, there wasn't. For him, Barney really wasn't there. No effort. No Barney.

Jude had managed, all through that summer, to hold onto some semblance of things being all right. But now, with Sam home and dragging around the place like a wounded buck and being the way he was, the semblance was gone for her and it hadn't ever existed for Barney.

He hung on for three weeks and it kept getting worse. Especially after Sam felt he could get out and around. All he did was wander. But he always stopped to talk to Paul and if Barney happened along and looked as if he might be going to stop too, Sam would turn around and walk away, slowly, deliberately, leaving absolutely no doubt in anyone's mind why he was leaving. Barney gave him the opportunity to do it twice. If Sam couldn't see him, he didn't know why he should bother to see Sam.

He was getting through the end of the month anyhow, he told himself. He hadn't said anything to any of them yet and he didn't intend to until the day he held his last paycheck for September right in his hand. What he couldn't figure was why Sam kept him on, feeling the way he did. Unless maybe they couldn't get along without him right now and that hardly seemed possible. Barney didn't want to give Sam the satisfaction, though, of being able to say he'd had to let him go because he wasn't holding up his end. So he held it way up over his head.

The hot spell ended the first week in September. The days were pleasantly warm, but the nights got chilly. It seemed to Barney the leaves began to turn early. By the second week in September the big elm outside their door—the one that had thrown such thick shadows over the road—was thinning out noticeably and turning color. The maples were yellow enough to make you think the sun was shining while you were underneath them, even when it wasn't.

He began to remember what the skeleton of the country looked like. Only remember yet, because it was still invisible. Not so much happened here along the coast in the fall because there were so many spruces to make the woods look still shaggy and living through the winter. In the hardwood country it was different, and the minute the first leaf fell it opened up a space you could look through and see a line of mountain or horizon you'd been missing all summer and there it was again. It made you know the bone was solid and there, even when you couldn't see it.

Barney was getting the get-up-and-go feeling and it would be only a matter of time before he had to do it. It would be different with a wife and two kids getting up and going with him. It was being made clear as it could be that he'd worn his welcome right down into the ground with Sam. He had Sam figured finally, though. *He* wouldn't ever be the one to tell Barney to get through. Barney had to do it himself, so he could never come back to Sam and say: Look what you did to me! Sam had to be the one, even at the end, who never shirked his responsibility or turned his back on anything he had ever thought to take care of.

They scraped and ground along and Barney wasn't saying anything but all the time he was getting further and further away from them and they from him. He felt as if they were looking at each other across a hell of a deep ravine. He was on one side and Sam and Jude on the other, and all the while it was getting deeper and wider and pretty soon they weren't even going to be able to see each other's faces.

He knew Cliff was still doing his visiting, but that didn't bother much either. It didn't matter even one afternoon along in the middle of the month when Cliff overstayed his time a little and Barney caught him. When Barney drove up the street, there was Cliff's car parked in front of the house. Barney had to grin, wondering how Cliff was going to feel when he walked in. Sixteen, Sabra'd said. Only sixteen!

Cliff was sitting alongside the table, big as Billy-be-damned. He didn't look half as upset as Barney thought he would and Barney wondered for a second how dumb he could be—if maybe he didn't realize himself why he stopped in every other day or so.

Sabra was sitting across from him and they were talking when Barney came across the yard: but it stopped when they heard him.

"Hey, Cliff," he said. "I'm just about ready for a drink. How about you?"

Sabra gave him a dirty look, but he wasn't getting it. She had stopped taking a drink with him back in the summer sometime. Said she didn't want the kids to see her drinking. It wasn't much fun drinking alone, so Barney thought: Well, here's Cliff. Maybe he'll keep me company.

"Why not?" Cliff said.

The first drink was a stout one because Barney wanted his that way and he didn't think he'd get any more than the first one into Cliff where he had to go home to Jude and probably she'd clobber him if she ever thought he'd been drinking. He put that one down quite fast and so did Barney, who then held up the bottle questioningly and Cliff grinned and shoved his glass across the table. His eyes were watering.

"Barney," Sabra said warningly.

"Cliff and I are thirsty." Barney didn't look at her. "Got to have another short one."

It wasn't short. The first one he'd given Cliff for the hell of it; but if he was willing to try and keep up, Barney thought it might be interesting to see at what point he'd fall by the wayside. So he made the second one as stout as the first.

Cliff didn't drink that so fast, and when he was about halfway through it he began to talk about Sam.

"You know," he said. "S a damn shame, the way he acts, Barney. S too damn bad he don't treat you decent."

"Isn't it?" Barney agreed. "But don't let it worry you, Cliff, will you? It won't be for much longer. I'm going to remove the irritation any day now."

"Whadda you mean?" He was slurring his words a little, but aware that he was and trying not to. Barney looked at Sabra and she had her mouth shut so tight her under lip looked thin and it wasn't really. At the rate Cliff was softening up, it wasn't going to take too long to find out what his capacity was.

"We're going to Connecticut this fall," Barney said. "Not enough to do around this place in the wintertime. Not now I've got a family to support."

He saw Cliff think: That means she'll go, too. When he looked at Sabra, his eyes knew what he was doing here. Barney didn't bother to offer him the third slug. Just reached across and filled his glass again.

"I didn't know you were having trouble with your brother," Sabra said.

"No. I didn't think it was worth mentioning. Where we're going so soon, anyway."

He was watching Cliff curiously. That made about six ounces of straight rum he'd put down without hardly stopping for breath. As soon as that hit bottom, he'd be about ready to be delivered. His eyes were glassy already and the pupils looked funny. He was going to be one surprised kid when he tried to stand up.

"Cliff," Sabra said. "Isn't it about time for you to be getting home to supper?"

She couldn't see his eyes or she wouldn't have said it. She'd have wanted to keep him there and sober him up a little before Jude got her eyes on him. But she was afraid if she didn't get him out of the house now, Barney would pour some more down his gullet. Cliff wasn't going to be sober for a long time, though. Barney *could* see him and knew he'd had plenty to serve the purpose. He supposed it was a dirty trick to play on the poor young devil; but Cliff should have had the sense not to put it down the way he had, as if it was water.

"Oh, my god, yes!" Cliff said. "Time *is* it, anyway? I ought to be there now."

He got up and made a beeline for the door and his momentum was enough to carry him out through before he realized he could hardly stand up. When he found that out, Barney was right behind him and ready. He edged Cliff over toward the car, with Cliff all the while making grabbing motions helplessly in the direction of his own.

"Got to go home, Barney," he was saying when Barney poured him into the front seat.

"Yeah, I know. That's where we're going."

"Can't leave car there."

"I'll take care of it," Barney said. "I'll pull it into the yard and you can pick it up tomorrow. You better not drive it tonight."

"Not drunk," Cliff said loudly.

"I know it," Barney told him soothingly. "It's all right. You just simmer down."

Sabra was watching from the door when they hauled out of the yard. Her face looked too white and her eyes too black for comfort. Barney could see he'd probably have a towse with her when he got back. *If* he got back, he amended, with a wry grin at the thought of what Jude would have to say if she caught him.

When he was trying to get Cliff unloaded again, he thought to god he'd never seen such long legs in all his life. And no more stiffening to them than there would be to so much macaroni. He got Cliff out of the car and of course his legs wouldn't hold him up, so he sat down in the driveway, laughing like hell. Barney was laughing too. Cliff looked damned funny, sitting there like one of those long-legged rag dolls. Every joint in his body would have bent one way as easily as it would the other.

They were making quite a racket and neither one of them heard Jude until she was right alongside them.

"What's going on here?" she said in a voice like a bucket of ice water.

"Having a little difficulty," Cliff said as clearly as Barney could have. "Nothing to worry about. Little knee trouble. Better call a doctor, though. Need a splint. Little arm trouble, too."

He tried to hold out his arm level with the shoulder and it went down as if it was melting like a candle over a hot stove, wrist first, then elbow, then shoulder. He giggled.

"He's drunk," Jude said.

"Yessir," Barney nodded. "He sure is."

"Barney Cousins," Jude said. "I want you off this place. And if you ever set foot here again, both you and I will be sorrier than we are now, if that's possible."

"I've got nearly a whole week's pay coming to me," Barney said combatively. That was the only thing left he cared about.

"Yes, and you've earned it, haven't you. I'll send it to you in the morning. I don't want to set eyes on you again in this life!"

"Okay, if that's the way you want it."

"Make no more mistakes about it. That's exactly the way I want it."

"Better help you get him in the house," Barney said. They both looked down at Cliff, who was still sprawled out there, limp and boneless, nearly underneath the car.

"Your kind of help I can do without. Now will you get the hell out of here?"

Barney got into the car.

"Hey, Barney," Cliff yelled. "Where you going? Hey, Barney, wait for me."

"You're staying right here," Jude told him. Cliff had no choice. He couldn't move; but he was still protesting.

"Barney's my *friend!* I wanna go *with* him. He's a good friend of mine."

"Yes," Jude said. "Barney's the best friend *you* ever had!"

Barney didn't tarry to listen to any more. He headed for home. He had another one waiting for him there. Once you get a woman stirred up, you might just as well try to cope with a nest of white-tailed hornets. It was funny, though, how he'd had to make Jude tell him, how he couldn't tell her. Now it was over, he knew he would have stayed on there, in spite of them all, in spite of all his thinking—safe job, safe pay, sure of everything—and taken whatever they wanted to dish out to him. But Cliff was a good excuse. He came in handy. He was another not-so-innocent by-stander.

Sabra was at the stove, back to, when he went in the second time. Usually the sight of the back of her neck made him want to go over and kiss her hard; but tonight he would just as soon have tried to kiss a porcupine. That was how she felt and could make him know she felt without saying a word.

So he grabbed the bottle off the table where she'd left it and went over and flopped down on the bed. There was either the bed or one of the straight chairs, and he was all of a sudden too damned tired to sit up straight.

She didn't intend to say a word, either, he discovered, and it didn't make him sorry. They were always so sure talking would solve everything and he had never seen it do it yet. You tried to say something and you found you were wound up even tighter in misunderstanding whoever you were talking with or listening to.

If she wouldn't talk, then he could just lie there and think how glad he was it was all over and they could go. It was as if he'd been chained down out there at Sam's—fastened to the paths where his feet had gone day after day until they could have found the way without his eyes to help them. Now he wasn't any longer. Jude had done for him tonight what he couldn't do for himself.

And they had been living in this jammed-up shack for six months and that was long enough in any one place.

That was what Barney was thinking, lying there, and the whole room was swirling with blue acrid smoke where Sabra had let the frying pan get too hot on top of the stove, when he began to hear the yelling. The minute he heard the first sound he knew what it was, but not where it was coming from, and he felt himself start to get tight and mad and disgusted. The back of his neck got tight first and his hands began to sweat.

Sabra had heard it too, and identified it. She was staring down at what she was doing; but her attention had gone right out of the room and down the street to meet whatever was coming, leaving her body standing there as still and empty as a deserted house.

Barney was looking out the window and he saw Ann when she turned the corner. She was coming as fast as she could leg it, hauling the bouncing cart behind her with Chris hanging on for dear life and yelling his head off. All that was visible of his face was open mouth and all that could be heard, once they'd got well into range, was the sound coming out of it.

Ann cornered across the ragged patch of grass toward the house and catapulted in through the door—Chris, wagon, and all—and pandemonium broke loose.

Barney bounced up off the bed, hanging onto his head with both hands. Sabra spun around from the stove, dropped her fork, and without a glance in Barney's direction, went over and picked Chris out of the wagon.

"What's the matter with him, Ann?" She wasn't looking at Ann, either. She straightened up with that screaming kid in her arms, staring at his face, running her free hand along his arms and legs. Apparently he was all in one piece, because she put her hand on the back of his head and thrust his face in against her throat, starting to make the crooning noise.

"For god sake!" Barney yelled. "Do we have to have that damn silly wagon in here, too?"

Sabra looked at him for the first time since they'd heard the screaming, looked at him as if she couldn't believe her ears. Right there he had a chance to go one way or the other; and he thought it might as well be now.

"I never intended to run a crazy house." He had to shout to make her hear him. "Shut that blasted kid off, will you?"

He turned his back on them and stood waiting and if he hadn't jammed his clenched fists hard against his thighs he thought he might have torn the place apart to let the noise out.

It sounded as if all three of them were going right round and round in the middle of the room. Actually it was only Ann who was. Ever since this fracas started, she'd been going around Sabra like a whirligig, pulling at anything that was loose—elbow, Chris's foot, Sabra's dress.

Barney heard Sabra say, "Oh, stop!" And then she said in a whole new voice that made him turn to look too: "Where did you get that?"

That kid was waving a five-dollar bill around her head like a flag and how in hell he'd missed it before he didn't know, because she'd been waving it, he realized now, ever since he'd first seen her turn the corner.

"A man!" she yelled. "A man gave it to me. A man gave it to me!"

After she'd said it the second time she stopped, and stopped moving too, staring at Sabra's face.

"*What?*" Sabra said. Her voice sounded frozen and her eyes looked frozen. Barney knew what she was thinking, because he was thinking the same thing and wondering what she was going to do about it. He could see what was going through her mind, what she thought she could see happening, see beginning for Ann.

When he looked at the kid, her exultation had changed to pure fright; but she looked as guilty as if she'd been thinking exactly what Sabra and Barney were.

"What man?" Sabra said and her voice was queer enough now to make Barney nervous. It was enough to scare the living tar out of Ann.

"I—I didn't know him." She began to blubber and her under-lip shook as if it wasn't even attached to her.

"Ann," Sabra said. "You stop lying to me and tell me who it was or I'll give you the worst hiding you ever had."

Chris had quieted down by this time and she didn't have to shout to make herself heard, so her voice was quieter anyhow; but there was no quietness underneath it and nothing in it to re-assure anyone, much less Ann.

"Honest, Mama. I didn't know him."

"What for? What did he give it to you for?"

It was lucky for Ann that Sabra had Chris in her arms. If she hadn't had, by this time, she probably would have hauled off and let her have a good one.

"Chris was mad and bawling and the man stopped his car and came back and gave me this. He said: Is he hurt? Is he all right?"

Ann held out the bill as if it being there in her hand would be all the proof she needed.

"You little liar!" Sabra said, and this time she did swing her hand back to let go. Ann opened her mouth and nothing came out but a squeak. Barney had been watching her face. There was a kind of dismay and astonished fright on it that made him think maybe she was coming as close to the truth as she knew how. It sounded interesting. Sabra twisted and tried to strike at him because he grabbed her hand before she could touch Ann. He had her too firmly, though, and she couldn't reach him.

"Wait a minute, Sabra. This sounds crazy enough to be true."

Barney wasn't thinking about Chris now, or that damned racket he made. He was too interested in what Ann was trying to say. He didn't let go of Sabra's wrist, but only because he'd forgotten he was holding it. He kept his voice quiet when he said to Ann:

"What was Chris doing?"

She swallowed before she could get the words out and when they finally came, they came fast and stumbling over each other.

"The car came up behind us quiet, see?" Her eyes on Barney's

face were saying a lot more than her tongue did. He never had
interfered between Sabra and the kids before, not where they
could see it, and having it happen now was another new thing for
Ann.

"Chris didn't hear it. I never neither. Then it honked loud
and scared him. He got mad and started flinging around and yelling the way he does, and tipped the wagon over. Then the man
stopped and came back and gave me the money."

"How—" Barney began and hesitated, thinking how to ask
what he wanted to know without telling Ann what it was. "How
did he look when he said: Is he hurt?"

"Awful funny. He kept shaking. His face was shaking."

Barney grinned at Sabra.

"He thought he'd hit them, see? He thought he'd knocked the
cart over and hurt Chris. God knows, if I heard him make that
noise for the first time, I'd think the same thing."

"You believe that wild yarn?"

She believed it, too. Barney could see that much in her face.
But there was something else, something funny that came from
her watching him. She still wanted to believe what she had at
first, she still wanted to think the worse story was the true one.

"It's *true*," he said. "Look at her! Look at her face! She
doesn't even know what you're talking about. Christ almighty, if
she got it the way you think she did, would she be foolish enough
to come home with it and tell you a man gave it to her?"

Barney let go her wrist and Sabra turned her back on him
silently, and over her shoulder there was Chris's foolish, blank-
eyed face. If it hadn't been for that stare, Barney might not have
said what he did then.

"Also," he said, "it's something to keep in mind. If one of us
had been with the kids when it happened, we might have par-
layed it into a little more than five dollars."

Sabra's body didn't move, only her head turned slowly as if
her neck felt stiff, until she was looking at Ann.

"You go up and go to bed," she said evenly. "I'll bring you
your supper later."

Well, Barney thought, she won't bring whatever it was she was frying when they came in. That had turned long ago to a black boot sole in the pan. The smoke in the room was thick enough to be nearly solid.

"Go to bed," Sabra repeated, when Ann didn't move.

"Hasn't Chris got to come too?" Ann said; but in the face of her mother's silence, she turned and went up the ladder without any more fuss.

After she'd gone, Sabra went over and put Chris down on the bed where Barney had been lying. There was something in the atmosphere of that room strong enough to get through to Chris and keep him quiet. He lay there with his light-blue eyes going from one of them to the other, his head moving a little on the pillow. When Sabra turned around to face Barney, her eyes looked swollen half-shut.

He was expecting almost anything but what she said.

"What are you trying to do to the kids?"

"Kids?"

"To Cliff? To *my* kids? What do you think you're trying to do?"

"Trying to do?" Barney was echoing again while he tried to figure out what she was getting at. "Nothing." He shrugged, thinking: Never mind Cliff. "I was just saying that them that has, might as well have a little taken away from them if we can get it. They all sit up there in their big cars, going fast. Go too damn fast anyhow. I've been eating their dust a long time. I'd enjoy it if I thought it was gold dust."

"For the love of god, Barney, are you *really* crazy?"

That touched him up. That made twice she'd told him he was crazy and look what she'd given him to take care of!

"Crazy? No," he said. "Nor foolish, either! But, by the lord, if I've got to take care of him, I might's well get a little back out of him."

Sabra knew what he meant without his having to point at Chris.

"You'll keep your hands off my kids!"

He could see he'd gone a little too far that time; but he still couldn't see what had made her so mad in the first place. She was more than plain mad, she looked sick and afraid of something, all at the same time.

"Oh, hell," he said. "Don't be silly. I'm just kidding. But I'll tell you one thing, Sabra, we've got to do something about that kid."

This wasn't the right time and he had had too much to drink. He knew the time wasn't right, and if he hadn't had the rum he could have held back. But he looked past her shoulder and there was that empty face on the pillow where he had been lying and would lie again, and before he could help himself, he shivered, and Sabra saw him do it. "He's getting worse every day. Pretty soon he'll be so big Ann can't handle him and neither can you." Barney didn't intend to make the noise he did; but looking at Chris, he couldn't help that either. You know how something'll make you gag before you know you're going to. "For god sake!" he said. "*Look* at him!"

Chris's mouth sagged open and a thin thread of water had trailed down across his face onto the pillow. He stared.

"He'll have me just as foolish as he is," Barney said, watching her lean over to wipe Chris's face. Her hand was shaking.

"He can't help it," she said.

"No. And neither can the rest of us. But we're the ones have to take it. There're places for things like that, Sabra, and you've got to come to it and put him there."

She reached out and put her hand on Chris's chest; but she was watching Barney and her eyes were black as coals after the fire dies for good and all.

"Barney!"

"That's all right," he said. "You've got to decide. It's beginning to get me down and I'm not kidding now, Sabra. I'm going out. By the time I come back, you've got to decide who's more important—me or that idiot kid."

"All right, Barney," she said quietly, and those eyes still watching him.

Her hand, though, was gentling Chris and all Barney could think of was a half-wild tiger cat he'd found in Sam's barn once.

He had found the kittens first and was leaning over them when something not like a real sound but as definite made him look up and right into the yellow eyes of the old she-cat. She was standing on a beam level with his head. Barney dropped the kitten he was holding and went out, not scared, but ready to go and leave her the field.

He was ready to go now, the same way. When he turned around, he tripped over the wagon still standing in the middle of the floor where Ann had left it. He put the sole of his foot against it and gave it a shove and it went over and lay with the wheels spinning unevenly. He didn't look back at Sabra before he pushed the screen door open and stepped out into the air and the being away from Chris and began to breathe again.

He started walking down the road fast and he was thinking, not about Sabra or Chris, but: I was happy once. Where the hell was it? Where— When was the last time I was happy?

When he went past each familiar house, it seemed to him he didn't see it the way it was now, but the way it had been years ago when he'd first looked, when there was nothing more important than what he was going to do tomorrow, or what he'd been doing today; and it was always fun and exciting and time had been a matter of day to day. Time, then, never meant anything as important as change—there wasn't any difference between one day and another, except on one day the sun might shine and on the next it might not. The days had been endless and forever; but now time was an express train and there weren't any station stops where you could get off for just a minute and stretch your legs and take one deep breath. Breathing was kind of a shallow business, because the train hadn't stopped, was pulling past the station before he'd had time to read the name on the sign and realize where he was.

When he'd been a kid he could remember waking early on summer mornings, with the first gray light before sunup, too early to go down to breakfast because nobody else would be up in the house. He could remember going over to the window and standing there in the before-daylight chill, shivering, looking up the road toward the still sleeping and mysterious town. And when he was looking in the direction of invisible life, he would feel himself begin to fill with a fizzy kind of expectation of the day— a whole day—not even touched yet and full of everything there was. And if nothing happened worth the fizz today, surely it would tomorrow.

That fizz, that feeling, was all happiness ever was. You had to be expecting something. You didn't have to know what it would be or anything about it; but you had to know it was bound to happen.

He was headed down the main street now and going fast, when all of a sudden he knew who he wanted to see, to talk to, and he made a sharp right turn under the familiar sign, so sharp he staggered and nearly lost his balance. The sign had Old English letters and all that, and it didn't say what it used to. The old sign was bigger and stuck out more. This one said: SAMUELS— ANTIQUES. The front of the store was different too, a sort of cream-white with black trim. In the window, the hodgepodge of truck that used to back up the SECOND HAND STORE was all gone and in its place were a couple of pieces of tobacco-colored pine furniture, the kind the old folks had replaced with golden oak and maple a long time ago—so long ago it was respectable now to have the pine back in the house, only they put the commode in the living room and made a bar out of it.

Inside, the long aisles were the same, winding back through what looked like an unclassifiable collection of everything under the sun. The thin brown man coming down the aisle toward the door was the same man who would have come, years back. But the last few years had put a gloss over him. He had a shine that meant success, meant money, and Barney thought maybe he'd made a mistake, maybe it wasn't the same man.

"Barney," he said and put his hand on Barney's arm and there wasn't any mistake. "You haven't been to see me in a long time. I've missed you, son."

Barney didn't realize how tight he was until Jacob touched him and that alone was enough to make him grope for balance. He put out one hand toward whatever there might be that would be solid enough to hold him up until he got the balance back.

The only thing handy was Jacob's shoulder and he shut to on that and leaned forward a little because it was hard to focus on Jacob's face, to make him look like anybody familiar. When Barney leaned forward, Jacob's eyes—eyes the color of the pine in the window—changed. He knew now what was the matter.

"Now, tell me," Barney said. "I got to see him. Where's Joe?"

"Barney, for the love of god," Jacob said. "Are you crazy?"

"Crazy? Everyone's telling me I'm crazy! I'm the only one knows I'm not. Hell, no! God damn—damn—not happy, see? Joe always happy. Thought he might tell me how to do it."

There was something awfully wrong with this; but he couldn't think yet what it was.

"Barney, let me." Jacob's voice sounded like a guitar string. "Maybe I could do something," he said. "I would if I could."

"Got to see Joe." That was the only idea in Barney's head and he couldn't let go of it.

"Stop, will you!" Jacob shouted. "Joe's been dead six years."

"Oh, my god," Barney said. "I—that's—I knew there was something, but I couldn't remember. *That's* what the trouble is. I couldn't remember."

He made a half turn toward the door to go, because that was a dead end; but Jacob had forgotten to move his hand and when he felt the restraint, Barney remembered the other question he'd intended to ask. The words came out bubbling because he had to hurry before he forgot this, too. Joe was dead and that was that and nobody could help it now. But maybe Jacob had the answer too, to this one.

"The last time he was home, you see—he never got where he wanted to go. Did you know that? That's what he said to me: 'Might's well leave one place to be the way you remember it.' And that's where I made my big mistake, Jacob. I tried to hold onto it. I tried to go back and see—and it wasn't the same. Why's that? *You* tell me."

"You want too much, Barney." Jacob was looking right at him and his eyes were brighter and Barney wanted to look away. Jacob was trying not to cry. Those were tears! And what did *he* have to cry about? "The place stays the same," he said. "It's the people who change and go. And even if you're right there, the way *you* are, Barney, you're changing. You're going."

"That's the god's living truth, isn't it?" Barney said. "I knew you would have the answer. I couldn't think what it was. So I thought I'd come in and ask you, just for the screaming hell of it. I will thank you for that profound truth all the rest of my days, Jacob. You've got it all!"

He could leave now because Jacob's hand was not holding him any longer, was hanging loose at his side, so Barney could walk to the door and go. But he had to tell Jacob something he knew and Jacob *didn't* know, no matter how sure he was about the answers. In the growing shadows, Jacob's face was all he could see, hanging in mid-air, with nothing under it like a man's body to hold it up.

Barney pointed one finger at the pale-brown blur to make sure it was there and he saw it.

"Be glad he died when you still had him, Jacob," he said. "Because he wasn't. You know god damn well he wasn't. He would have been just like me and look at me! You've got a lot to be happy about. You're a lucky man! And now you've got the answers, too."

Jacob's voice followed Barney out through the door. Barney thought he said:

"I haven't any answer for you, Barney."

But that didn't make sense. That was the obvious thing. Barney could have told Jacob that himself. There wasn't one. That was why. All the answers except the one there wasn't, and nobody could have that. You didn't have to say something everybody already knew.

He walked a long way. It was hours later and full moonlight before he came back to the house where Sabra would be waiting for him. His shadow got across the yard to the door first, longer and taller than he was. He stopped outside and hauled the bottle out of his pocket and up-ended it. Silvery moonlight slid along its side and nothing else.

"Empty," he said and pushed it away from him. He watched

the twinkle of the twisting glass, following its arc of flight until it disappeared in shadow and then he stood listening for the sound it would make hitting the ground. No sound came.

"There's a hole in the bottom of the sea," he said, considerably sobered because there should have been a sound and wasn't. He opened the door into the dark room and said: "Sabra?"

"I'm right here, Barney."

Her voice came at him out of darkness, from the direction of the bed, quiet, without the expression he'd been expecting. Everything was something he hadn't been expecting, different, and each thing that happened sobered him a little more. He reached up, groping, for the string to turn on the naked ceiling bulb. He felt revealed, betrayed, outlined there against the brilliant moonlight in the doorway and he had to see her, he had to do more than merely hear her voice out of darkness.

"Yes, turn it on," she said levelly.

Barney was directly underneath the light when it came on, shedding its unshaded brilliance down over his head like water. Sabra saw his face eyeless, because the heavy ridge of his brows shaded the deep eye sockets; and it seemed to her that he had been that way for a long time. He saw her sitting on the bed beside Chris, apparently exactly as she had been hours ago when he'd left her. Chris was asleep; but he was there and that was the focal point for all Barney's troubles.

"Well," he said bitterly. "You been sitting there ever since I went out?"

Sabra shook her head. She was breathing fast as if she'd been running. For a second it seemed to Barney almost as if she was talking to him without words, trying to tell him something; but whatever it was, it didn't get through. He needed the words.

"You make up your mind yet?"

Sabra closed her eyes, and when she did that all the youthfulness went out of her face.

"Yes."

"Well?"

"Barney," she said quickly, "you listen. You're the most important person in the world for me; but you'll never believe it. I think you've gone crazy. I don't know what's wrong, but it's too late to do anything about it."

"Too late?" he said stupidly, feeling as if he were talking to himself. How did she know, anyway? How could she always tell what he was thinking?

"You can't be contented with anything—once you get what you want, it's never enough. You want to ruin everything and everybody and I'm not going to let you do it to my kids."

"What're you going to do?" Barney stepped back out of the light and Sabra could see his eyes now; but he still looked blind to her. There wasn't a shadow of expression on his face, not an indication of what he might be feeling or thinking. The lack was frightening.

"I'm through. I'm going to leave you."

Barney laughed.

"Where the hell d'you think you can go with two kids?"

"Pa'll let me come back there, with the kids. He had to work late tonight or I'd be gone right now."

"You mean you'd have walked out of here and let me come home to find you gone?" His eyes blazed suddenly into expression.

"I meant to."

Barney, watching her face, saw it sharpen suddenly to attentive listening. He turned his head slowly to listen, too. He felt as if he were doing everything very slowly, considering every move with great care. So he listened carefully and heard what she had, the inevitable footsteps coming up the long stone corridor.

"That's what he's been waiting for," Barney said aloud, but to himself. "That's what he's been hanging around for. It wasn't me, after all."

He thought he was still moving slowly; but he had the gun in his hands and loaded before Sabra realized what he was doing. Methodically he came back to the center of the room and stood looking down at her horror-stiffened face. One corner of his mouth twitched upward; but his eyes were still unseeing.

"No need for you to be afraid," he said.

"What're you going to do?"

"He's coming up the path now," Barney said quietly. Arthur's footsteps had changed—no longer loud on cement, but softened on grass. "I'm not going to let anyone take you away from me, Sabra. The minute he sets foot inside that door, I'm going to kill him. I don't see anything else to do."

"*Oh my god*," Sabra said despairingly and flung herself at him. Barney felt her hand on the muzzle of the gun.

"Don't, Sabra," he said desperately, loudly, doing his best to be reasonable with her. He saw her face in a lot of little pieces, each one with a separate life of its own. She had both hands on the gun now. "Don't," he yelled. "That's *dangerous*. You'll make me shoot *you*."

Arthur had his hand on the latch and when he opened the door, the deafening blast of the shotgun in confined space rolled out at him, drowning the words he'd heard just too late.

"Sabra?" Barney said, as if he didn't believe it, as if she had just stepped out the door for a minute and he had to know where she was. But the door she'd stepped through was the one that had to close between them and the whole world before everything would be all right and the way Barney wanted it. There was something wrong with it, though—she'd left him on the wrong side of the door.

It was almost too late to hold onto what he really wanted any longer; she'd almost found the one thing that could take her away from him forever, and forever was too long.

"You see, I'll have to hurry," he said to Arthur in a low reasonable voice. "I'll have to step on it. I can catch up with her. Wait just a second."

Arthur stood stricken and horrified in the door, helpless and old, with his chance gone forever, unable to move, knowing he wouldn't have moved if he could. He stood and watched Barney turn the gun with careful shaking hands and put his thumb on the trigger. The second blast, as deafening as the first, Arthur was expecting when it came.

It seemed to Arthur that Barney had simply moved to one side, leaving him to stare without surprise past the place where Barney had been to the place where Sabra was with her son.

He heard a whimpering noise and thought at first Chris was making it, until he took a shaking step closer and saw that Chris couldn't be making any kind of a noise at all. So he had to be making it himself.

In the quiet house on the hill looking down across the moon-silvered summer fields to the ocean, the phone spoke its summons to wakefulness. Jude, out of years of habit, awoke instantly at its first ring, glanced at the radium dial of the clock on the dresser.

"Quarter of two," she said to herself. "Now, what?"

Knowing what, even as she said it. She was halfway across to the door before she remembered that it didn't matter to her any longer—that it didn't matter to Sam. They were free not to answer because it was no longer important. As long as Cliff was in the house, and she had good reason to know he was tonight, then those who were wandering in the darkness could manage for themselves.

She spun on her heel and thudded back to bed. As she sat down to take off her slippers, the phone rang again.

"Might's well answer it," Sam said wearily. "Want me to go?"

"No. I will." The man on the other end of the articulate wire would know she heard the ring—would keep ringing until she spoke to him.

"Just tell him not to call again," Sam said levelly. "Just tell him once and for all, we're through."

Jude stooped slowly to put the slippers back on. She didn't hurry down the stairs. She picked up the phone and said: "Kermit?"

"Yes."

"I don't care what it is or anything about it. I told Barney today we were through with him and I meant it. He had no right to have you call us."

"Wait," Kermit said into the spate of her denial. "Wait just a minute." There was a note in his quiet voice that turned Jude off, left her clinging to the phone with her breath cut off, beginning to shake uncontrollably.

"I can promise you this will be the last time," Kermit said levelly. "He's taken care of everything—but one. There's just one thing and I need your help. He doesn't. *I* do."

Quietly, in direct simple words, he told her what had happened, what Arthur had stood and watched.

"Barney's dead," he said. "The boy is, too. She died on the way to the hospital. But I need some help."

"All right," Jude whispered into the phone and let it fall to hang dangling at the end of its cord just short of the floor. Sam was sitting up in bed with the night light on when she went back into the bedroom and at the sight of her face he lurched out of bed and reached her just as her knees buckled.

"No," Jude said.

"What? What?" he said wildly.

She told him the way Kermit had told her and saw color drain out of his face leaving the eyes dead-black against dead-white.

"What's there left to do tonight?" He stammered a little, getting it out, trying to think.

Staring at him, sick at heart, Jude had no words for the emptiness inside her that must have been a greater emptiness in him. He would feel that the fault, or the responsibility, lay with him and he would try to see where he'd gone wrong. Already he was trying, and he didn't know.

Maybe it's just as well, he was thinking, when something goes this far wrong, that you can't ever really know where you made your first mistake. It would probably be some god-damn little thing you did without even thinking and just happenstance that you did or didn't do it. And if you ever found out what it was, in case it should turn out to be something like that, it would be enough to drive you crazy. But it seemed as if there ought to be some way you could tell the difference between a lost pup and a mad dog.

They drove together and in silence up through the white town, quiet in moonlight, clinging to the shoulder of the mountain, with its wharves fingering out into the bold water of the Sound; the town across whose daily life Barney had written with hasty fingers the scrawling foolish violence he called living now for twenty-three years; the town he might have made a good man for because his father and his grandfather had, back before they produced this ending for generations of good men.

Kermit was standing on the sidewalk waiting for them, caught in the clash of yellow light that spouted out the open door, light like a yell in the darkened street.

"I hate to ask you to go in," he said wearily. "We've cleaned things up the best we could tonight. But you've got to."

"Why?" Sam said desperately.

"There's a loose end," Kermit told him. "There's a piece left over."

They followed his broad back numbly up the path to the door, dreading what they might find.

"Does Jude—" Sam said at the door. "Couldn't she wait out here?"

"I need her more than I do you," Kermit said stiffly, and shouldered his way in, as if he felt himself he was passing from normal night into an atmosphere heavy enough to offer physical resistance.

The place was a shambles. The floor had been scrubbed and was still damp. The bed, stripped of clothes, offered nothing but the jangling springs to sit on. The Medical Examiner sat there, a young man, his face honed down and tired-looking with shock. He was still young enough to be shocked at intentional violence. He kept sighing and looking at his hands spread out on his neat tweed-covered knees.

"I don't think I can pick up any more pieces," Jude said numbly, following the two men into the shoddy little room. She couldn't even make herself look around, she could only stare directly in front of her.

"Take a look," Kermit said and jerked his thumb toward the ladder that led to the loft where the two children had slept. Jude's glance, in spite of herself, followed the direction of his gesture and she looked squarely into the eyes of the small girl who sat on the lowest rung of the ladder staring, blindly, her hands covering her ears.

"Oh, my god!" Sam said.

Kermit nodded.

"The old man just walked out," he said. "He just walked out. Said he couldn't do it. Have her around, that is."

"Can you?" Sam looked at Jude.

Kermit started across the room toward the child who, for all the look in her eyes changed slightly, didn't even see him coming; but when he put his hand out to touch her, she opened her mouth like a mechanical child, and screamed.

Jude felt as if a hand had closed around her heart. She went past the trooper's big back swiftly and stooped to Ann, holding out her arms, waiting to let Ann do what she would, not offering to touch her first.

Doubtfully, not going all the way, Ann put out one hand and took hold of one of Jude's and her hand *was* like the claw of a bird. Jude felt it close coldly around her own large warm one.

"You're coming home with me tonight," she said quietly. "Tomorrow we'll think what to do."

Obediently Ann got up off the ladder rung and started for the door. Kermit was watching them hopefully.

"I haven't been able to get a word out of her," he said. "Nor anywhere near her, either. *You* saw."

At the door Ann thought of something and, turning, went like a somnambulist back to the table, took her book off it, and headed for the door again.

Going back home through the quiet night, its quiet lately destroyed for them all, but how much more for one of them, with the staring child between her and Sam in the truck seat, Jude could think only of the sick kitten. But the kitten was well grown now and happy and sleek and at home, and if you could do that for a sick cat, maybe you could do it for a sick child too.

Trying to make a whole thing out of one piece, though, was a hard job. Barney had been that, she could see now, only part of a whole. And what he didn't have was something nobody, with all the will in the world, could ever have created out of thin air and grafted onto him. Seeing that, Jude had to hope that the little girl wasn't what they'd all been calling her—the piece left to be picked up.

Seven years with half-people—her mother, her grandfather, at last, Barney—would be hard to erase, and Jude looked at the necessity with a sinking heart, knowing she would always be watching, would be prone to see what she was expecting whether it was there or not.

I cannot, she thought wildly. I cannot do it again. I'll just take care of her tonight and in the morning—

But in the morning, what? Have Paul put her out of the way? Animals you could handle that way—and seldom did.

Suddenly Ann, who hadn't moved a muscle since she climbed into the truck, lopped over without a sound into Jude's lap and started to cry. Tears, without noise, poured out of her. Slowly, cautiously, Jude put her hand down flat on the bony little shoulders, feeling the flat scapulas sticking up like bird bones, too, feeling the long shuddering silent sobs. Children weren't supposed to know how to cry like that.

The minute she touched the defenseless thin little back, she knew what she was going to do, could see herself, and knew there wasn't any other possible course.

Sam glanced over at her worriedly.

"She's all right now," Jude said quietly. "Let her cry. She'll be all right now."

www.ingramcontent.com/pod-product-compliance
Lightning Source LLC
Chambersburg PA
CBHW070749280626
47162CB00018B/2816